the used women's book club

the used women's book club

PAUL BRYERS

BLOOMSBURY

First published in Great Britain 2003
This paperback edition published 2004

Copyright © 2003 by Paul Bryers

Bloomsbury Publishing Plc, 38 Soho Square, London W1D 3HB

A CIP catalogue record for this book is available from
the British Library

ISBN 0 7475 6827 8

10 9 8 7 6 5 4 3 2 1

All papers used by Bloomsbury Publishing are natural, recyclable
products made from wood grown in well-managed forests.
The manufacturing processes conform to the
environmental regulations of the country of origin.

Printed in Great Britain by Clays Ltd, St Ives plc

www.bloomsbury.com/paulbryers

CHAPTER ONE

Precipitation In Sight

THE POLICE DO NOT clean up the mess left by the Dead. But they know a woman who does. A detective had given Larry her card. 'In case you don't fancy doing it yourself,' he had said.

The card was in the inside pocket of the black weatherproof jacket Larry did not call an anorak, though he had heard it described as such by former work colleagues – people he did not quite count as friends. He had called the number twice but both times he had been put through to voicemail. He had left his own number but the woman had yet to return his call. No one had phoned or texted him for two days now and he was starting to feel bad about it. He felt that he was becoming invisible. That having cut the ties to home, job – family? – he had slipped through the cracks in the paving stones and entered some shadowy domain between the living and the dead.

He felt invisible now, despite the gaudy red-and-yellow placard in front of him. Certainly he had failed to attract any attention in the ten minutes he had been standing here.

'You can get up to seventy punters on a good night,' Jud had assured him. 'That's two hundred quid for two hours. Cash down.'

But it was not a good night. Visibility was not its strong point. Dirty drabs of cloud had been gathering through the day and now, under cover of the dark, they gobbed a thin, bitter drizzle on the streets of London.

Larry had been expecting it.

Since the murder he had become a regular listener to the

weather forecast on Radio Four. Knowing the weather at the time of the murder would not have helped, so far as he was aware, either to avert it or to mitigate the horrors of its execution, but he derived some comfort from the knowledge that some things – like the wind force off Ushant – could be predicted with a degree of accuracy. He also found the voice of the forecaster comforting – and somehow directed at him personally, like the coded messages the BBC sent out during World War II to spies and resistance fighters in Occupied Europe.

At five to seven two people turned up. A man and a woman in their twenties, wearing stylish raincoats and carrying umbrellas. Larry knew they were foreign tourists even before he heard the man's accent. It was partly the raincoats, partly an air of optimism, bordering on the desperate or insane. He thought they might be Danes. After they had bought the tickets they stood in the entrance to the Tube station, just out of the rain. Larry avoided looking at them but he sensed their unease, like a couple who have entered an otherwise empty restaurant and lack the confidence to leave but would like to summon it up. Then, just on the hour, a party of six arrived, all women of middling age, all wearing anoraks. (Anoraks that, unlike his own, could not be mistaken for anything *but* anoraks.) They, too, were foreign and determinedly cheerful. The woman who bought the tickets told him they were from Iceland.

Larry hung on for a few minutes past the hour before he decided this was as good as it was going to get. He folded up his placard and left it just inside the station entrance, facing the wall. If it were nicked the replacement cost would be deducted from his takings – which would leave him considerably out of pocket. Then he stood in the middle of the pavement and summoned his thin band of followers.

'OK, if you wouldn't mind gathering round.'

The rain had intensified slightly. Larry could see it in the street lamps. He thought of alluding to it, making some cheerfully

'British' remark that would reduce it to the insignificant, or at least the merely tiresome, but nothing sprang to mind.

He asked them if they all spoke English. Nods all round, confident from the Icelandic contingent, cautious from the Danes. Were these national characteristics? Larry wondered.

'Good,' he said. 'Because I don't speak Icelandic.'

His first joke of the night.

The Icelanders smiled. The Danes looked mystified for a second and then, seeing everyone else smiling, they smiled too.

Larry led them into the rain.

His first location was just a short walk down Whitechapel High Street. It was a stone drinking fountain set in a wall. Larry described it as the outlet of an ancient spring, long since dried or diverted. He pictured the cool, clear water bubbling up from the rock and tumbling down a leafy glade to the River Thames half a mile to the south. Druids might have sacrificed here, he said, and archaeologists had found the remains of what might have been a Roman temple. In later years Christians had built a church, the original White Chapel from which the district took its name. Then the terrible city had spread beyond its walls, defacing the outlying meadows and woodlands and turning them into the infamous Victorian slum that was the Ripper's killing field.

He pointed out the inscription.

To one unknown yet well known.

There were some, he said, who thought this referred to the Ripper, even though the fountain and its inscription pre-dated him by many years. As if the anonymous mason had some inkling of the terrors that were to come, some foreboding of their unknown perpetrator. Two of his followers began to nod wisely. The others peered blankly at the inscription and then, more hopefully, at Larry. He began to feel a little sorry for them, though not as sorry as he felt for himself.

In fact, the reference was to Jehovah, he told them, and not uncommon. Most of the drinking fountains on the streets of

London had been erected by religious, or charitable, foundations. He paused a moment, wondering whether to push it. On his previous tours he had expressed his opinion that the fountain was like an altar to more primitive gods, the gods of the Druids perhaps, gods who demanded and received the sacrifice of human blood. If the neighbourhood of Whitechapel had a spirit, he would say, then this was where it resided.

It was a small theatrical touch though Jud said it was lost on anyone but himself. *Keep it simple*, Jud had instructed him, *don't go off on one of your bloody tangents.*

Tonight, Larry decided to give the god of the Druids a miss. But he would remind them of the sacrifice. Of the blood. This, after all, was why they came.

Within half a mile of this venerable marker – to the north, south, east and west (he makes a weather vane with his umbrella and they follow with their eyes, squinting into the rain) – in the space of thirteen weeks in the late summer and autumn of 1888, six women had died in a way that ensured they would live for ever. Their throats slit, their bodies ripped from crotch to breast, their womanhood extracted and ritually displayed. The ultimate expression of man as predator; woman as prey. *And he gets away with it.* That is the final obscenity. He is never caught. His identity never satisfactorily revealed. There is no Retribution. No Avenging Angel.

As yet.

Several of his audience were now looking restless. One of the Icelanders was muttering in the ear of another, hopefully a translation rather than a critical aside. Either way, judging from the expression on the face of the recipient, she didn't get it. Larry pressed on regardless. This was his justification, his personal prayer for pardon from the exploited dead.

There has to be a point.

But there is no point. Don't kid yourself. We do no good, we merely record. If you want to do good, join a charity, join an aid organisation. In the meantime just fucking get on with it.

Larry shook away the memory and soldiered on.

All terror has its context and in this case it is poverty. Imagine it, just over a hundred years ago ... The heart of the greatest empire known to man. To the west – he sweeps his umbrella in the direction of the City – the richest square-mile in the world. Here – a single stop on the omnibus – the very pit of penury. Ninety thousand no-hopers crammed into a warren of diseased, rat-infested hovels, seventy thousand of them women and children. Twelve hundred prostitutes, *known to the police*, and at least as many unknown. Pallid street moths fluttering in the gaslight. Tired butterflies decked in the faded finery of their betters plucked off a barrow in Petticoat Lane: the limp feathers and stale fur, the threadbare velvet, the tarnished lace ... A macabre pageant performed in the darkest, dirtiest theatre you can imagine. Try. Not so difficult on a night like this. Picture a typical London pea-souper of the 1880s. Kill the lights, drop the curtain of cloud, paint the set: one part fog to two parts smoke, flecked with soot from a million flues, add the night ... And bring on the star.

There was no applause.

'We will now cross the road,' said Larry. 'Look out for the traffic.'

Twenty minutes – and three murders – later they stood at the entrance to Larry's street. He did not tell them this, though they would almost certainly have been interested. Given the context.

It was a narrow street – little more than an alleyway, really – cobbled and pedestrianised. The absence of traffic, the period street lamps and cobbles, even the rain, all combined to give it a quaint, Dickensian charm. Or so Larry had been told. To him there had always been something of the Jekyll and Hyde about it, even before the murder. During the daylight hours through most of the year it attracted a fair number of tourists, on their way from Liverpool Street Station to the shops and stalls around

Spitalfields Market. The wine bars and restaurants were usually packed at lunchtime and well into the afternoon with men and women from the City. But late at night – when the shutters went up and the rats came out to scavenge among the rubbish left on the corner for the weekly visit of the binmen – it took on an altogether more sinister aspect. It was a street that wandered like a geriatric between past and present, as if it didn't always know where or what it was.

Larry's house was the third from the end. All the curtains were drawn and there was a light in his bedroom. For a moment this startled him, as if someone might be in there. But he supposed the police had left the light on, either accidentally or as a deterrent to intruders.

It was actually the only 'house' as such in the entire street – all the others were business premises with flats in the rooms above. It was a very small house. A two-up and two-down with a converted loft. The estate agents had advertised it as 'a Huguenot silk-weaver's house' – built for the Protestants exiled from France by Louis XIV in the seventeenth century – but Larry knew this was unlikely. There were *real* Huguenot silk-weavers' houses a couple of blocks away that were two or three times the size and four times the price. Rob had said it was probably where they kept the silkworms. Larry liked to think it had been a farm cottage back in the time when Spitalfields was open countryside. In the sixteenth century, Henry VIII had permitted the Honourable Artillery Company to practise firing their cannon here, in the fields outside the city walls. One of the reasons Larry had taken to the area was that it had a lot of history. Now it had a little more.

He turned his back on his house and drew the attention of his followers to the much larger building on the corner, in the process of being restored as 'courtyard offices'.

It had once been a Victorian flophouse, he told them. At the time of the Ripper, it provided shelter for down-and-outs – or prostitutes who hadn't earned the necessary fourpence that would have purchased a bed in a cheap lodging house. Some of Jack's victims, he told them, might well have spent the night here. If you couldn't afford a bed, you paid a halfpenny to take your place along a rope stretched between two hooks in the wall. You put your arms over the rope and you just flopped. Larry mimed how it was done. Several of his increasingly bedraggled flock looked as if they would be grateful for the privilege.

He had a sudden, bizarre thought – an inclination – to lead them across the street and into his house. He had the front-door keys in the pocket of his jacket – the skin of his thumb was broken where he had been nervously rasping it along the teeth of the Yale. One glance into the hall, or beyond into the horror that was his kitchen, and they'd have a night to remember. Certainly they'd have had their money's worth.

But of course he didn't. He took them to the pub instead.

CHAPTER TWO

Trial Run

IT WAS NOT PART of Jo's plan to spend a quarter of an hour in a wine bar being ogled by men in suits. She had, she frankly admitted to herself, panicked. The light had thrown her. She had not imagined that anybody would be there. Probably nobody was there – they'd just left the light on – but her immediate thought, feeling exposed, out in the open, unseen eyes watching her, had been to run for cover. Kind of insectile, really. Was there such a word as insectile in the English language? Even now, in such circumstances, in her present state of mind, Jo could not help but consider the question. She decided there was not. Insect-like, then. Scuttling, furtive, diving under the nearest stone.

Or wine bar.

And now she was stuck here, with a glass of wine she didn't want to drink, attracting unwanted attention. Exactly what she didn't want to do.

She was sitting at a table by the window. She leaned towards it and pressed her forehead up against the glass, making a shade with her hand to cut down on the reflections. The men at the bar would think she was looking for the imaginary friend she was pretending to be waiting for.

The light was still on, a single light in an upstairs window.

She sat back and took another sip of her wine.

So what? Even if somebody *was* there, it was unlikely they had been looking out of the window at the exact moment she arrived in the street. Even more unlikely that they would have recognised her. Or concluded that she was the killer returning to the scene of her crime.

They said people always returned to the scene of the crime. The police would be on the lookout for it.

She was useless at this game. She should leave. Go home. Forget about it.

There was nothing to stop her from leaving except the fear of bringing further attention to herself. Making herself *remembered*. The woman who came in the bar, stayed five minutes *alone*, and left without finishing her drink. She snatched a furtive glance at the men. Could they be *policemen*? The police station was just around the corner on Bishopsgate.

She would stay here for fifteen minutes. In the role of a woman waiting for her friend. Who doesn't turn up. She took a book out of her handbag, *The Volcano Lover* by Susan Sontag, the group choice for the month. Jo's choice, in fact. She had read it twice already – once many years ago – and had no intention of reading it now, but on the random page she had opened, her fleeting glance was caught and fixed by the words of a sentence.

Moments of slippage, when anything seems possible and not everything makes sense.

She read more, no longer feigning interest. It was the bit where the Cavaliere's wife has died and he is in mourning. He shares his house with a painter who fills small canvases with what seem to be studies in emptiness. *Everything rhymed with the Cavaliere's condition*, Jo read.

She was not a superstitious woman, or one who finds significance in small coincidence, but these words seemed strangely appropriate to her own condition.

Well, she *had* a condition, that was for sure, and paranoia was a part of it. Deceit, also. Or was that a symptom?

Jo did not like telling lies but on the rare occasions that she did she liked to cover every angle, to be sure that she was not going to be found out.

As a teacher of English literature, Josephine Connor was

an accomplished and unforgiving critic. She subjected the details of plot and motive to rigorous analysis, posing questions which never occurred to her more charitable friends, pulling at the threads of the narrative until it frequently fell apart in her hands. Unhappily, her infrequent attempts to tell a lie tended to be at least as fragile and often more elaborate than any plot in fiction. *Keep it simple*, her friend Meg had told her on more than one occasion. *Don't go into too much detail. People don't expect you to explain yourself.*

Which was all very well but Meg was, at times, hopelessly naïve. If Jo *had* been seen – if she was being watched *now*, by someone in the bar – it was necessary to have an explanation for her presence here, in this street at this particular time.

With her head bent over the book – no longer seeing the words – she rehearsed the possible explanations. A ghoulish curiosity seemed to be the most plausible. She wanted to see the house where it had happened. That was simple. And if she didn't go gabbling on it would do very well, except . . . Inevitably her mind ran on to a possible line of questioning that she would find uncomfortable . . .

A movement at the bar caught her attention. One of the men had knelt down, as if to tie his shoelaces, and was clearly trying to look up her skirt. His companions were enjoying the joke. Jo did her best to ignore them and concentrated on her book. If she didn't leave soon they'd be over here, hassling her.

She recalled that her situation resembled a sexual fantasy of her husband Michael when they had lived together. Perhaps it still was. He liked to imagine her alone in a bar, wearing a coat over a short black dress, stockings and high heels. When she crossed her legs she would reveal a small triangle of flesh on the underside of her thigh between stocking tops and skirt. She would not, of course, be wearing knickers.

He always made up an elaborate plot – as elaborate as Jo's lies – to explain what she was doing in the bar. The most imaginative of these was that he had confessed to an affair which had begun in the same place and that she had gone there to be revenged – at his own suggestion.

'I don't want you to leave me,' he would explain. 'So I invite you to even the score.'

The location of these fantasies was as important to him as the clothes Jo wore, or didn't wear. He would describe it with as much attention to detail as if it was the setting for one of his plays. He had a soft spot for English kitsch. Sometimes he chose an airport hotel with canned music and very bright lighting and dark-red upholstery that stuck to her naked bottom. But more often it was a wine bar in the City. This place was perfect for him: traditional oak panelling, oak floorboards, oak casks behind the bar, the inevitable quotation from Dr Johnson above it. Even the Christmas tree with its twinkling fairy lights was a prop he might have imagined. The clientele would have pleased him, too. Heavily built men in suits, in their late twenties and early thirties.

Football teams were a favourite choice, particularly if it was an airport hotel. *French* football teams stranded between flights. But in the City wine bars he favoured English public-school types, the kind of men he despised.

Jo was never consulted in the composition or casting of these scenarios, although they were supposedly designed to turn her on while making love. In fact, it was Michael who was turned on. He invariably wrote himself into the script – in the role of the husband forced to watch at a discreet distance, sometimes in the role of her chauffeur, while she was chatted up at the bar, or talked into playing pool so they could watch her climb on to the table to reach for a shot. The fantasies always ended with him driving them to another bar, or hotel, while she disported herself in the back of the car wedged between two men kissing and groping her while stripping off her clothes. He frequently climaxed while describing how he opened the door for her to climb out, naked save for her high heels and stockings.

Michael's presence – as writer, director, stage manager and

extra – in what were meant to be *Jo's* fantasies was, she considered, significant. Once, shortly before their final parting, she had attempted to instruct him on the difference between male and female fantasies, a subject on which she was not nearly as expert as she had sounded at the time. It had fooled him, though. He had sulked for days.

She glanced at her watch again. Just after seven. Time to go. She turned up the collar of her overcoat before she emerged into the little street, resisting the temptation to glance back towards the house, and set off at a brisk pace toward Bishopsgate. There was a thin drizzle but she didn't bother to take her folding umbrella out of her handbag. She wore a black beret which kept most of the rain off her hair.

What was the quickest – a cab or the underground and a short walk along the river? The cab almost certainly. But speed was not the only consideration. The driver might remember picking up a single woman. The underground was far more anonymous.

At exactly eighteen minutes past seven, she emerged from the Tube station at Tower Hill and headed south towards the river. The rain seemed colder now and slightly heavier, hinting at snow or sleet, but she still didn't take out her umbrella. She walked briskly, her hands in the pockets of her leather coat and her handbag wedged in the crook of her elbow. Her shoulders were slightly hunched and she kept her head down, butting into the rain. When she reached the bridge she stopped and looked at her watch again. Twenty-five past seven.

She knew how long it would take from here to her apartment. Ten minutes. Twelve at the most.

So it was possible.

She had a sudden mental image. The face of a watch, but not hers. The glass was smashed and the minute finger was broken.

She turned and put both hands on the parapet of the bridge and was violently sick.

The wine. On an empty stomach. Or the panic.

She waited for the wave of nausea to subside. After a moment she felt the cold sweat on her forehead. It was oddly comforting. She wiped her mouth with the back of her hand and looked around to see if anyone was watching.

Cars swept past with a hiss of tread on the wet road, headlights cutting through the drizzle. But she seemed to be the only one *walking* across the river. Nobody was watching, that she could see.

She found a tissue in her bag and blew her nose. She felt better now, or at least not nauseous. She walked on, more slowly now, taking comfort from the feel of the rain on her face. Her temperature seemed to have gone back to normal but she was sticky with sweat. She took the steps down to the riverside walk on the south side and stopped again at Butler's Wharf to look out over the water.

The tide was up – almost up to the level of the walkway. Jo watched the river sliding past, like the black back of some monstrous mammal, streaked with lights from both embankments. There were cranes on the north side, all lit up, with Christmas trees tied to the very tops. Another riverside development. She didn't know the north side, not very well. She thought of it now as hostile.

This was her territory. The south bank from Tower Bridge to Jacob's Island. A stretch of waterfront. She felt like a cat, a stray that had made its home here. And for a while she had been safe, but not any more.

CHAPTER THREE

The Quick and the Dead

LARRY TOOK THEM TO the Ripper pub in Spitalfields, the Ten Bells. For half an hour they could buy drinks and souvenirs from behind the bar – a Ripper T-shirt or a tea towel, a mug or a tankard with the supposed signature, written in red . . .

Jud was sitting at a table in the corner with a couple of the other guides. Larry bought a pint of bitter and joined them.

'God awful night for it,' Jud said, not quite catching his eye. He would have seen how few punters had followed Larry into the pub.

'I thought you had a job,' said Larry disagreeably.

Jud, in common with most of the tour guides, was an actor. He only did this between *acting* jobs. But he was supposed to be rehearsing for a Christmas pantomime and Larry was one of the lucky few he'd persuaded to stand in for him with his promise of untold riches.

'Cancelled,' Jud said, 'due to poor advance bookings.' His tone was devoid of surprise or disappointment as if this was the fate expected of pantomimes in which he had a part, or indeed any other form of public entertainment. He could have been the weatherman on Radio Four announcing there were gales off the Faroes.

'Great,' said Larry. 'You can have your walk back.'

Jud regarded him thoughtfully but said nothing. Larry had the impression that Jud had already written him off as a worthy replacement. Whatever his failures as an actor, Jud's perform-mance as a tour guide was reckoned to be spot on – at least according to the other tour guides Larry had met. But then Jud was on the management committee that sorted out the schedule and the publicity – and took 10 per cent of the takings.

Jud was more of an acquaintance than a friend, the brother of a woman Larry had been out with once or twice. When Larry gave up being a television cameraman and started the course at art school she had suggested he might pick up a bit of extra cash doing the walking tours.

'You're good at bullshit,' she had assured him.

Larry saw the two Danes looking at him from the bar. The man said something to the woman and then came over. He was very sorry, he said, but they would not be able to finish the walk. His wife did not like the rain, he said.

'We are from Luxembourg,' said the man who Larry had thought was a Dane, by way of an explanation.

As if it never rained in Luxembourg.

Larry said that was all right.

He thought of giving him his money back but was inhibited by the presence of Jud and the other guides.

When the couple had left, Jud shook his head sadly. 'You give them too much of all that pseudo-socialist-feminist crap,' he told Larry. 'All they want is the blood and the guts, man.'

When Jud did the tour he carried a book of photographs with him that showed the Ripper's victims. He held the photos up under a flashlight so everyone could see them. And he always wrapped up the tour with his own pet theory on the identity of the killer.

'I'm not so hot on blood and guts at the moment,' Larry said. 'Sorry.'

He saw the other two guides exchange a glance. He wondered if any of them knew about the murder.

'What's the problem?' said Jud.

Perhaps they *didn't* know. His name hadn't appeared in any of the press reports – none that he'd seen, anyway – though he had seen pictures of his house. But he had no intention of telling them now.

'I just can't hack it,' he said. 'Any chance of something a bit less ghoulish?'

It was probably not the best word to use in the circumstances. The two guides looked distinctly miffed. They said nothing but they drank their beer in a stiff silence.

'Like what?' said Jud.

'Oh, I don't know – the Fire of London, Guy Fawkes, London of Doctor Johnson, something like that.'

'D'you know anything about them?'

'I didn't know much about Jack the Ripper until about a week before I did the tour.'

'Yeah, well, maybe that's the problem, mate.'

But he promised to ask around and give Larry a ring if anything came up.

At nine o'clock Larry delivered his group back to the underground and took his placard back to the pub to stash behind the bar.

It was not so easy to dispose of the bodies. They were in his head and under his feet. They would follow him home and crawl into his sleep and he would wake from some terrible dream that one of them was lying beside him. And so they paid him back.

He cut down the back streets towards the river, then across Tower Hill with its monument to the men of the merchant navy who had died in the war, the great black wall of names, and the site of the block where condemned prisoners from the Tower of London were hung, drawn and quartered or, if they were lucky, merely beheaded. And waiting for him on the river, down by Tower Bridge, was Dead Man's Hole where the jumpers were fetched up by the tide. He knew them all, all the favourite sites, the blocks and the scaffolds and the ditches, the mass graves where the plague victims lie. He had a morbid preoccupation with Death, the doctor said, when he was a child, but the way

Larry felt about it, Death had a morbid preoccupation with *him*. For some reason Death had singled him out for a witness and when he stopped looking, when he stopped taking pictures, when he walked away, it sent them drifting back, piling up in some dark backwater of his mind. At night he is like old Captain Cat in the lee of Milk Wood, hearing them calling to him above the sound of the waves.

Remember me, Captain? I lost my step in Nantucket . . .

But Larry hears a different voice.

Remember the first one we ever saw, down at Rotherhithe, down by the old Dog and Duck?

The first of many. If only they'd known then just how many. But they'd sat, in their ignorance, on the Bermondsey Wall watching the river police drag it up on to the deck of the launch and Larry had made a remark about 'something looking a bit fishy', the kind of naff remark a twelve-year-old kid *would* make to hide his shock and distress. *No offence, mate*, he'd thought at the time. And imagined the reassuring reply: *None taken, guvnor.*

But he sometimes wondered if the outraged ghost *had* taken offence. And tolled on some hidden bell to summon all those other corpses Larry had encountered over the years . . .

You think I'm *funny, take a gander at this.*

It came at him then – the first glimpse of Rob's body through the half-open door into his kitchen – and he almost cried out, stopping in his tracks, before he pushed it back to where it must stay – in the backwater with all the others.

His dad's tug, the *Lady Jane*, was moored to a floating jetty about twenty metres out into the river. To reach it, you had to use a trio of rubbish barges as a bridge. At high tide, as it was now, the deck of the first barge was almost level with the embankment and Larry could step down on to it easily from the riverside walk. The decks were greasy with rain but he crossed confidently from barge to barge until he had almost reached the jetty. There was a gap here of four or five feet – deliberately left by his dad to deter vandals – but he kept a plank under the gunwale to use as a gangway.

The plank was damp and slimy to the touch and he disturbed a rat pulling it out. When he reached the boat he couldn't get his wet hand into the side pocket of his jeans where his keys were. And then he dropped them. Larry swore out loud and the waterfowl gave it back to him like irate neighbours in a tenement slum, disturbed by the local drunk.

There were easier homecomings.

Once he was in the wheelhouse he put the electric heater on and dried out for a few minutes in the blast of hot air. Then he went down to the galley to light the stove. It was black and old and ugly, like the tug itself, and had a mind of its own. It only worked when it felt like it. He stacked it with kindling and coal as his dad had once shown him – a long time ago – and coaxed it into flame.

While it was drawing he made himself a mug of tea and took it back up into the wheelhouse and sat in the dark, hunched over the chart table with both hands wrapped round the mug, feeling lonely and sorry for himself.

There was a time when he might have considered this a bit of an adventure, though perhaps not in winter. When his dad first bought the *Lady Jane* in the late 1970s he'd let him spend the odd night here with Rob, supposedly doing paint jobs. Once they'd brought a couple of girls back, student nurses from Saint Thomas's a year or so older than themselves, a major coup at the time. He had an idea it was Rob's first. It would have been Larry's, only *his* wouldn't let him go all the way. He'd spent most of the night trying.

In those days, all of this land on the north bank had been derelict, apart from a couple of bonded warehouses still used for storing wines and spirits. A fire had gutted most of the wharves in the 1930s and the rest had been flattened by bombs during World War II. Larry always remembered it as a dark, silent place, a backwater even when the rest of Docklands was thriving. Now it was a building site. Three new apartment blocks were nearing completion, with curved balconies overlooking the river and wooden decking to resemble a luxury cruise liner. The developers called it Hermitage Wharf after an old medieval retreat that had once stood on the site and they'd agreed to build a memorial garden dedicated to the Londoners who'd lost their lives during the Blitz. Larry doubted if the old mooring figured in their plans, though, with its scruffy little flotilla of rubbish barges and the old tug. He figured that pretty soon they'd be wanting them to move on and his dad would have something else to moan about. Old Scrooge, as Larry's Auntie Ethel called him, though not to his face.

Old Scrooge – the real Scrooge, not Larry's dad – had been in Larry's thoughts of late. Partly because it was the season for it but mostly because, whenever he returned to the mooring after dark, it put him in mind of the miserable old miser trudging back from his office on Christmas Eve, to his cheerless chambers and his thin gruel and the ghost of Jacob Marley.

Larry rubbed a hole in the condensation on the window of the wheelhouse and pressed his face up against the glass, making blinkers with his hands, so he could see out over the river to the south bank. Directly opposite were the lights of the Conran development at Butler's Wharf but over in Bermondsey it was darker, more like the waterfront he remembered from his childhood, except there were no ships. He thought of his dad and his Auntie Ethel sitting in front of the television in their flat on the Dickens Estate, just back of the river. Or maybe she was out walking the dog along the Bermondsey Wall, even in this weather, taking him out 'to do his business', as she put it, and looking out over the river to see if there was a light on in the tug. She didn't like to think of Larry staying there by himself. She wanted to put him up on the sofa bed in the living room but he resisted, telling her he was allergic to dog hairs. He was, too. It gave him symptoms similar to a bad cold. But this wasn't the only reason.

He knew she was worried for him, worried about him being alone, worried that he didn't have any friends he could stay with.

'I have plenty of friends,' he had told her. 'I just don't want to burden them at the moment, that's all.'

He had ended up snapping at her, which was presumably why she hadn't rung him for a day or two.

He was thinking about this when the phone rang.

But it wasn't Auntie Ethel. It was the woman from Crime Scene Restoration returning his call.

What was the precise nature of the problem? she asked.

Larry told her. He had not expected the solution to be simple and it wasn't. In the first place, she told him, she could not agree to anything on the phone. He would have to make an appointment and bring written evidence that he was the owner of the house along with a release note from the police.

'We don't want to be accused of cleaning up before forensics are through with it,' she told him – somewhat primly, he thought, but he had no objection to that. Prim was what he wanted. She sounded Scottish, too, which was also reassuring. It made him think of a competent housekeeper in a doctor's practice, or a presbytery. Then there was the question of payment, she said. He would have to pay for the initial 'survey' in advance – in cash or with a banker's draft.

'We have to assess the amount of work involved,' she said, 'and as I'm sure I don't have to tell you, this can often be a somewhat traumatic experience, hence the high premium, you understand?'

Larry said he understood, wondering where he had heard the voice before.

She asked him if the victim was a relation.

'No,' he said. 'A friend.'

'I see.' A small silence. He wondered if this made a difference. To the price perhaps.

'And I take it your intention is to move back into the premises?'

He told her he didn't know.

'The only reason I ask,' she said, 'is that in such cases many of our clients prefer a complete interior decoration – which is something we can arrange for you if you so desire. Is that something that you might consider?'

Her voice reminded Larry of someone but he couldn't quite put a face to it. There was something familiar about the phrasing, a certain delicacy of expression – and the way her voice rose on the last word of the sentence. He thought of the several Scottish women he had known but still couldn't place her.

'I'll think it over,' Larry told her and they fixed an appointment. The moment she rang off he remembered.

The waitress in the tea-shop in Peebles.

He was with Rob at the time. They had been filming in the area and were driving back to Edinburgh to catch the shuttle. They were in no hurry and Rob, who had been drinking at lunchtime, announced that he needed tea and cakes.

The waitress had been coyly attentive and there was a wide choice of teas on the menu. Larry had felt he owed it to the woman, and the establishment she represented, to be more than usually *selective*.

So he had selected Lapsang souchong, not because he particularly wanted it but because it sounded sufficiently exotic to reward their obvious endeavour.

But there was no Lapsang souchong.

(*Lapsang souchong's off, dear*, Rob had said, enjoying the discomfort of both Larry and the waitress.)

Larry, of course, had been mortified for her but she swiftly recovered her poise.

'I think you'll find Orange Pekoe very refreshing for the time of year,' she had told him. 'Is that something you might consider?'

Rob had been delighted. It had made his trip. On future occasions when offering Larry an alternative – usually the lesser of two evils – he would add, in his simpering version of the waitress's Peebles accent: 'Is that something you might consider?'

CHAPTER FOUR

The Used Women

IT WAS THE FIRST meeting of the book club since the night of the murder.

'She can't possibly want to talk about *books*,' Liz had said, phoning Jo to discuss their strategy.

But Jo wasn't so sure. Jo knew Meg of old and her immense capacity for what Meg's mother called 'displacement activity'.

'It's the only thing that keeps me sane at the moment,' Meg had said. 'Losing myself in a book.'

Jo sat down in Meg's kitchen and watched her carefully while she opened a bottle of wine. Meg wasn't wearing any make-up and her hair needed washing but she still looked beautiful. She looked less like a grieving widow, Jo thought, than a schoolgirl in a sulk, but then Jo could often see the schoolgirl in Meg, even at thirty-seven.

Put a brave face on it, girls, the nuns used to say to them at school. Sod that, they used to think. For them, being miserable was an act of subversion.

Jo drank her wine in silence, waiting. She'd assumed that the reason Meg had asked her to come over early was because she wanted to talk about something in particular, before the others arrived, but if this were the case she seemed to be in no hurry to begin.

'Where are the girls?' Jo asked, after a moment.

'Mum's taken them for the weekend. She said they needed a change of scene.'

Then she was crying. Jo went to her and put her arm round her and held her.

'I know, I know,' Jo crooned.

Thinking, almost at the moment of speaking, that it was a very strange choice of vocabulary in the circumstances. Given how little she knew about anything at the moment, not least the true nature of Meg's feelings on the subject of her husband's violent death.

But whatever her own feelings she would be upset for the girls.

Rob had been a good father. Ironic, thought Jo, that a man could be so foul to women, so accomplished a *user* of women, and yet so good with his own daughters, so keen for them to stand up for themselves.

When Meg had blown on a tissue and dabbed at her eyes, Jo asked her if she'd thought about Christmas.

'Rob's parents want us to go down to them,' Meg told her. 'Same as always.'

Jo shook her head in despair. 'What? As if nothing's happened?'

'You know his father,' Meg said.

'It will be awful,' Jo said.

'I know.'

Well, *do* something about it, Jo thought. Put your foot down, for once. Do what *you* want to do.

It was not the first time she had thought this of Meg. But all she said was, 'What do the girls think?'

'Sophie thinks we should ignore Christmas. She told me she doesn't want any presents. She said she couldn't bear to open them. I don't know about Kate. She hasn't said anything. This is the first year she's stopped believing in Santa Claus.'

Jo thought she was going to cry again but she tugged at the black ribbon that tied her hair back, shaking it loose so that it fell down around her face. Drawing the curtains. She used to do this at school sometimes when she'd been told off for something or other. You'd see her sitting there behind that veil of hair and never know if she was laughing or crying.

'What about you?' Meg said. 'Are you going back to Boston?'

Jo had her ticket booked for the 19th. It felt like a betrayal.

'If I don't do Thanksgiving I always do Christmas,' she said.

She had a sudden fantasy of taking them with her, Meg and the girls. Walking along the shore on Cape Ann. Hard rocks and a harsh wind and the waves grinding up the shingle, scouring away all the grief and the pain – and the guilt.

'Mum wants us all to go down to Cornwall with her,' Meg said. 'She's rented a big house on the cliffs with some friends.'

'You should go.'

But Jo was already thinking about flights to Boston, wondering if she could find them somewhere to stay this close to Christmas. It would be good for all of them.

'No thank you,' said Meg. 'Can you imagine it? She'd have us walking along the beach every day, wrapped up against the cold. "Come on, girls, this is just what you need." I think I'd rather be with Rob's parents.'

The phone rang from somewhere inside the house and she went off to answer it, leaving Jo to contemplate the grim possibility that after the best part of a lifetime trying to be as different as possible from her *own* mother she had ended up like Meg's.

Meg's mother – the Termagant, as they had called her since their adolescence – was a successful businesswoman, an organiser of international conferences and a writer of self-help books. She was also a bully. She had bullied her former husband until their divorce – he had gone off with a younger woman – and she had bullied Meg and her sister all their lives.

But she had always liked Jo. She *respects* you, Meg had told her once. She thinks you've made something of your life. The implication being that Meg had not.

Jo filled her wine glass and cast her eye over the interior of the kitchen.

Meg had become a creature of the kitchen. It was her private domain, her den, just as for some women it is the bedroom, or the bathroom or the garden. (In Jo's case it was a close contest between the bathroom and the study.) It was a large kitchen with a terracotta tiled floor and a Welsh dresser and an Aga and one of those cast-iron things hanging from the ceiling like something in a medieval dungeon, hung with the instruments of torture.

Jo's mother would love a kitchen like this.

Oh stop sneering, Jo scolded herself, stop *condescending*. It was a fine kitchen. It even had books – and they weren't *all* cookery books. You could almost call it a study with an Aga. Meg read books here, at the kitchen table, head down, shutting out the world with that curtain of pale-blonde hair. Shutting out all the bullies who tried to make her do things she didn't want to do, be something she didn't want to be.

As long as Jo had known her, people had tried to bully Meg. They bullied her because she was beautiful and good-natured. A fatal combination. Even Jo felt like bullying Meg sometimes – the wilful Cinderella who *will* not go to the ball. *Leave me alone*, she'd have told the fairy godmother, *I'm happy where I am.*

Slowly, year by year, Jo has seen Meg wrap herself up in this kitchen. Wrap it around her, like an invalid who surrounds herself with the necessities and the indulgences of her proscribed existence – the drugs, the books, the flowers, the chocolates – so she doesn't have to move or make an effort. You look around the kitchen and you see what Meg is – what she was, even what she could have been. A framed photograph of her directing a shoot when she was at film school – where she had met Rob; a couple of watercolours she had painted when she was pregnant with Sophie and been persuaded to have framed. The three Victorian champagne flutes left from the set of six Jo had bought her as a wedding present – had she thrown the rest at Rob, Jo wondered, or smashed them in despair when he hadn't come home at night? Jo hoped it was the former, but thought the odds were against it. The hand-painted dishes Meg had bought in Amalfi where she went with Jo during what she called a 'trial separation'. (It was significant – Jo had thought at the time and did now – that she had bought a dinner set during a trial separation.)

Jo stood up and carried her wine glass over to the cork-tile notice-board where Meg kept the ongoing record of her life: the telephone numbers and invitations, the bits of useful and useless information, postcards and photographs . . . an open scrapbook of memories and memorabilia.

Among the postcards were two that Jo had sent her a long time ago, both from art galleries. The first one she'd sent – it must have been while they were both at university – showed two young women in ball gowns: healthy, rosy, well-upholstered young women with an air of slightly self-mocking assurance. One of them, the older, more confident-looking of the two, had one hand resting on the top of a large porcelain vase, the other was clasped around the other's waist, as if she was cupping her drooping breast. On the back of the card it said: *Ena and Betty, Daughters of Asher and Mrs Wertheimer, John Singer Sargent, 1901.* Jo had sent it to Meg as a joke, an ironic comment on their social pretensions at the time. For a while they had called each other Ena and Betty.

The other had been sent a few years later, not long after Meg was married. It was a detail of a painting by Degas called *Absinthe* and it showed a woman sitting next to a man in a bar. The man had a glass of beer in front of him and a pipe in his mouth and he was looking away from the woman, out of the picture. The woman had a glass of absinthe in front of her and she was looking at nothing in particular, or at something deep within herself, something that touched the heart of despair. She was probably much the same age as the older of the two daughters of Asher and Mrs Wertheimer but in the downturn of her features and the slump of her shoulders you could already see the tug of the grave.

Jo had sent this as a joke against herself – she had been dating some pretty awful men at the time – she had never intended that it should be taken as a comment on Meg, or her marriage. You only had to look at the photographs of Meg to see how different she was from the woman drinking absinthe. But Meg had clearly taken it as such. And if you put the two postcards together, as Meg had, they could be seen to be making a statement about expectation and actuality that seemed deliberately personal and desperately sad.

There were photographs of Rob here, too. Rob and Meg together, Rob and Meg with the two girls, and a few more of Rob on location with a film crew. Jo was looking more closely at one of these when Meg came back.

'Is this Larry?' Jo asked, without turning round.

She sensed Meg behind her.

'Yes.'

'Have you heard from him yet?'

'No.'

There was something in the way she said these two words – yes and no – that made Jo turn to look at her.

'You'd think he'd have been in touch,' she said.

'Why?' Sharp, almost a snap.

'Well, to say how sorry he is. To see you. To see the girls. I mean, given how *close* he and Rob were.'

Meg turned away and started to pour a packet of nuts into a bowl. That seemed to be all they were having to eat. Pistachios.

'Maybe he's ashamed,' Meg said.

'Ashamed? Why should he be ashamed?'

But she knew at least one reason why he might be ashamed. Meg spoke with her back turned.

'Oh come on, Jo. Do you think he didn't *know*?'

'Know what?'

'That he was with someone.' She turned round and Jo saw the anger now, undiluted by grief or any other sentiment. 'You don't give someone the key to your house when you're not there without asking what he wants it for.'

But was she angry with Larry – or Rob? Or both of them?

'And it wasn't the first time, by all accounts.'

Jo was frightened – by her anger, or something else?

'By whose account?' she said.

They heard the front-door bell.

'Will you get that?' Meg said. She let the curtain of hair fall down.

They had arrived together. When Jo opened the door they looked startled, as if they had been surprised in some illicit transaction. Liz was carrying a bottle of wine and Amy a bunch of flowers and Jo had the absurd idea they were hiding behind them. Sometimes, when Jo saw Liz and Amy together, she thought of the 'lame' fox and the 'blind' cat in *Pinocchio*, the confidence tricksters who tempt the wooden boy with dreams of fame and fortune and sell him to a travelling puppet theatre. Not that they were ill-intentioned or even cunning, but they had the same air of mischief about them, of having a secret agenda. *Hey diddle de dee, an actor's life for me*. Tonight they looked like the fox and the cat after they'd been *found out*. Jo loved Liz. She even had a soft spot for Amy sometimes. But she didn't really *know* either of them, she didn't know what was going on in their heads. They hugged Jo like the mutual survivors of an earthquake or some other natural disaster and Jo led them through to the kitchen and watched them hug Meg the same way. Then Liz picked up the book on the table, as Jo had.

'You cannot be serious,' she said.

She still had her coat on. She had a bottle of wine in one hand and the book in the other and she wore an expression of pained incomprehension, like a drunk at a bible reading. Or the member of a Used Women's Book Club, Jo thought, who has lost the plot.

The Used Women's Book Club was Jo's idea. The title was not. The title was a mistake: a typing error, Jo insisted, though there were those who suspected a measure of intent, even if it existed solely in the subconscious.

For many years she and Meg had swapped novels. Or rather, the novels that Jo was reading were invariably acquired by Meg.

'What are you reading at the moment?' Meg would ask, and the conversation would follow a well-charted route of explanation and appropriation satisfying to both parties. Talking about books was as much a part of their friendship as talking about their friends and families – perhaps more so, because they were on safer ground.

It was only when Meg started lending Jo's books to other friends, notably Liz and Amy, that Jo raised a mild objection. Jo liked to get her books back. They were a part of her life. They had become a part of *her*. The characters in them were the grown-up equivalent of the dolls and cuddly toys and imaginary friends of her infancy, as real – sometimes more real, certainly more understood and often better liked – than the people she encountered in her own life. She did not want them to disappear for ever or to return, after a long absence, looking like something the cat brought in.

'What do they *do* with them?' she would demand of Meg when she surveyed the mangled remains of what had once been a pristine paperback. But she knew what they did with them – the evidence was on the pages. They spilled wine on them or dropped them while reading in the bath (Amy); they left them overnight on a heap of compost or used them to swat wasps with (Liz). Only Meg could be trusted to treat them with the respect they deserved. Amy and Liz treated books like men they wished to be revenged upon.

It was Meg who came up with the radical idea of taking turns to buy the books, though she requested that Jo, to whom they all deferred in matters of literary taste, provide a list of the books she considered worth buying. It was Liz – recently divorced and obsessed with imposing a new structure, a new formality on her life – who suggested that they also take turns to host a regular supper evening at which the said books could be exchanged and debated. And it was Jo who typed out her first list under the heading *Women's Used Book Club* and e-mailed it to her three friends. Except that when the e-mails arrived the heading read: *Used Women's Book Club*.

Jo swore that it must have been changed by malign spirits in cyberspace but when she looked in her 'Sent Items' there it was, just as she had typed it. Meg thought it was deliberate. Liz thought it was wonderful. On her own initiative she had it printed up as their letter heading.

'She means "used" in the sense of "second-hand",' Amy assured Jo, who expressed her doubts about the choice and was not overly reassured by the explanation. Besides, she had a suspicion that to Liz it meant a lot more than 'second-hand'.

'So?' said Liz.

'It's *irony*,' said Amy, as if Jo didn't know what irony was, or that it could be double-edged at times.

So there it was. They were the Used Women's Book Club.

Like the Prayers for Pardon, Jo thought – the four sad sisters created by Zeus to alert mortals to the dread consequences of infatuation, blind folly and delusion. *Lame, wrinkled things with eyes cast down*, whose sole purpose is to warn: Look at us; avoid our fate.

Jo was distressed, not only that they should accept such a description of themselves, even *ironically*, but that they should consider *her* to be a member of the same club. *They* might think of themselves as having been used and abused by the men in their lives but they could hardly say the same for Jo. Or could they?

It was even more distressing – when she put this question to herself – to conclude that they could – and probably did.

The thing that qualified Jo for membership of the Used Women's Book Club was her marriage.

Jo's marriage, like the title of the Used Women's Book Club, was a mistake. In her more confident, light-hearted moments she would describe it as a whim, inconsiderately indulged, swiftly regretted, painlessly abandoned, a foolish but ultimately harmless fancy comparable to that of the teenager on her seventeenth birthday – or the senior citizen on her seventieth – who fulfils a frivolous ambition to go bungee jumping. At other times she compared it to a disease, one of those childhood afflictions that recur more virulently in later life, like shingles.

'I caught it from a book,' she would say, mysteriously, and change the subject.

When Jo was a child her mother had warned her about the germs she could catch from reading other people's books. Jo's mother imagined the unwashed and contaminated fingers turning the pages, the germs mingling with the sweat and grime in some toxic ferment that was imbibed by the pages, saturating their fibres, a dormant virus waiting for the next unwary reader.

Jo's mother was not a frequenter of public lending libraries. She would not have become a member of a Used Book Club.

While never, even as a small child, endorsing her mother's opinions on the spread of diseases – or indeed on any other subject of note – Jo conceded that there *were* some things you could catch from books and one of them was Love. Or to be more precise, the desire for *Romantic* Love. There was nothing wrong with this, of course, in its place, but it could sometimes cause complications. It could sometimes recur in later life – like any childhood disease – in the more virulent form of Infatuation, accompanied by its terrible sisters, Blind Folly and Delusion.

Jo had first caught the disease at the age of ten from a novel by Georgette Heyer called *The Convenient Marriage*. She was captivated by the stammering heroine, Horatia – not least because as a child Jo, too, had a stammer – and by the dashing, supremely sophisticated hero, the Earl of Rule. (The Earl of Rule remained a model of the romantic hero for Jo well into her teens and even when she was older she would often – with a pretence of self-parody – submit her own and her friends' lovers to the simple test: how did they compare to the Earl of Rule? The answer was invariably not very well.)

Between the ages of ten and twelve, Jo read every book by Georgette Heyer that she could lay her hands on. Then she graduated to Jane Austen. In swift succession she read *Pride*

and Prejudice, Emma and *Sense and Sensibility*. She had since
read that the novels of Jane Austen were basically Mills & Boon
written by a genius. At the age of thirteen, Jo's own verdict was
that Jane Austen was Georgette Heyer without the schmaltz.
She had later attempted more detailed appraisals but this, she
considered, was the definitive word on the subject. 'Never mind
the social comment, the irony, the piercing observation,' she
would tell her students, 'Jane Austen wrote a bloody good
love story.' Jane Austen made romantic love *real*. And she
did a nice line in romantic heroes, too. Darcy, Mr Knightley,
Colonel Brandon. They weren't quite the Earl of Rule but their
flaws made them more lovable, more attainable.

The main thing Heyer and Austen's heroes had in common, Jo
thought, besides extreme wealth, was that they were *solid*. They
were not flaky. They might condescend at times, they might be
a little lacking in a sense of humour, a little hard on frivolity,
but when the chips were down, when your father was a bit short
of the readies, your mother an imbecile and your younger sister
ran off with Sholto the Shagger, you could trust them to rally
round with a helping hand, twenty thousand a year and a large
estate in the Peak District.

In her paper on the *Victorian Literary Hero*, Jo had written:

> It has been said that Jane Austen's heroes have that affliction
> known to the British as 'a poker up the bum'. To me, as an
> American and an Anglophile, this is less of an affliction than
> an attribute. It speaks of consistency, integrity, dependability,
> a sense of honour. Call me old-fashioned, but I am of the firm
> belief that a degree of stiffness is a good thing in a man . . .

When Jo had first presented this paper the last line had brought
the house down. Jo had been gratified but slightly surprised at
the level of hilarity until a friend had explained the ambiguity
in the word 'stiffness'. Jo had been mortified and even more
distressed that the laughter had entirely obscured her own

intended punchline that the one thing that neither she nor Jane Austen could stand in a man was *looseness.*

Which made it all the more surprising, all the more ironic, all the more *tragic*, that Jo had chosen of her own free will to marry a man as selfish, as capricious, as dishonourable, as flaky and as *loose* as Michael Geraghty.

One of Jo's small vanities, when she was feeling particularly pleased with herself or with something she had written, was to script the conversations that her friends and family, students and fellow tutors had about her when she was not present. But this was accompanied by the suspicion that whenever her modest achievements as academic, writer, critic and woman were discussed among her circle of intimates, someone or other, sooner or later, would raise the question of her marriage. At which point there would be a collective sigh of regret, a rueful shaking of heads. Even a woman like Jo, they would agree, not without satisfaction, could find herself hitched with a man like Michael Geraghty.

Jo had not suffered as her fellow members of the Used Women's Book Club had suffered. She had not been bullied and humiliated as Meg had been. She had not been robbed blind and left for a younger woman as Liz had. She had not been beaten, turned out of doors without a stitch of clothing or subjected to unspeakable sexual practices, as Amy claimed to have been on several occasions by several successive partners. She had not been *Used*, not at least to the same extent. But she *had* been damaged. She had been diminished. She had lost faith in her own judgement – which was as important to Jo as faith in herself. She had earned her membership of the club.

They gathered at the table in Meg's kitchen, waiting for someone to start. Normally, they'd all be chatting away about this and that, pouring wine, eating nuts and olives, dipping into dips, until whoever's turn it was to host the meeting would call them to order and then they'd launch straight into the discussion. But not tonight.

Tonight it felt more like a seance, Jo thought, than a book club. Any moment now, Meg was going to ask them to join hands.

Jo glanced covertly around the table at her fellow members. Liz was staring at the back of her right hand where she'd grazed the knuckles – gardening, Jo thought, or hitting someone; it could be either with Liz. Amy was dabbling with her finger in a small puddle of red wine that she had spilt while pouring. Meg had her head down, staring at the closed book on the table in front of her, a book they should by now all have read (they had moved on from sharing the same book – the original *purpose* of the club – and now they all purchased a copy. Unfortunately, in Jo's opinion, they stuck to the original *name* of the club).

Meg looked at Jo.

'I'm interested,' she said, 'in why you chose this for us.'

Jo was suddenly wary. She had chosen the book for *herself* for a number of reasons, not least because of the author, but she had chosen it for *them*, she supposed, because of its heroine – or anti-heroine – Emma Hamilton.

Emma Hamilton was a famously *Used Woman*. She could have been their mascot, their figurehead. Born a humble blacksmith's daughter, she had progressed from prostitute through kept woman to wife of Sir William Hamilton, the British Minister to the royal court of Naples in the late eighteenth century and the Volcano Lover of the book's title. Emma was the trusted friend of the Queen of Naples and a leading hostess in what was then the second largest city on the continent of Europe. Then she met Admiral Lord Nelson and became his lover.

As the mistress of England's greatest hero, Emma became immortal. She also became – in her lifetime – the most grossly caricatured woman in Europe, an object of ridicule and hatred, and a gin-sodden wreck who ended her days in a cheap boarding house in Calais where she had fled to escape her debtors.

Jo was both repelled and fascinated by Emma Hamilton.

During her time in Naples, she had supported one of the cruellest and most corrupt regimes in Europe. When the people rose up against their rulers, she urged her husband – the Ambassador – and her lover – the Admiral – to support a Royalist Terror that subjected thousands of men, women and children to appalling scenes of slaughter, rape and torture.

Why? How *could* she? A woman whose background and experience should have put her firmly on the side of the oppressed, to ally herself so totally with their oppressors? These were questions that tormented Jo, perhaps because she feared the answers.

> Another talented, overwrought woman who thought herself valuable because men she could admire loved her. Unlike her husband and her lover she had no genuine convictions. She was an enthusiast and would have enlisted herself with the same ardour in the cause of whomever she loved. I can easily imagine Emma Hamilton, had her nationality been different, as a republican heroine, who might have ended most courageously at the foot of some gallows. That is the nullity of women like her.

Thus had Sontag described her, in the voice of her true heroine, the revolutionary and poet, Eleanora de Fonseca Pimentel – who was as much a role model for Jo as Emma was not.

Was it shame? Did Emma, the used woman, finally turn – not on her oppressors – but on those like Eleanora who dared to challenge their oppression, and in so doing revealed *the nullity of women like her.*

> I sang my song and my throat was cut. I saw beauty and my eyes were put out. Perhaps I was naïve. But I did not give myself to infatuation. I did not drown in the love of a single person.

Eleanora and Emma, the two faces of woman? Discuss.

Jo could have said all of this and more. In another place, at another time, she might have. But not now.

Now she said, 'I don't know. I've forgotten.'

'I suppose,' said Meg, 'you identify with Eleanora and you see me as Emma.'

The charge was so unexpected, so *challenging*, Jo could find no immediate words of denial. As she sat, stunned, searching for the words of rebuttal and confronting the terrible fear that Meg was *right*, Liz spoke.

'You cannot seriously expect us to talk about this,' she said. 'Not now.'

Meg looked at her for a moment and then she stood up and walked out of the room.

They sat there at a loss.

Then Liz said to Jo, 'You'd better go and talk to her.'

'I don't know,' said Amy. 'Maybe she's best left alone.'

Slowly, reluctantly, Jo stood up but before she could move Meg swept back in, as abruptly as she had left, and dumped herself down in her chair. Jo almost expected her to fold her arms as she had when she was a child in sullen defiance of teachers or nuns or parents.

'All right,' she said, 'as you obviously don't want to talk about books, let's talk about Rob.'

As if that would teach them. That would make them sorry they'd interfered with her agenda for the evening. But Jo knew that Meg didn't want to talk about Rob, any more than she wanted to talk about books. Not really.

They all looked at her. She looked at them, from one to the other.

'I was thinking of having a memorial service,' she said, 'as they won't let me bury him.'

Silence for a moment. Then Liz said, 'I think that's a very good idea.' She looked around the table with evident relief. 'Don't you think so, Jo?'

'Who won't let you bury him?' Amy said.

'The police.'

'Why not?'

'Apparently, they hang on to the body for a while,' said Meg as matter-of-factly as if it had been a book she'd lent them. 'In case they have a suspect and the defence want to conduct their own post-mortem.'

'*Do* they have a suspect?' Amy asked.

Meg appeared to consider this. 'Only me,' she said. She looked at their shocked faces. 'Well, they always suspect the partner. I mean, if it's the wife who's killed they always suspect the husband, so I suppose if it's the husband . . .'

'How could they suspect you?' asked Amy. 'Given that you were with *us* at the time.'

Now, Jo thought, *if you're going to tell us at all, now is the time.*

'So, where shall we hold it?' Meg said. 'Any ideas?'

Later, when Jo was leaving, Meg followed her to the door.

'I wanted to ask you something,' she said. Jo nodded, waiting. 'I was wondering if you'd mind telling Larry. About the memorial service.'

Jo had run through a number of things that Meg might want to talk to her about privately but not this. She could think of nothing to say.

'He should be invited,' Meg said. 'Given they were so close. He might want to say something.'

'About what?'

'About Rob. At the service.'

'But I don't know Larry. Why don't you invite him yourself?'

'I just don't want to talk to him at the moment.'

Meg held out a scrap of paper.

'This is the number of his mobile.'

Jo sighed. 'All right,' she said. She took the paper. 'Of course I'll tell him. And Meg . . .' She held her arms out to her. 'I never for a moment thought you were like Emma Hamilton.'

'Liar,' said Meg. But she hugged her all the same.

CHAPTER FIVE

The Cleaner

THE CORPORATE HEADQUARTERS OF SOCARE (Crime Scene Restoration) Ltd were above a video-rental shop in Camden. Larry speculated that the two businesses were linked by more than the same address. Judging from the recent releases in the front window, they could certainly have shared the same promotional material. They did, however, preserve separate entrances. SOCARE's was distinguished by a brass nameplate, a plastic speaker next to the bell, and a surveillance camera. Larry rang the bell twice before the speaker responded with the single interrogative 'Yes?'. A woman's voice. Larry gave his name and the door opened to reveal a small hallway and a narrow staircase.

Larry went up the stairs and entered a kind of lobby or waiting room, not much bigger than the hallway, but with a small sofa and two upright chairs and a table covered with what looked like trade magazines, neatly arranged, and a copy of the *Financial Times*, prominently displayed. (The *FT* troubled Larry – and would continue to trouble him vaguely throughout the forthcoming interview, like the odd one out in a Spot the Odd One Out picture in a child's comic. Later still, he would worry that he had spotted only *one* Odd One Out, with so many others staring him in the face, as it were.) There was a window, overlooking the street, and a door – directly opposite the stairs – with another brass nameplate that read *M. Hoffman, Director*. Larry was wondering whether to sit down or to knock on this door when it opened and a young woman emerged. She had blonde shoulder-length hair and an unseasonable tan which was probably fake but applied with expertise. She was attractive enough for him to pull in his stomach.

'Mr Hunter?' she enquired. A *serious* enquiry, as if he might have been substituted between the front door and the top of the stairs.

He confirmed that it was indeed he.

'Please come in,' she said.

Larry entered the inner office. She shut the door and gave him her hand.

'Muriel Hoffman,' she said.

Her married name, presumably, unless there was a Clan Hoffman in some obscure region of the Highlands that Larry hadn't heard about yet. She was younger and smaller than her voice had indicated. (Larry had imagined a *big* woman.) She was in her mid- to late-thirties, he judged – with surprisingly large breasts for so slight a frame. She wore pale-blue jeans and a white T-shirt with an illustration that, at first glance, appeared to be from Aubrey Beardsley's *Lysistrata*. There was also a logo that Larry couldn't quite make out without staring overlong at her breasts which he did not want to do.

Larry noted another surveillance camera high in one corner behind her desk. One on the front door and one in the office suggested an above-average level of paranoia to Larry but perhaps in the Crime Scene Restoration business you had to deal with the kind of clients that *made* you paranoid. He wondered if she had colleagues in an adjoining room watching the monitors, ready to rush in if there was a problem. Or perhaps they were down below in the video-rental shop. Larry did his best to reassure her – and the hidden watchers – with his relaxed manner, though in truth he was far from *feeling* relaxed. Mostly this could be attributed to the peculiar nature of his visit but the T-shirt didn't help.

. . . ball me for . . . ugh girls . . . able . . . defecate, he read,

as he reached to place a copy of his mortgage agreement on the desk.

'I brought the documentation you wanted,' he said. 'The police said they'd fax you direct with the clearance.'

Ms Hoffman confirmed that everything appeared to be in order as far as the paperwork was concerned. Perhaps he could take her through the relevant circumstances, she requested.

Larry considered what might, and might not, be considered relevant.

'Well, the . . . *victim* was staying at my house,' he said, 'in Spitalfields.'

'And I take it you were away at the time?'

'Yes. I came back the next day. He was in the kitchen.'

She nodded. He noticed that she had some newspaper cuttings on her desk and wondered if they were of the murder. *His* murder.

'Stabbed to death,' she said. 'I believe.'

'In a manner of speaking,' Larry said. The word *stabbed* – even with the addition of *to death* – seemed inadequate, somehow.

He could read more of the lettering on her T-shirt.

. . . *game for rough girls, suitable . . . boys . . .*

'So it's just the kitchen area?'

'And in the hall. The police think he was attacked when he opened the front door.'

He realised he was staring directly at her breasts now and that she could hardly fail to have noticed.

'I'm sorry, but what *does* that say?'

She sat up straight and put her shoulders back, holding the T-shirt so he could read it.

Football
is a game for
rough girls,
not suitable for
delicate boys

'Oscar Wilde,' she said.

She swivelled round in her chair so he could see the back.

Wilde, it read, with a number 8. In pink.

'Do you play?' he asked her, adding, with some embarrassment if perhaps unnecessarily, 'Football?'

'No,' she said. 'But I'm a Chelsea fan. At least since I came down to London.'

'Right,' he said.

'And you?'

'No,' he said. 'I used to but . . . no, not lately.'

'So, the kitchen and the hall.' She wrote it down. 'And it's mostly bloodstains?'

'Yes. There was a bit of, you know, tissue and that, but I think the police took it away with them, most of it.'

'And nowhere else in the house?'

'Well,' he said. 'The police think they might have used the shower.'

She looked up from the pad.

'The shower?'

'To wash the blood off.'

'*They*?'

'*He*. Whoever.'

'Strange thing to do,' she said.

'Well, he'd have been covered in blood,' Larry explained.

'Yes but . . . I mean I can understand him having a wash, hands and face and that, but a shower . . . Don't you think that's strange?'

What seemed strange to Larry was that someone should hack his friend Rob to death in the hallway and kitchen of his house. Having a shower afterwards seemed normal, at least in comparison. But he knew why she was looking at him in that way. She was thinking it was the kind of thing you did if you *lived* in the house.

The police had looked at him like that, too.

One of the reasons Larry hadn't been to see many of his friends since the murder was because he didn't want *them* looking at him like that.

'Well, I just think they found traces of blood in the shower, that's all, or traces of *something*, and I'd like to be sure there aren't any left.'

'Of course,' she said, and made another note on her pad. 'We always put something down the drains in any case,' she said. 'Just to be thorough. It's the thought of what might be down there that often distresses people.'

She had a sympathetic professional manner – rather quaint and old-fashioned for someone who was not on the wrong side of seventy. He was concerned that she should not consider him too delicate – either to play rough games or to stand in a shower recently used by the killer of his best friend to wash off the blood. He was reasonably confident he could cope with living in the house – drains and all – he told her, but he had a six-year-old son . . .

'And I don't want to expose him to something so . . .' He could not find the word for it.

'Gross,' she supplied.

Gross would do.

'I quite understand.' She held his glance for a second longer than was comfortable and he had an idea she had made some kind of judgement about him. 'And does he know what happened there?'

Larry shook his head.

'And your wife? Does she have any views on the subject?'

'We're divorced,' Larry told her, though he was aware that this in no way answered the question. The truth was he did not know Ruth's views on the subject.

'I understand,' Ms Hoffman said again. She, too, was divorced, she told him, but there were no children.

'My ex would not have considered this a suitable occupation for a woman. I am aware that many people feel the same way. They wonder how on earth a woman such as myself can do such a thing.'

It had followed directly on her divorce, she said, leaving him wondering for a moment if she had intended it as some kind of therapy. But no, she meant it was a way of earning a living.

'Not that it came to me immediately,' she said. 'When I started the agency it was more general – domestic and commercial, that kind of thing – but then I read about this line of business. It's getting very big in the States; they have their own lobby. The American Bio-Recovery Association. I went to their conference last year in Vegas. As an observer.' She pointed to a framed photograph on the wall. 'That's me with some of the delegates. We're nothing like so advanced over here. It's a niche market, of course.'

She had long been on the lookout for a niche market, she said, though it wasn't simply a business decision. She did think they performed a valuable social function, a *service*. It was asking a bit much of the family to expect them to clean up after a loved one had been murdered in their own premises and she had never been what you might call a squeamish person. When she was younger she had always wanted to be a nurse.

'But I married young and alas it was not to be. He was in the meat trade. All his family are.' She reflected on this, as if it had been something she should have thought about more carefully at the time. 'I'm a vegetarian now, of course. Well, it would be hard not to be in this business.'

'You go out yourself then . . . to the scene?' Larry blundered a little late into the space she'd left for him. He was having problems keeping up.

'Oh yes,' she said firmly. 'Oh yes. Never expect anyone to do something you won't do yourself. I don't mind telling you, the first one I did, I was sick. I cried. It was seeing the pictures of the family; that's what gets to you. Of course, the protective clothing helps. And I've a very good team, very professional. You've not seen our brochure . . . ?' She slid it across the desk to him and he studied it dutifully. Muriel Hoffman figured prominently in a number of different outfits. She succeeded in looking fairly alluring in all of them. 'Fourteen staff on call, twenty-four hours a day, seven days a week. And we use the very latest technologies – chemicals, detergents, enzymes, insecticides . . .' She noted his reaction with approval. 'Oh, believe you me, some places you need it. You throw in the bug bomb and in you go, over the top. It's no place for sissies.'

'Bug bomb?' he said.

'For the bugs,' she said. 'There's always bugs. But it's much worse in the summer. You shouldn't have much of a problem with bugs. Unless you left the central heating on. I take it you're not living there at the moment?'

Larry confirmed this was the case and told her about the boat. She could contact him on his mobile number, he said, but she seemed reluctant to bring the interview to an end. She asked him how did he find living on a boat at this time of the year.

'Cold,' he admitted. No bugs. Only rats. He didn't tell her that. It seemed inappropriate to be flippant and he did not think she would take it well. But there was a stove, he told her, and even a shower. And he belonged to a nearby gym where he could use the facilities.

'A gym,' she repeated. 'You work out?'

Her eyes, once more, seemed to appraise him.

Muriel Hoffman, too, was the member of a gym. The same chain, they discovered.

'But I've never been to the one in Cousin Lane,' she said. 'Does it have a pool?'

Larry confirmed there was a pool. He was thinking that they were getting a bit off the subject. Divining this, she resumed her professional manner.

'If I could just take a few personal details,' she said.

Larry wondered how these might differ from the personal details she already *had*.

From among the papers on her desk she produced some kind of a form.

'Age, occupation, marital status, that kind of thing . . .' She smiled a little coyly. 'I can fill in the bits I already know.'

He told her his age was thirty-nine and his occupation art student.

She looked up from the form.

'Before that I was a television cameraman,' he said. 'But I gave it up.'

He thought for a moment she was going to pursue this further but she looked down at the form again.

'Average monthly income?'

'Nothing,' he said, adding, 'I'm living off savings.' He didn't tell her about the money from the Murder Walk. He took the envelope out of his pocket with the cash advance she had asked for and put it on her desk.

She glanced briefly at it but didn't pick it up.

'You should be able to claim it on your house insurance,' she told him kindly. 'Or, if you're eligible, you can apply for a grant from Victim Support.'

Would he want to be there for the survey, she asked, or would he just leave them the keys?

'I'll meet you there,' Larry said. He hesitated and then added, 'But I may not want to come in.'

'I quite understand,' she said again.

They arranged another appointment, outside the house, at eleven-thirty on Monday morning.

Outside, he hung around for a moment to gaze in the window of the video shop. His first impression had been correct. It was entirely stocked with horror and gangster movies. In the latter, Larry recalled, a contract killer was often referred to as a 'cleaner'. He saw that he was being watched by two men from inside the shop. Muriel Hoffman appeared beside them. She saw him in the window and waved. Larry waved self-consciously back and turned away.

CHAPTER SIX

Wives and Lovers

THERE WERE VARIOUS ARRANGEMENTS for the hand-over. Usually it was the school playground. Sometimes, in the summer, they met at the swings. In the winter, at the local leisure centre. The one place they did not meet, ever, was the place they had once called home.

In the five years since their divorce, Larry had not once been back to the house he and Ruth had bought together when she was pregnant with Ben and where she now lived with Ben and her new husband, Oscar.

Larry acknowledged that this was inconvenient at times. He accepted Ruth's charge that his refusal to meet the man who, like it or not, was his son's stepfather was, to say the least, unhelpful. He had no answer to this, none that stood up to any modern test of mature and responsible parenthood. All he could do was point out that Ruth had only once been to his house in Spitalfields, presumably to inspect it for vermin, and left with indecent haste. It was as if neither of them was willing to confront the reality of their lives without each other. So they met on neutral territory, no man's land.

This Friday it was the leisure centre. Larry arrived first and sat alone in the miserable coffee bar with his undrinkable coffee. This was his least favourite of the venues for the hand-over but he accepted that he had no right to object – any more than he had a right to object when his wife chose to have an affair with another man – but he didn't have to like it, he didn't have to *approve* it.

The reason Larry felt he had no right to object to his wife's adultery and subsequent remarriage was that he had brought it on himself. From the moment that he had proposed he had been running away from her.

One step forward and two steps back . . .

Larry had met Ruth in Palestine, or the West Bank as they called it then, meaning the land occupied by Israel to the west of the Jordan River. She had been a field worker with the Save the Children Fund and he was covering the uprising of the Palestinians known as the intifada. The first intifada. He had fallen in love. Not for the first time, admittedly. Uniquely, however, when he left, he found he could not rid himself of the sensation. In fact it was worse. He wrote to her. They spent a long time speaking on the telephone. He rang her from hotels in other battlegrounds and sometimes from his flat in London. Finally he went back – on holiday, because the belligerents had called a truce and, temporarily at least, had no need of his services. He stayed at the American Colony Hotel in Jerusalem, his favourite hotel in the world. They were having lunch there, on his last day, when he asked her to marry him.

It was not something he had planned.

They were sitting in the courtyard of the hotel, which had once been a Turkish pasha's palace. There were palm trees and flowers and a fountain. There were lizards, darting in and out of the sun. And there was a cat – one of those half-starved, half-wild street cats that had somehow found its way into what was normally a cat-free zone. Ruth was feeding it surreptitiously under the table. This would not have been encouraged by the Swiss management but Ruth was a cat lover. She could not see a cat without wanting to take it home. Larry wasn't so keen. He didn't dislike cats as such but he sometimes thought they should re-assess their position in the scheme of things. He was beginning to dislike *this* cat intensely. Irrationally, he saw it as a rival for Ruth's affections – or at least a distraction, mewling in on what might be their last lunch together.

It had been a wonderful two weeks but it did not seem likely that their relationship would survive a long separation. This made him sad. On the other hand he did not think he was ready for the alternative. Two weeks was too short, a lifetime unthinkable. And yet the occasion seemed to call for some kind of a statement. The story needed an ending, even if it was not a happy one – he was sure his proposal would be rejected. He never seriously considered any other possibility. He imagined a time in the distant future when Ruth would dangle a child on her knee – her granddaughter – and tell her that once, a long time ago, a man had asked her to marry him in Jerusalem.

But she said yes. She looked a little surprised but she said, 'Yes, if that's what you want.'

It seemed to Larry, thinking about it later, that this was a strange answer.

Not as strange as the fucking question, Larry's friend Rob had said when Larry told him this, *in the circumstances*.

Even Rob, who knew Larry of old, thought that Larry's thinking on this occasion had been especially woolly. Larry admitted that he hadn't thought it through. He stressed the influence of his sadness and sentimentality and the added distraction of the cat. Rob acknowledged that the cat could have been the significant factor. As he put it, *nothing else makes any sense*.

After lunch Larry and Ruth had returned to their room to make love. Later, Larry left her sleeping and went to the pool. He swam for a while and then sat at a table with a beer thinking about what had happened. A young woman appeared wearing a bathrobe which she removed to reveal a fine body in a bikini. Larry did not consciously watch her but he knew she was there. She piled her hair on her head and tied it in some kind of a knot – she didn't have a bathing cap – and lowered herself into the water and swam carefully with her head up. Larry did watch her while she was swimming but he was really thinking about Ruth. Ruth would have dived in, he was thinking, and swum in a fast crawl with her head down, even without a bathing cap. But then the woman climbed out of the pool and, aware of his interest, shot him a familiar look as she sat with long brown legs dangling in the water, pulling her long blonde hair free of the topknot and shaking it so that it fell around her bare shoulders. And Larry had thought, *What have I done?*

It wasn't that he was a womaniser, like Rob, he told himself, it wasn't that he wanted every good-looking woman he saw – or thought he could *have* every good-looking woman he saw – but he didn't want to exclude the *possibility* of having them. And the one thing that could be said to his credit, he thought, was that he never for a moment thought he could have them after he had asked someone to marry him. The problem, as he acknowledged, was that he felt so depressed about it.

They were married in Hampshire, where Ruth's parents lived. Ruth had worked a transfer to the London office, and Oscar – her new boss – was one of the guests at the wedding. Larry remembered him as being somewhat withdrawn, which he put down to shyness. Physically he hadn't made much impression on Larry except that he had dark hair and pale skin and there was something rather catlike about him, a soft, heavy cat somewhat running to fat. Ruth was clearly fond of him. She felt sorry for him, she had told Larry, because although he was good at his job and seemed sure of his position in the scheme of things he was really quite vulnerable – and he was not very happy in his marriage. Perhaps, even then, Larry knew there was something between them. Nothing sexual, not then, but *something*. Possibly he was over-sensitive to such matters. Larry's mother had left his father – and therefore Larry (he always put it in that order) – three years after their marriage. He was aware of feeling vulnerable himself, less aware perhaps of the walls that were going up all around him.

Rob was the best man. He made a speech. Then Larry did. They were both funny speeches. There was a demand for Ruth to make a speech but she wouldn't. She was shy of public performance, a private person. Foolishly, Larry tried to persuade her and she rebuked him sharply: '*You* might not mind making a fool of yourself but *I* do.'

Larry was shaken. So much so he had to go off for a while and walk by himself in the darkness outside the hotel where the reception was being held. I don't know this woman, he thought. I have married someone I don't know. But this did not worry him half as much as the thought that he had married someone who could hurt him with a few sharp words.

After a little while he began to think more reasonably. He thought of the things he or Rob had said in their speeches that might have hurt *her* and conceded that it was not inconceivable that some of them had. Later, she apologised, saying she had just panicked at the idea of being made to speak and said the first thing that came into her head to make him back off. He knew that he had been over-sensitive. But he became convinced that she thought him a clown, a buffoon. A lovable clown perhaps, but still a clown.

Most of her friends, he had discovered, were serious. Oscar was serious. No one would ever call Oscar a clown. Over the next few months Larry noticed himself acting more and more *clownishly*. He couldn't seem to help it. It was almost as if he was standing in the audience watching himself perform. He couldn't stop the performance any more than he could explain it. Ruth kindly thought it might be a release from the tension of his job. Larry knew it was something other than that but he accepted the excuse. The current battleground was Bosnia and Larry was spending weeks there at a time.

When Ruth discovered she was pregnant, he was in Sarajevo. He was away for most of the pregnancy. He didn't have to go. He could have had time off; he could have changed jobs. Rob's view was that Larry hated being married so much that, all things considered, he'd *rather* be in Sarajevo. But Larry knew he didn't hate being married, not as such, he just hated feeling vulnerable. He felt less vulnerable in Sarajevo. Sarajevo wasn't *personal*, at least not to him.

He was home for the birth.

It was a Caesarean and Larry stood by Ruth's head holding her hand while they cut her. She'd had an epidural so she couldn't feel anything – though she said later she could feel the knife if not the pain – and they had put up a small screen over her abdomen so she couldn't see what they were doing to her. Larry could see the baby coming out but Ruth could not. They lifted it free of the gash they had cut in her abdomen. It looked red and raw and appeared to be bleeding. Larry thought it looked like the infant Alien bursting out of John Hurt's stomach. The first thing that was recognisably *human* – that Larry noticed – were its balls. They seemed overlarge. It was all head and balls. Then they handed it to him. He only held it for a moment before he passed it to Ruth but in that moment he was lost. The walls had come crashing down. He went back to Bosnia but he was a changed man. He was already planning ways of changing his life.

When he came back Ruth had started her affair with Oscar.

Larry did not say anything but he *knew*. He knew as soon as she met him at the airport. How is it you always know? You doubt your own perception, you put it down to all kinds of insecurity, but you know. He said nothing for several months, even when she spent nights away – at conferences – and he knew she was with Oscar. When he finally challenged her she curled herself up into a huddle on their bed, a foetus. She was raw and bleeding, too, but Larry didn't see that.

'What are you going to do?' she said.

'I'm going to leave you,' he told her.

'If you loved me,' she said, 'you wouldn't say that.'

She was right. He hated himself for saying it and even worse for meaning it.

'I love you,' she said. 'You know that, don't you?'

He did know that but it didn't stop him from leaving her. His friends thought he was crazy. Even Rob, who thought he was crazy to get married in the first place, thought he was even crazier to walk out on it just because she had an affair. He listed the advantages of staying:

'A, there's Ben, B, there's the house and C, there's Ruth who's going to be so riddled with guilt from now on you'll be able to screw whoever you like.'

This, to Rob, constituted the perfect marriage.

Larry told him it was some working-class thing. This was always the way to shut Rob up. You don't put up with that kind of thing in Bermondsey, he said. You thump the bloke or you leave the wife, maybe both. Even if you get the worse of it, even if it hurts you more than in hurts them. Male pride, male ego, you can't do anything about it, mate, it's your nature.

He reminded Rob of the story about the scorpion and the frog.

'The scorpion wants to cross the river but it can't swim so it asks the frog for a ride. Fuck that, says the frog, you'll sting me. But the scorpion says, Don't be fucking stupid, if I sting you I'm going to drown. So the frog takes the scorpion on his back and halfway across the river the scorpion stings him. And just before the paralysis sets in, the frog says, Why did you do that? Now we're both going to die. And the scorpion says, It's my nature.'

Rob was confused.

'So who are *you*,' he said, 'the scorpion or the frog?'

Rob thought the scorpion was always the woman.

'It's just your vanity that's hurt,' he said. 'Get yourself laid a few times, you'll feel better about it. It will restore your sense of perspective.'

Larry acknowledged that vanity played a large part in it, though the word 'just' seemed a little inappropriate, especially coming from Rob. But it was also the question of forgiveness. It wasn't that he couldn't forgive Ruth for fucking Oscar, he told himself. It was because he couldn't forgive himself for being in a position where a man like Oscar could fuck *him*.

To Larry, Oscar was like one of the cats Ruth wanted to

bring home. And home he had come, while Larry was away, purring sympathy, support, sincerity – most of the words Larry associated with Oscar began with the letter S – easing himself into the places that Larry, in his vanity, had expected to be exclusively Larry's.

In truth, and as he later admitted to himself, Larry knew very little about Oscar. He didn't want to know about Oscar. He didn't want Ruth telling him that Oscar had been unhappy, vulnerable, needy – as if Larry was none of these things and this counted against him. All he knew was that Oscar had padded into his life and left his cat's paws all over it. He had rewritten the story of Larry's romance just when Larry had worked out the happy ending.

Larry knew his feelings about Ruth were confused, ambivalent, downright perverse at times, but he had no such doubts about his romance with her. He had *loved* his romance. He had loved the feeling of being in love and he had particularly loved the feeling that she was in love with him. Then she had fallen in love with Oscar. It didn't matter to Larry that this was a 'temporary weakness', as she had put it, or that she herself had been particularly *needy* at the time. 'Where *were* you?' she had said tearfully.

You take one step forward and two steps back.

Larry knew she was right. But at the time, all he could think of was that she had conspired with this man to wreck their romance. Not their *marriage* – that could have survived, even become stronger, maybe, if he had let it. But their *romance*, or at least Larry's perception of it, was destroyed for ever.

Since then, of course, people had told him how he had brought it on himself. They had practised their psychobabble on him and in truth it wasn't difficult. He had tested her to see if she would abandon him – as he felt his mother had abandoned him. He had made it very difficult, some said impossible, for her to pass the test. He had practically *forced* her to have an affair and then refused to have her back again when she clearly wanted to come back.

On the whole Larry agreed with this analysis. He had come to terms with what had happened, he told himself – and anyone else who cared to ask. Sometimes he was even embarrassed by how much he had cared about it at the time. It was as if it had happened to a different person. He hated the memory of how he had behaved – when they were married and when they were breaking up – but he hated more the memory of the nights he had been at home with Ben knowing that Ruth was with Oscar. That was why he never wanted to go back to the place that had been their home. He did not want to be reminded that it had happened to *him*.

They arrived in a bustle of coats and scarves and hugs and excuses, their cheeks cold against his. While Larry fussed over Ben he felt Ruth's eyes scanning his face, searching for damage.

'I got a new pair of swimming trunks,' Ben told Larry. 'They're red and they've got a frog on the side, diving.'

Ben had been able to swim since he was four but he still had classes. Ruth wanted him to be a *better* swimmer. They both did. They wanted him to be able to keep swimming even after the scorpion stung him. Normally, when they met at the leisure centre, Larry would pick him up after the class. They only met *before* the class when he and Ruth needed to talk – usually about Ben.

Larry took him into the men's changing room and watched him while he changed into his new swimming trunks. Ben's balls had long since shrunk to insignificance, or possibly his body had outgrown them, Larry was never quite sure how it worked.

'Are we still going on the boat?' Ben asked.

'Yes,' said Larry. He had told him about the boat on the phone. He had said his house was being redecorated and they needed to stay somewhere else for a while. Ben knew they couldn't stay at Larry's father's house because Larry was allergic to dog hairs. He never asked why Larry couldn't stay at Ruth's house but he might have thought he was allergic to Oscar.

'Is it going on the sea?' Ben asked.

Larry told him no, it was staying on the river.

'I can do two widths now,' Ben said, 'without putting my foot down.'

Larry wondered if this betrayed an anxiety. 'That's very good,' he said.

'So if I fall in I'll be fine, won't I?'

'Fine' didn't sound quite right to Larry, it didn't seem like the word a six-year-old would naturally use. It sounded like a word he had overheard an adult use after another adult had raised an objection. *Don't worry, he'll be fine.* So who had done the objecting – Ruth or Oscar?

'You'll be fine,' said Larry, 'but you won't fall in.'

When he had left Ben with the swimming instructor Larry joined Ruth in the public gallery above the pool. It was as good a place as any to talk about his best friend's murder and better than some, better than the coffee bar anyway. The splash of water and the echoing shouts of the swimmers effectively drowned their own more intimate dialogue.

'You look better than you sounded on the phone,' she said.

He thanked her. She looked beautiful, he thought. She always looked beautiful when they met. He wondered if she made a special effort. *Of course she makes a special effort*, Rob had assured him. They might not want *you* but they sure as hell want you to want *them*.

The demon voice in his ear – or his head. Larry heard it as clearly now as when the speaker was alive, with its rasping note of sarcasm – or irony – or *wonder* that anyone could be quite so naïve. Death had not blunted its edge. There was no sign yet that Rob would sink gracefully into the silence beyond the grave. Perhaps because he wasn't in a grave. He was in some frozen drawer of a police morgue with a tag on his toe.

She asked him if he'd heard any more from the police.

'Only about the weapon,' he said.

'They've found it?'

'No, but they think it might have been some kind of a hook.'

'A *hook*? Oh my God.'

'Well, *curved* like a hook. Or a fish gaff . . . or a scythe.'

She covered her face with her hands and he warned her that Ben was looking at them. He waved to reassure him.

The instructor had them sitting on the edge of the pool. He was teaching them to dive. Ben was not as tall as some of the boys but stockier than most. He was at ease with his body. He looked like he would not be an easy child to break.

'They wanted to know if I had anything like that in the house,' Larry said.

'And *did* you?'

'I don't know. I might have. But it's not there now. They've searched the place from top to bottom.'

'You might have?'

He sighed. 'I think I did have one once. A bale hook. It was my dad's. He used it when he worked down the docks – to haul bales around. All the dockers did. They stuck the hook through the bale and heaved it on to their shoulders.' He looked at her. 'Do you remember me having a hook?'

She shook her head. She was looking at him with an expression in which he recognised elements of horror and disbelief. It had become familiar of late and was not confined to Ruth.

'I vaguely recall seeing it somewhere,' he said, 'but I can't remember whether it was *after* I moved to Spitalfields or before.'

He might have been talking about some tool he had mislaid, he thought, something he found useful for the odd bit of DIY.

He watched Ben stretch out his arms and tuck his head down and fall into the pool. His first dive. Or the first Larry had ever seen him do. Seconds later his head came bobbing up. As soon as the water was out of his eyes he looked up at the gallery. Larry gave him the thumbs up.

'Are you worried they might think it was you?' Ruth said.

It was a question you could interpret in several different ways. One of them was: '*Was* it you?'

'Not exactly,' he said. 'They're bound to think it was me.'

'Why?'

'Oh come on, Ruth. It was in *my* house and *I* found the body.'

'But – what possible reason could you have had for killing Rob?'

'He told Alice Oakley I fancied her,' he said.

'What?'

Larry shook his head. 'I'm sorry. I don't know why I said that.' Alice Oakley had been in their class at Bermondsey Comp. She had the biggest tits in the first year. Rob had fancied her, too.

Ruth was looking at him with concern.

'Are you all right?' she said.

'No,' he said. 'Not really.'

'You're probably still in shock,' she said. 'Finding him . . . like that.'

'I loved him,' he said. 'He was my best mate.'

'I know,' she said. She took his hand in both of hers and began to rock slightly backwards and forwards on the seat as if she was rocking a baby. He knew she had never liked Rob.

'I feel as if I betrayed him,' he said.

'In what way? It wasn't *your* fault.'

'I always watched his back.'

'Even when he was with some woman?'

He said nothing. He kept his eyes on Ben in the pool.

'You couldn't help what happened, Larry.'

But he'd been watching Rob's back since they were kids. Just as Rob looked out for him. If Larry had his eye pressed to the viewfinder, filming what was going on in front of him, Rob always watched his back.

'I just keep thinking I let him down,' he said. 'Especially . . .'

He didn't know if he should say this, even to Ruth. 'We weren't getting on so well lately.'

'You hadn't fallen out with him?' He detected the note of alarm.

'Not exactly.'

'You weren't seeing the same woman?'

It was like a sixth sense. She let go of his hand.

He shook his head. 'It wasn't that. It was more about women in general. It's like he knew I wasn't on his side any more.'

He had once told her – just before they were married – that whatever happened he and Rob always knew they were on the same *side*. And Ruth had said, 'And we're the enemy, I suppose.'

Now she said, 'You were never *really* on his side. Not in *that* war, at least.'

'I was once,' he said. 'But I changed.'

'And that's why you think you betrayed him?'

Larry shrugged.

'So where *were* you at the time?' He knew that she would have been thinking about this – maybe even talking it over with Oscar – and that she was trying to keep her voice light.

'On the boat,' he said.

'By yourself?'

'Unfortunately.' And then, because she might misinterpret that, 'So I can't prove it.'

Surprisingly she didn't ask him what he was doing alone on his father's boat on a December evening.

'Do they know exactly when it happened?'

He nodded. 'They think so. His watch was smashed. The hands were stuck at a quarter-past seven.'

'His watch?'

'I expect he was warding off a blow,' he said.

'Oh God, Larry.' She put her hand up to her head, shielding her eyes the way she did when she was praying in church.

Then, after a moment, she said, 'Have you spoken to Meg yet?'

'Not yet.'

'And you still haven't any idea who he was meeting?'

'No.' Naturally, when he had first called Ruth and told her about the murder, she had asked him what Rob was doing in his house when Larry wasn't there. Larry had told her that Rob had been using it to meet a woman. Like the police she seemed to have difficulty believing he hadn't any idea who the woman *was*.

'I wonder if Meg knows,' she said.

'Why wouldn't she say?'

Ruth had no answer to that but after a moment she said, 'If he had to meet this woman at your place it suggests she couldn't take him back to hers. So she must live with someone.'

'You think he found out and came round instead?'

'Or followed her,' said Ruth, 'and caught them together.'

Ben shouted something up at them that they couldn't hear. They both smiled and waved.

'How does he feel about the boat?' Larry asked.

Ruth wasn't clear what he meant, or pretended she wasn't. But Larry knew she'd be worried about Ben going back to the boat. She didn't like the river. She'd heard talk from Larry's father of the currents that dragged you down and spewed you up five miles from where you'd gone under. Of the diseases you caught from rat's piss. Other things. Larry had told her it was more dangerous to let Ben play in the park, with all the dogs that were about, and the paedophiles – Battersea was a bad area for both, he maintained, with no evidence whatsoever – but he wasn't sure she was convinced and nor was he. They passed the child back and forth like a priceless piece of porcelain, terrified that one of them was going to drop it. Whenever the phone rang and Ben wasn't with him, Larry always thought it was going to be Ruth with the news he dreaded. He had imagined all the scenarios, rehearsed all the scripts. He knew she had a long list of her own.

'I thought he might be a bit apprehensive,' he said.

'He's been on it before, hasn't he?'

'Not to sleep on.'

'Well, I think he's all right.' He could tell she was being careful with her words. 'He's a bit . . . anxious at the moment. He senses something's not quite right. Kids always do. I told him Rob had died, by the way. Not . . . how he died or anything, just . . . I thought I should.'

'What did you say happened to him?'

'I said he was in a fight. It's sort of true, really.'

'Did you say where?'

'No. I thought I'd leave that one to you.'

Thank you, he thought.

How do you tell a six-year-old child your best friend was butchered in the kitchen where he has his Weetabix in the mornings? Larry didn't know if he was ever going to be able to tell him that.

'He'll be quite safe on the boat,' he said. 'It's not as if it's going anywhere.'

Larry had grown up on the waterfront in the early 1960s when the river was still full of ships and the docks full of dockers. Charles Dickens may not have known it, after the Blitz, but he'd have known the faces hanging around the pubs and the back alleys. When he was a kid, Larry knew at least three dead ringers for Bill Sikes and his school was full of Artful Dodgers. Larry knew the river was dangerous and the riverside worse but he had no fear of either. This was his adventure playground, then and now.

But it was different for Ben.

Larry would have preferred to take him back in daylight – the first time, at least. In daylight it was trendy Docklands, nothing to worry about. Tourists taking snapshots on Tower Bridge, the old sailing ships in St Katherine's Dock, the Dickens Inn, a stroll through history. In daylight, even the old mooring at Hermitage looked picturesque. But not in the dark.

Larry paused at the top of Hermitage Stairs with Ben on his

shoulders and viewed the mooring as a child might. A haunted harbour filled with shipwrecks and the ghosts of dead mariners. Larry wished now he'd not told him the story of Captain Kidd, hanged in chains on Execution Dock until the body was covered by three tides – to make sure he was dead. Or of Hanging Judge Jeffreys, who sat on the balcony on the pub over the river and watched the condemned men dangling and thrashing there while the waters rose. Safe stories they'd seemed in the house in Spitalfields or eating ice-cream on a summer's day over on the Bermondsey Wall; not so safe now with a loose rope tapping in the wind like bony fingers on a coffin lid and a lone water hen keening in the darkness.

The tide was out – they'd have to go down the steps to reach the barges.

'It's easy enough,' Larry assured the boy as he took him down off his shoulders. 'It just looks a bit more scary in the dark.'

Ben said he wasn't scared but Larry saw him looking down at the river and saw it briefly through a child's eyes, a slick black beast lapping at the bottom steps.

For once he was glad Ruth wasn't with them.

'I'm a bit worried about Monks, though,' Ben said.

He was clutching one of his toy animals – a monkey called Monks – and Larry wondered if he should put it in the backpack. There wasn't a lot of room. He said he thought Monks would be all right if Ben kept tight hold of him. Larry had a backpack on his shoulders with Ben's things for the weekend and the fingers of his right hand were hooked through a plastic bag with the fish and chips he'd bought for their supper. He'd left the stove drawing to keep the boat warm for them when they got back. Or they could sit up in the wheelhouse and eat straight out of the newspaper wrapping while they watched the lights on the waterfront. But first they had to get there.

Larry switched the plastic bag to his left hand and took Ben's hand in his right. The deck of the first barge was level with the sixth step down and the gap between them was no more than two or three feet. Larry lifted Ben over with one hand locked into his armpit and set him down gently on the deck. A few roosting gulls took off into the darkness, shrilling their complaints. Ben gave a yell and raised a hand to shield his face as he cowered away.

'It's only seagulls,' Larry told him.

'I don't like birds,' Ben said. There was a break in his voice.

This was a surprise to Larry; he'd never heard this one before.

'Well, they've all gone now,' he said.

He took the boy's hand again and led him across the barges. The difficult bit was the gap between the last barge and the jetty. Larry had lashed three planks together to make a proper gangway for the boy but when he edged it into position it still seemed narrower than he would have liked.

There was a scuffling in the hold of the barge.

'What's that?' Ben said.

'Just a rat,' Larry told him, thankful again that Ruth wasn't here. He stepped on to the gangway and tested it for movement. It felt firm enough. He stepped back on to the barge and told Ben he wanted him to walk in front of him on to the jetty. It seemed safer than the pair of them shuffling across holding hands. Ben appeared hesitant.

'There's no birds left, is there?' he said.

'Honest to God, there's no birds,' Larry said. 'You saw them all fly away.'

But he was wrong. They were halfway across when Larry's phone rang in his coat pocket. He did not try to reach it but it distracted him for a moment. And in that moment, maybe triggered by the sound, a lone gull, too careless or cussed to leave with the others, screeched a raucous protest and launched itself from the shadows. Ben made his own noises and turned to run. It would have been funny in daylight on a beach. He crashed into Larry and bounced off into the dark gap between the barge and the jetty.

CHAPTER SEVEN

Sleeping Beauties

JO LEFT HER NAME and number on Larry's voicemail and asked him to ring her back. She didn't know if he would remember her. They had met only once, at Rob and Meg's wedding. Or so she had been told. Jo herself had no recollection of the encounter.

You talked to him, Meg had insisted. *You took his tie off. You said it didn't suit him and you rolled his trousers up to his knees.*

If this was true, it must have been stimulated by a considerable amount of alcohol. It was not the sort of thing Jo would have done sober. She wondered if Meg was confusing her with Amy. It was much more the kind of thing Amy would do, drunk or sober.

You said he was gorgeous. We thought you'd hit on him.

But Jo would have remembered *that*, however brief the encounter. She could never have been that drunk, surely, not even in her early twenties.

In the pictures she'd seen of him he had a beard. It comes and goes, Meg said, a bit like the man himself. He was a television cameraman who worked a lot with Rob, usually on foreign assignments. But now he had given up the camera, apparently, and become an art student. He seemed pretty old to be an art student but, like his friend Rob, there was a suggestion that he'd never quite grown up.

'Why won't she speak to him herself?' Amy said.

'Because she's pissed off with him,' Jo said. It was better not to explain too much to Amy whose indiscretions were legendary.

'But she wants him to go to the funeral?'

'Apparently so.'

If you could call it a funeral without a body. You probably called it a Celebration of his Life or something, Jo thought.

'I suppose *we'll* have to go,' said Amy doubtfully.

'Yes,' said Jo firmly. She didn't want any backsliding from Amy. Not that Amy was much use in the role of Pillar and Support for the Bereaved. Jo just didn't see why *she* should wriggle out of it when everybody else would have to go.

'What if she makes a scene?' said Amy.

'Meg won't make a scene,' Jo told her, with an assurance she was far from feeling.

For an actor, Amy was strangely nervous of 'scenes' if they occurred in real life. The only other actor Jo had known well – her husband, shortly to be ex-husband, Michael Geraghty – had relished them.

They were in the Actors' Centre in Covent Garden, not a regular haunt of Jo's, but Amy was a member and it was conveniently close to Birkbeck where Jo had lectures on Fridays.

'I just *have* to talk to you,' Amy had insisted on the phone. But as usual when there was something *desperate* she needed to talk about she would lead you up several false trails before you realised exactly where she was taking you.

Although they saw quite a lot of each other, Amy was not a close friend. She had come second-hand, as it were, on the back of the Used Women's Book Club, introduced by Liz who was herself a friend of Meg's.

Jo had her doubts about Amy's oft-expressed passion for literature but as a Used Woman she appeared to have the best membership credentials of them all. Men used Amy the way Amy used books. For the first few pages they couldn't put her down and then they suddenly lost interest or turned into violent critics. The plot got too complicated for them, or too silly. They left her in hotels or airports or railway stations. They discarded her, face down on a bed, crumpled and tearful. And sometimes they threw her across the room.

Jo was wary of the glib assertion that Amy was a woman who *invited* abuse but she certainly seemed attracted to men who went in for a bit of physical from time to time.

And yet . . . Jo was not entirely convinced by Amy in the role of victim. She suspected – without a shred of evidence – that Amy gave as good as she got. And that the men often ended up being more damaged than *she* was by the relationship, at least mentally.

Amy was an actress by nature as well as by profession. You could never be confident that her love – or friendship – was based on true affection or on the supporting role you had been allocated (or as likely a seat in the stalls) in whatever 'real life' drama she had currently scripted for herself. You might not hear from her for weeks on end – her attendance at meetings of the Used Women's Book Club was erratic – and when you did it was often because of a particular need she had at the time of calling, usually emotional. This 'neediness' was hard for Jo to resist – and Amy was always endearingly grateful for the support and advice you gave her, even if she frequently took the opposite course from the one you had recommended.

Amy was impulsive. She suffered from frequent rushes of blood to the head. She developed sudden, intense passions – for people, places, fashions, food . . . the list was a long one – and equally intense dislikes. She was invariably engaged in some obscure and complicated feud, usually with another actor, or a director or stage manager.

Jo had few illusions about Amy – she was hopelessly unreliable and totally self-obsessed – but whenever anybody else pointed out these shortcomings Jo invariably had a good word to say for her, even if it was simply 'insecure'. Geraghty, who claimed to despise Amy, said this was because she always told Jo what she most wanted to hear about herself. That she was the Goddess of all the Virtues. Jo the Good, Jo the Wise, Jo the Beautiful.

'She reinforces your good opinion of yourself,' he told her snidely.

Which was probably a useful social function if you lived with a man as devastating to the morale as Michael Geraghty.

Even so, Jo was increasingly wary of being cast as Amy's Oracle.

She sat with her at a table in the corner of the bar and toyed with a mineral water until Amy revealed what it was she wanted to talk about. It came out a good deal quicker than usual. Amy wanted to talk about Meg.

'How does she seem to *you*?' she wanted to know.

'Bereaved,' said Jo unhelpfully.

'Not – angry?'

'I don't suppose *she* knows at the moment,' Jo told her. 'Certainly *I* don't.'

'She hasn't talked to you, then – about what he was doing that night?'

'Well, she knows he was seeing a woman. Or, at least, that the police think he was seeing a woman.'

'But she doesn't know who?'

'No.'

'Where did she think he was, then?'

'Where he *said* he was. In Darlington. Doing a recce for some film.'

'Yeah, sure.'

'Well, why not?'

'Because . . .' Amy shook her head impatiently. '*No one* goes to Darlington. I mean, you might as well come right out with it and *say* you're screwing someone.'

Jo felt too uninformed – too much of an outsider – to comment. Her knowledge of the North of England, outside the realms of literature, was uncertain, to say the least.

They were both silent for a moment. Then Amy said, 'It's funny to think of us all being together when it was happening.'

'Why funny?'

'Well, just the idea of it. You know. Talking about some book while he was being . . . I mean, I suppose it's lucky really.'

'Lucky?' *Funny, lucky*?

'Well, if we hadn't been with her – I mean, if Meg hadn't been with us at the time – the police might have thought it was *her*.'

Jo wondered for a moment if Liz had said anything to her. She looked carefully into Amy's eyes, as if there was the slightest chance they would reveal what was going on inside her head. Amy's eyes stared guilelessly back. Violet eyes, like Elizabeth Taylor, with long dark lashes.

That was as much, and as little, as you could say about them.

'How could they have possibly thought it was *her*?' Jo said.

'Well, if she'd *known* . . .'

'I told you, she *didn't* know. Besides . . .' Jo had seen the photographs. The police had shown them to her, hoping, no doubt, to shock her into candour or compliance. The idea of Meg – even in rage – doing that to Rob, or anyone, was unthinkable. Almost.

'I'm not saying she's capable of such a thing,' said Amy, 'but the police are bound to think the worst, aren't they?'

'Well, as you say, lucky she was with us at the time,' Jo said. Her tone and expression conveyed a warning. There was no indication that it had been received, let alone acted upon.

'She did seem a bit strange that night, don't you think?'

'What do you mean – *strange*?'

'Well, a bit off.'

'Off?'

'Moody. Irritable. Even a bit – *hostile*.'

Jo shook her head. 'I didn't notice that,' she lied. 'She might have been a bit hostile to *you*,' she added, 'because you hadn't read the book.'

'I had read the book.' Amy went for aggrieved indignation but it didn't quite come off and she caught Jo's eye and shrugged. 'Well, most of it, anyway.'

'You didn't even bring it with you.'

'Honestly, Jo, you're not going to talk to me about books. God. Talk about school prefect.' She was much better at petulance – and she knew the accusation would sting. Jo hated being called a school prefect. She was aware she did, sometimes, act like one.

Amy looked at her watch. 'I've got to go,' she said. 'Jud's got me doing the walks again.'

Jo didn't know what she meant at first. Then it clicked. Amy's brother, Jud, was involved with some group of out-of-work actors – although they didn't call themselves that – who did historical tours of the city and he sometimes fixed Amy up with a job as a guide. She did the Bloomsbury Walk: a tour of the streets and buildings associated with Virginia Woolf and the Bloomsbury set. Jo had been on it once with Meg and Liz. A Used Women's Book Club outing. It had been rather good. That is, *Amy* had been rather good. A better guide, they had all agreed – not at all bitchily – than she was an actor. Amy had once played the young Virginia Woolf in a fringe production that they had also faithfully attended (as they did all Amy's performances). This had not been good – in fact it had been so unbelievably bad that even Amy had noticed – but it had sparked a lasting interest and given her a profitable sideline.

She had borrowed a couple of Woolf's novels from Jo – which Jo had never got back – and then immersed herself in the biographies. She now considered herself an expert, though Jo privately wondered if she had ever read more than the two novels she had borrowed – if, indeed, she had ever finished them. Jo had once heard Amy telling someone it was Woolf's *life* that interested her, not her *writing*. It had taken all Jo's restraint not to make the obvious retort. She sometimes felt she knew how Amy's lovers felt.

They parted outside the Actors' Centre and went their separate ways – Amy to join her group at Russell Square and Jo to return to her flat on the river.

*　　*　　*

Jo's flat was in a large modern block on a stretch of waterfront known as Jacob's Island, a half a mile or so to the east of Tower Bridge. When she had bought it – with her husband Geraghty – Jo had been favourably impressed by the information that the block in which it stood was on the site Charles Dickens had used for the murder of Nancy in *Oliver Twist*.

She had not, at the time, considered this ill-omened.

Now, returning alone after her meeting with Amy, Jo found herself thinking about her own role as a victim of male aggression.

Not that she had been assaulted physically – as Amy had by several of her lovers, or Nancy had by Bill Sikes. Geraghty's speciality was verbal abuse – and ever more refined degrees of mental cruelty. But it still made Jo feel that she had been a victim. And she despised herself for it.

It was ironic, she often considered, that she had met Geraghty for the first time shortly after the success of her book on the use and abuse of women in fairy-tales.

And she had failed to recognise him for what he was. The Wolf. Her own particular Wolf.

Naturally one of the fairy-tales that Jo had been told as a child was 'Little Red Riding Hood'. It was a particular favourite because it was said to originate in the forests of Bohemia, on the German–Czech border, where her mother's family came from. But it came in two versions. In the version Jo's father read to her – the *Hollywood* version, as Jo called it in her book – just as the wolf is about to gobble up the little girl, the woodsman rushes into the cottage and kills it with his axe. Then he cuts open the wolf's stomach and out jumps the little girl's grandmother, alive and kicking. Then Little Red Riding Hood marries the woodsman and they all live happily ever after.

But in the version Jo's mother told her – the *Bohemian* version – the wolf eats both the grandmother and the little girl and that is the end of them. No woodsman with his axe, no marriage, just a blood-soaked hood and a well-fed wolf. Jo's mother – who was born in Marienbad – assured her this was the *true* version and that it was meant as a warning, so that pretty little girls like Jo didn't stop to speak to strange men.

This was probably the first time that Jo realised there was more to fairy-tales than a good story. Years later, when she was a student, she discovered there was an even deeper meaning. The wolf, she read, represented female sexuality and by *surrendering* to it, the little girl brought about the death of her grandmother and herself.

Like most women of her generation, Jo was aware that fairy-tales had been used for centuries to produce what most men regarded as the right kind of woman. A woman who was beautiful, elegant, gracious, a little stupid and, above all, submissive, a woman who lived in the hope of marrying the right kind of man. Jo's own contribution to the subject was to show how the original tales – often designed to empower women – were twisted by a succession of writers to turn them into victims. Victims whose only chance of survival was to use their beauty, grace and submissiveness to hook a handsome prince, or the nearest equivalent.

Jo called her thesis *Sleeping Beauties*.

To Jo's surprise and gratification it was published to a degree of critical acclaim and for a while she became a minor celebrity, interviewed on TV and radio, and invited to give numerous readings to literary societies and women's groups. And at this high point in her life – single, independent, reasonably successful and with a cause to promote – she had met Michael Geraghty.

It was as if he had been tracking her all along, keeping his eye on her, running ahead of her through the forest, his red tongue lolling over his terrible teeth, waiting for her to arrive at the end of her journey: relaxed, off-guard, vulnerable.

There was, of course, a more rational explanation. That after ten years of dating fellow academics she was ready for something different – and Geraghty was certainly different – or that in the euphoria of her literary success she was ripe to fall in love. But either way, she now considered, she might have been a little more astute, a little more wary, a little less inclined to self-destruction than to fall in love with a man like Michael Geraghty. Let alone marry him.

The flat was what she had saved from the wreck. But it had cost her dearly. It was still costing her.

It would have made financial sense to sell it – pay off Geraghty – and find somewhere rather less exotic, and expensive. But Jo loved her flat. Or rather, she loved the location.

In Dickens's day, Jacob's Island had been a notorious sink of depravity. Bounded by a rambling stream – a filthy open sewer – that fed into the Thames, it had contained some of the worst and most overcrowded housing in London, a jerry-built rats' nest of slums piled up, one against the other, behind the wharves and warehouses of the waterfront. A thieves' kitchen, a fever swamp, a mockery of a refuge for the most destitute and desperate of London's immigrants: the Poles and Hungarians, the Russian Jews, the Slavs and Latvians, the Bohemians . . . The ones who hadn't made it and probably never would.

Now the best part of the site – the part along the river – was occupied by luxury apartments. Where the foetid waters of the sewer had once bred typhoid and cholera there was a landscaped water garden with elegant fountains, floodlit at night, and slatted wooden walkways winding through strands of bamboo and pampas grass. When Jo entered the brightly lit lobby she exchanged greetings with the night porter who sat before a bank of monitors linked to security cameras that scanned the surrounding area. From the windows of her second-floor apartment she could look out over the water garden towards the river and the lights of Wapping on the far side. Brought up in a series of US Air Force bases in Germany and East Anglia, Jo considered this the first place she had truly thought of as home; the main reason, far more than her job, more than her friends even, for staying on in London. In Jo's own private, romanticised story of her life, Jacob's Island was the place her immigrant ship had landed, where she had planted her roots.

When she shut the door behind her she kicked off her shoes, poured herself a glass of wine and sat in the window, with the light off, trying not to think of how little a time she might have left to enjoy it.

CHAPTER EIGHT

Playing in Duggan's Yard

LARRY LAY FULL-LENGTH ON the gangway. His phone was ringing but he didn't have a free hand with which to answer it. Nor was this a major priority. With his left hand he was holding the edge of the planks and with his right he was holding the hood of his son's coat. His son, judging from the weight, was still wearing it. With a bit of help from the Almighty and the L.L. Bean stitching he might stay wearing it for a little while yet. Larry judged that his feet would be just above the level of the water.

Slowly and with great care Larry began to haul him in.

He raised him high enough for the boy to grab the strap on Larry's rucksack with both hands and then Larry let go of the hood and seized him under the armpit. When he had him safely back on the planks he told him to crawl on to the jetty. Larry crawled after him. He didn't trust either of them to stand up.

When they were safely on the jetty he knelt and held the boy by the shoulders.

'Are you all right?' he said.

'Yes,' said Ben. 'But I dropped Monks.'

'Shit,' said Larry. He stood Ben as far from the edge of the jetty as possible and went back to have a look. The river was running like a millrace between the barge and the jetty. There was no sign of the toy monkey.

Larry returned to the boy and knelt down again.

'I'm sorry,' he said, 'I think he's gone.'

'Will he be all right?'

Clearly Larry should have been more explicit. But now he prevaricated.

'Probably,' he said. 'Monkeys are very good swimmers.'

He wasn't at all sure if this was true. He remembered taking Ben to a zoo where they had monkeys on an island in the middle of a lake – the obvious implication being that they could not escape by swimming.

It took a moment for Larry to recall that Monks was not a real monkey.

'We'll look for him in the morning,' he said.

'Where do you think he'll be?'

Dead Man's Hole, Larry thought, the backwater at the side of Tower Bridge where the jumpers were washed up by the tide. There had once been a morgue at the base of the northeast tower where they stored the bodies until they were claimed by relatives – or surgeons from the medical schools.

It was worth a look, anyway – but not until morning.

Ben was shivering, with cold or shock or both. Larry picked him up and carried him to the tug.

For once the stove had behaved itself and the saloon was blessedly warm. Larry sat the boy down and put his arm round him and held him tight.

'Bloody hell, Ben, I thought we'd lost you,' he said.

'Like I lost Monks,' said Ben. He looked upset now.

'It wasn't your fault,' Larry assured him.

'We'd better not tell Mum,' Ben said. Larry saw he was trying to fight back the tears.

'No,' said Larry. He kissed him on the cheek. 'Tell you what – I'll make you some hot chocolate to warm you up. And how about some cheese on toast?'

He had dropped the bag of fish and chips in the river.

Ben nodded.

'Good boy,' Larry said. He felt like crying himself.

Later, when Ben was asleep, Larry sat alone in the wheelhouse.

He had the lights off so he could see out on to the river. The tide had turned and he could hear the hollow booming sound the rubbish barges made when they banged against each other. There were times when he had found it a comforting noise – it had often lulled him to sleep – but not now. Now it sounded like the knocking of doomed sailors, trapped in a sinking ship.

He and Rob used to come here when they were kids. Not to the tug – which was a working boat then – but to this part of the docks. The whole area east of Tower Bridge had been razed during the Blitz and was still pretty much of a bombsite in those days and an ideal playground – for them, anyway. They didn't call it the Hermitage, they called it Duggan's Yard, after an old boatyard that was there. They would sit at the water's edge at the end of a summer's evening watching the sun go down beyond Tower Bridge. It was hard for Larry to describe how he had felt on those evenings. He knew he had not often felt it since.

It was forbidden territory of course. They were supposed to stay on the south bank, or – to delineate the precise boundaries of their mischief – between Tower Bridge and Rotherhithe. The river was the border. Crossing it was like escaping into Badlands, where they could hide out like the Wild Bunch, beyond the jurisdiction of the law. Once, late one evening, they had watched Larry's Auntie Ethel looking for them over on the Bermondsey Wall. Larry had felt sorry for her but he managed to hide it. Rob would have scoffed.

They were hard cases, all right. There wasn't a water rat in Wapping that could match them for villainy. The only thing that let them down was their accents. They both spoke 'posh'. Posh for Bermondsey, at least. This was because Larry had been packed off to elocution lessons at an early age by the aunts and Rob *was* posh – his father was the local vicar. Rob only went to the same school as Larry – Bermondsey Comp – because his father was a socialist and didn't hold with private education.

Larry's aunts blamed Rob for being a bad influence. 'He might be a vicar's son,' they said, 'but he's got the Devil in him, that one.'

Whatever Rob had in him it found expression in rebellion. He was at war with Authority, whether represented by his parents, his teachers or the lollipop lady who stopped the traffic for children to cross the road. *Women* in authority seemed to upset Rob most of all (even lollipop ladies). The one thing he could not stand, he told Larry quite early in their acquaintance, was being bossed about by a woman

The strange thing was – his mother was not at all bossy. In fact she was a bit of a doormat. Hopelessly out of her depth both as a vicar's wife and a mother. She let everyone bully her. Rob was an only child, conceived late, and it was as if the effort had drained her of all her remaining energy.

The first time Larry met her he thought she was Rob's grandmother. She was thin and frail and fretful. She pulled and picked at her clothes like a bird making a nest and whenever she could get her hands on him she pulled and picked at Rob – or Robin as she called him. Larry could see he didn't like it.

Rob's father, the vicar, looked a lot younger and he was certainly a lot more dynamic – it would have been hard not to be – but he was a self-contained intellectual whose idea of relating to young boys was to crack the occasional feeble joke and make awkward conversation about football or cricket. Mostly, if he was at home at all, he was holed up in his study writing the next sermon, or an essay for the Fabian Society, leaving the domestic arrangements and whatever parenting had to be done to Rob's mother.

Which was presumably why she became the Authority Figure – though it was difficult to imagine her ever putting her foot down.

To Larry, at age eleven, Rob's home life seemed infinitely preferable to his own. The vicarage was an old Victorian pile that had miraculously survived the Blitz. The first time Larry saw it he found it somewhat forbidding, all elbows and chins and chimneys and high attic windows like hooded eyes that seemed to be peering down at you from their lofty heights as if you were something nasty it had nearly stepped in. Years later, when they were old enough to see Hitchcock's *Psycho*, they called it the

Adams Motel. But by then Larry had come to love it. It had all the space and freedom his own home lacked and a kind of seedy gentility that he found strangely comforting, like the stuffy old leather armchairs and the old bookshelves with hundred of back copies of the *National Geographic Magazine*.

The two boys had the run of the place, with minimum interference from the old folk. The one thing Rob's mother could do well as a mother was make a good tea and to Larry, lacking a direct comparison and chafing at the more interventionist approach of the aunts, this seemed a perceptive analysis of the job requirements. Later he would form a different view.

In the first year of their friendship, before they found less innocent amusements, Larry and Rob would roll up from school at around four o'clock in the afternoon for sandwiches, buns, cakes and a suitable drink before Rob's mother retired for a nap, presumably in the rocking chair down the cellar. Then they would run riot for an hour or so until it was time for Larry to go home to the more frugal and disciplined world of the aunts.

It was not fair, Larry knew, to blame Rob for leading him astray. It was never a question of leader and led. Larry's father had it right when he commented, with weary acceptance, that they were each as bad as the other. He knew Larry needed no tutoring in perfidy. He was his mother's son.

Larry had been raised by his father and his father's sisters because his mother had left home shortly before his third birthday. Her name was Connie and she came to Bermondsey in the early 1960s to take photographs of the dockers. She was applying to go to art school, she told people, and needed the photographs for her 'portfolio'. Because she was young and attractive the dockers didn't put up too much of a fight about it.

Years later Larry found a few of the pictures she took of his dad. They were grainy and faded and she hadn't always got the exposure right but Larry could see why she had been attracted to him. He looked a bit like the young Albert Finney.

Larry was supposed to look more like his mother. He had seen a picture of her, too – just the one – taken a year or so later, when they were married. Auntie Ethel, who was the only member of the family to have a good word to say for her, insisted she was beautiful but it was difficult to tell from the black-and-white photograph Larry had seen. She looked better in colour, his aunt told him. She had red hair and blue eyes and a lovely smile, she said. But in the photograph, Larry thought she had a slightly foxy look. Something about the eyes, something about the lips – parted to reveal her teeth but not quite enough to call a smile – made Larry think of a cornered vixen. But this was doubtless his own colouring, through the tinted lens of hindsight.

She had left them in November 1963, a few days after the death of President Kennedy.

'She was very upset,' Auntie Ethel said. 'Out of all pro-portion.'

'I expect I was teething at the time,' said Larry, who was damned if he was going to be upstaged in his own life's drama by the death of a President.

So Larry lost a mother and gained two. As partners in parenthood the aunts were a perfect match. Auntie May looked after the practical things – like feeding him and clothing him and dosing him with Vitamin C when he had a cold. Auntie Ethel taught him to draw and to dream. And they both constantly told him what a lovely boy he was. Which was probably why – in spite of his mother and his father and his best friend Rob – Larry grew up loving women. The only problem, from a woman's point of view, was that he preferred them in the plural.

And the other thing was: he couldn't help wondering if he was so irresistible how come his mother could bring herself to leave him and never come back?

Larry was about nine or ten when he first began to wonder if she'd been murdered. Not necessarily at the time she had disap-peared and not necessarily by his father but at some subsequent date by person or persons unknown. It was strange, after all, that she had disappeared so completely. Whenever he read about serial killings that involved the digging up of numerous, mostly female, corpses, Larry would wonder if they would find the remains of his mother among them. Whenever it was suggested that the police would never uncover the true extent of the killer's butchery, Larry would wonder if the reason for his mother's continuing absence lay in some unmarked grave in someone's cellar or field or backyard among the bones of the nameless dead.

The disappearance of his mother did not leave Larry with a lasting hatred of women or even his father's deep, disturbed distrust, but she did leave him an abiding sense of doom. He was always imagining the unimaginable. When Larry returned to his house in Spitalfields and saw the mutilated body of his friend Rob on his kitchen floor he was shocked and he was horrified, but he was not *surprised*.

A cry from the cabin below had Larry on his feet in a flash, hurrying down the companionway.

Ben was fighting monsters in his sleep. Larry stroked his forehead and soothed him until he stopped. Then he stayed for a while, kneeling by the bunk, watching the boy's face by the glow of the stove. Larry could never imagine not loving his son, much less leaving him. And yet sometimes he was so afraid of losing him . . . The fear ate away at him like a cancer. He could imagine someone wanting relief from that. He wondered if his mother had ever watched him like this when he was sleeping, perhaps on the night she left. One last look.

He went back up to the wheelhouse to lock up before he turned in.

Then he remembered he'd left the gangplank in position. In the past he wouldn't have worried about it but the murder had made him more security-conscious, especially with Ben there. He decided to go out and pull it up on to the deck.

It was bitterly cold and the birds were back. Larry saw the dark, huddled shapes on the barges. They did not move even when he hauled in the gangplank. Sounds carried on the river. He could hear the hum of traffic on Tower Bridge and from somewhere closer the throb of music from a car, up and past. And then, closer still, close and loud enough to startle him, he heard a woman's laughter. Mocking, almost demonic in its disdain. Larry looked out across the barges towards the wharf but there was nobody there that he could see. The laughter had stopped almost immediately. He shivered and turned back towards the wheelhouse.

Rob always thinks of women as the enemy.

The thought hit Larry at the door of the wheelhouse and he turned round as if someone had come sneaking up behind him.

But it was only his ex-wife, ambushing him with a memory.

Rob always thinks of women as the enemy. When Ruth had told him this Larry had disputed it but later he had decided it was probably true.

Why *was* that?

Once, quite recently, when Larry had gone round to Rob and Meg's for dinner he'd seen a quotation from some newspaper or magazine highlighted and pinned on to the noticeboard in the kitchen.

A man who hates his own mother will sooner or later end up hating you.

It seemed an odd thing to stick up in your own kitchen. Larry thought it odder still when he discovered Rob had stuck it up there and not Meg as he had imagined.

Rob thought it was an amusing thing to do. He made out it was just to tease her – and her friends, he said, the harridans of the Used Women's Book Club who thought he was such a misogynist.

He didn't hate women, Rob said, but he was damned if he was going to let them control him. They all tried to control you, he said, if they could. They all tried to get their hooks into you.

Sometimes, when Rob told Larry he was having an affair, he called it Playing in Duggan's Yard.

Larry stepped into the wheelhouse and turned the key in the lock and slipped the bolts on the top and the bottom of the door before he joined his sleeping son in the cabin.

CHAPTER NINE

La Ronde

LARRY'S SLEEP WAS DISTURBED by frequent cries of gibberish from the next bunk. He would open his eyes to see Ben in the ghostly gleam of the nightlight lying flat on his back and waving his arms in the air like some demented beetle. The only word Larry understood was *No!* repeated many times. Each time this happened, Larry would crawl out of his bunk and kneel down beside the ranting child and smooth his forehead and whisper: *It's all right, it's all right* until he stopped.

Larry had his own nightmares. The restless pattern of his sleep was stalked by corpses. They either came popping up out of the river or they were lying in neat rows in the morgue at Dead Man's Hole. Sometimes Larry was lying among them, other times he was looking down on them like one of the relatives – or one of the surgeons – wondering which one to choose. Their faces were covered with sheets to make it difficult for him. He knew that one of them might be Monks, laid here by mistake, but he didn't want to pull the sheet away in case he saw the face of Rob, looking like he had on the floor of Larry's kitchen with one eye missing and the other staring up at him as he walked in through the door.

In the morning he felt terrible. Ben seemed quite refreshed.

'When are we going to look for Monks?' he said.

It was a fine December morning – brighter than it had been all week and with a healthy bite in the air. Larry decided to take the workboat and search the shoreline – west to Tower Bridge and then downriver for a mile or so to the Limehouse Cut.

He tied Ben into a lifejacket and lifted him down into the boat.

'What if they attack?' Ben said.

'Who attack?' Larry looked at him warily, wondering if he was still locked in one of the nightmares.

'The birds,' Ben said.

Larry followed the direction of his gaze and saw maybe three or four herring gulls, perched on the piles that rose out of the river at low tide.

'They won't attack,' he said. 'Birds don't attack people.'

Ben looked as if he knew better but didn't want to start a row about it.

'Have you seen the film or something?' Larry asked. He meant the Hitchcock movie, *The Birds*.

'What film?'

If he didn't know, Larry thought it better not to tell him. But what had made him so frightened? Clearly this was something to be discussed with Ruth.

It took a few pulls to spark some life into the outboard and then they were heading upriver towards Tower Bridge. Larry felt the wind on his face, a hint of spray as the bows bit into the current, a sudden, satisfactory sense of detachment from the city that had now opened up around him on both sides of the river. He didn't feel happy, exactly, but it was a reminder of what happiness *used* to feel like.

There was nothing resembling a body at Dead Man's Hole, man or monkey. Only a Christmas tree.

Larry came alongside and hauled it aboard. It was barely four feet high but with a good spread of fir.

'How did it get in the river?' Ben wanted to know.

Larry looked up at the Gothic folly towering above them.

'Fell off the back of a lorry,' he said. Like most of the things his dad brought home when Larry was a kid.

'Or maybe it jumped,' he told the boy. 'Like the one in the book. Trying to get back to the forest.'

Ben looked at him, wary of deceit. He had a book about a Christmas tree that ran away; Larry had read it to him. Ben was at that age when he still *wanted* to believe what he read in books but he was beginning to have his doubts: the first hint of a suspicion that someone might be making all this shit up.

'We'll tie it to the mast for Christmas,' Larry said. 'Boats are supposed to have Christmas trees on their masts at Christmas time.'

They didn't find Monks but, as distractions go, the runaway Christmas tree was a reasonable success. Ben wanted to know how they were going to get it up the mast and would it have Christmas decorations.

'No,' said Larry, 'Christmas trees on boats don't have decorations.'

'Because the birds would take them?'

'No, it's got nothing to do with the birds.' What the hell *was* this? 'It's because it might rain and spoil them.'

The real reason was that Larry didn't want to draw attention to the boat. A Christmas tree twinkling with fairy lights and laden with decorations would be a standing invitation to every wino on the waterfront, every band of drunken bums staggering back legless from an office party. They'd be lining up on the wharf in their paper hats waving bottles at him and singing 'Silent Night'.

Larry was up the mast lashing the tree in place when he saw the police launch coming alongside. He didn't take much notice at first – the river police headquarters was just downriver at Wapping Pier – but then they called his name and he saw that beside the usual crew there were two others in plain clothes – a man and a woman. They wanted to come aboard.

Larry left them in the wheelhouse while he took Ben down into the saloon and gave him some paper and coloured crayons.

'What shall I draw?' said Ben.

Larry found *The Observer's Book of Birds* on a shelf where his dad kept a few reference books on the river. He opened it at gulls. He had a vague notion this might help tackle what was clearly becoming a phobia.

'D'you think they've found Monks?' Ben wanted to know.

Larry told him no, he didn't think that.

When he went back to the wheelhouse, the man introduced himself as DI Stone and his colleague as DS Harris. Stone had recently been assigned to the case, he said, and there were a few things he wanted to go over 'just to bring him up to speed'.

This seemed excessively diligent of him on a Saturday morning and Larry suspected they must have some new information. He asked them if they'd like a coffee but Stone declined for both of them.

He was tall and angular with a long nose that had a slight kink in it – as if he'd broken it and never had it set properly – and sharp, excessively bright eyes. A crane, Larry thought, *The Observer's Book of Birds* still in his mind, or a heron. In the cramped wheelhouse he was like a bird in a cage, folded in on himself. His dark hair had receded almost to the crown of his head and he'd had what was left shaved to a number one with a small patch of stubble left on his forehead that looked like dirt, as if he'd recently headed a muddy football. He looked about Larry's age, late thirties or early forties.

They fenced around a bit, talking about the boat and what it was like to live here in the middle of winter, covering much the same ground as Larry had covered with Muriel Hoffman. Larry told him it was just a temporary arrangement until he got the house cleaned up. Stone gazed about the nondescript interior of the wheelhouse.

'And this is where you were on the night of the murder?' he said, as if passing the time of day.

'That's right.'

'Doing a bit of DIY.'

There was nothing in his tone you could call objectionable but he managed to convey a note of scepticism.

'Painting, actually,' said Larry.

Stone sniffed.

'The for'ard cabin,' Larry told him. 'D'you want to take a look?'

Stone turned his head slowly to look at his sergeant. She stood up.

'Where would that be exactly?' she said.

Larry showed her. He'd only half finished. There was a tin of paint and a jar of paintbrushes standing on a newspaper. Larry knew he could have made it look like this in half an hour. Probably the sergeant did too. She was younger than them both, boyishly attractive with short blonde hair, quite stocky. Sporty-looking.

When they went back up to the wheelhouse she nodded to the inspector. He scarcely looked up. He was reading a document that could have been a copy of Larry's statement.

'You left the keys in a wine bar,' he said, as if seeing this for the first time. It wasn't quite a question.

'That's right,' Larry told him again.

Stone looked at him.

'Was that the usual arrangement?'

'I wouldn't say it was usual.'

'So why didn't you give them to him personally?'

'I just didn't want to hang around,' he said.

'Anxious to get started on the boat.'

Again there was that faint suspicion of mockery in his tone. Larry said nothing.

'And I gather this was a fairly regular occurrence. I mean, using your house for the purposes of sex.'

He made it sound like a crime. Perhaps it was, of sorts. Larry saw that the sergeant was taking notes.

'I wouldn't say it was *regular*,' Larry corrected him. 'But if he was seeing someone and for some reason or other he couldn't go back to her place, sometimes he'd ask if he could use mine.'

'Sometimes. How *many* times, would you say – in the past . . . six months or so?'

'I think in my statement I said about eight or nine times.'

'Eight or nine times, eh? Not bad. Not bad at all.' He seemed to consider this and then have second thoughts – as if it might reveal too much of his own sexual expectations. 'Well, not if it was a different woman every time. Was it a different woman every time?'

'I don't know,' said Larry.

'You didn't ask?'

'He'd have told me if he'd wanted me to know.'

'I'm surprised you didn't let him have a key of his own.'

'I did. He lost it. I had to get the locks changed.'

'Really?' Stone looked at his sergeant as if this was something he should have known. 'And when would this have been?'

'Early summer. July maybe. We decided after that it was better if he didn't keep the key. There was always a danger of Meg finding it, anyway, and wondering what it was.'

'His wife?'

'Yes.'

'You know her quite well, I believe.'

'Quite well. I was a friend of the family.'

'And yet you didn't mind him using your home to screw other women?'

He smiled as if to take the sting out of it. He smiled a lot, Larry had noted. He had a wide mouth that stretched easily into the shape of a smile without at all capturing the spirit.

'It would have been difficult to object,' Larry said. 'I've known Rob since we were kids. I've only known Meg as his wife.'

'So you *did* object?'

'I didn't say anything but I might have wished it wasn't happening.'

'I take it she didn't know about it? His wife.'

'She might have known he was seeing other women. But not *where* he was seeing them. No, I'm pretty sure she didn't know that.'

'So you felt like an accomplice?'

'I suppose you could say that. It wasn't something I was very comfortable with.'

'And is that why you preferred not to be there?'

'I think that was probably the case, yes.' Larry sighed. He felt that some explanation was called for. 'Look, Rob had some difficulty with monogamy – like a lot of people – but he loved his kids, he loved Meg. He just didn't like to be tied down. And he made the most of whatever . . . opportunities he had.'

Stone stared at him blandly throughout this little speech.

Then he said, 'Well, let's get back to the night of the murder, shall we? You leave the keys at 6 p.m. and you arrive here, according to your statement, at about six-thirty, having walked from Spitalfields. You didn't stop on the way? Didn't see anyone you knew? Didn't drop in a pub for a quick pint?'

He watched Larry carefully as he shook his head to all of this.

'You're sure about that? Because, you see, obviously there's a bit of confusion here . . .'

Here it comes, Larry thought, this is why they're working on Saturday . . .

'One of the bar staff, in the Town of Ramsgate, back on the waterfront there, clearly remembers you coming in for a drink at about nine o'clock. She remembers the time because there was a match on Sky and it was just before the second half. You were practically one of the regulars, she says. She knew you by your first name, at any rate, and she's convinced you were on your way to the boat. When you'd finished your drink she says you borrowed a flashlight they keep behind the bar so you could see your way down to the pier. You'd done this before, apparently. Now is she making this up or what?'

Larry shook his head. 'She's not making it up,' he said. 'I did drop in that night. I took a break from painting and went to have a quick drink. And it *was* half time. West Ham were on.'

'I see.' The detective screwed his face up and rubbed his nose with a knuckle as if it was itchy or he'd smelled something bad.

'So, let me get this straight – you left the boat to go ashore to the pub but you didn't take a flashlight with you. However, you *did* need a flashlight to get *back* to the boat. Was this because you'd had a bit too much to drink or had it suddenly got darker or what?'

'No,' said Larry, to both of these. 'I can manage without a light – there's lights on the shore, there's lights on the pier – but when the tide's coming in and there's a bit of movement on the barges it makes it a bit easier, that's all.'

'So why didn't you take a light to go ashore?'

'I would have, but the battery was out.'

'The battery was out.' He held Larry's gaze for a lot longer than was comfortable, at least for Larry. 'You didn't think to mention this earlier, to put it in your statement or anything?'

'I didn't think it was relevant.'

'I see.' He rubbed at his nose again. Perhaps that was why it was bent – a lifetime of pressing his nose into his face so he would not have to smell the bad smell of lies. 'So why do you suppose the barmaid is convinced you were on your way to the boat at nine o'clock? You had a chat to her about it, she said. She said it must be a bit monkeys out on the river and you said it was all right once you'd got the stove going.'

'I can remember talking to her about the cold,' Larry said, 'but I'd definitely been working on the boat for a couple of hours by then. She must have got confused.'

'You wouldn't care to come over there now to clear this up?'

'Well, quite frankly, no.'

Stone raised his eyebrows. 'May I ask why not?'

'Because I don't want to go barging in there with two police officers and call the barmaid a liar.'

'Well, you can understand why we might have some doubts about this.'

Larry nodded. 'Well, I'm sorry about that,' he said, 'but there you go.'

Stone carried on as if Larry hadn't spoken. 'Because you see, at this crucial time, from 6 p.m. to 9 p.m., you don't have anyone to confirm your whereabouts.'

'Unfortunately not.'

The DI looked at him for a moment as if weighing something up. Then he said, 'Well, Mr Hunter, I'm afraid we're going to have to ask you to come into the station to make a new statement.'

'What about?'

'About your visit to the pub.'

This sounded crap to Larry. 'Right now?' he said.

'No, I think Monday will do.'

They arranged for ten o'clock on Monday morning. Larry wondered if he should have a lawyer with him. He escorted them up on to the deck and watched them climb aboard the police launch and head back downriver towards Wapping Pier.

Previously the police attitude towards Larry had been one of sympathy and understanding. The officer who appeared to be in charge of the case – DI Dent – had been benign, even avuncular. He had treated Larry as a victim rather than a suspect. Not so much of a victim as the corpse but on the same side of the fence, as it were. Clearly Stone represented a different view.

The City of London police were not, as DI Dent had been at pains to point out, the Met, that much larger force that policed the seven million citizens of Greater London. It was a small independent body responsible for the ancient area of the City, formerly bounded by the City walls and including that unique area of wealth and privilege known as the Square Mile. (DI Dent came over to Larry more as a tour guide than a police officer, a Beefeater in plain clothes, perhaps.)

The City was a place where people worked. They did not live there. At least, not many of them. By day, it had a population of several hundred thousand, ferried in by bus and train and car to work in the banks and insurance houses and the hostelries that serviced them. Between the hours of four in the afternoon and seven in the evening this vast floating population drained down subways and across bridges until the City was almost empty – the size of a small market town in the provinces. By night, the streets of the old City were silent, deserted; the majority of their ten thousand citizens safely tucked in their beds with the combined resources of two small police stations to keep watch over them. There was relatively little crime in the City of London, Dent had told him. Murder was a rarity. When Larry alerted the City of London police to the horrors on his kitchen floor it was as if he had brought them an unexpected piece of exotic trade.

He considered – not for the first time – the possible lines of enquiry they might be following. They would almost certainly have begun with Meg. Where adultery was a factor, Larry knew, it was always the wife, or the husband, they looked to first, if only to eliminate them from their enquiries. But presumably Meg *had* been eliminated. She had been with friends at the time, Dent had confided: members of some book-reading circle. (This would be the Used Women's Book Club that Rob had told Larry about.) So they were focusing on 'the girlfriend' – the mysterious woman Rob had arranged to meet that night. They might have thought, as Ruth did, that she had a partner – a husband or boyfriend – who had discovered the assignation, maybe even followed her to Larry's house and killed in a fit of jealous rage. Or maybe it was the woman herself, though Dent himself clearly did not believe a woman capable of inflicting such injuries. Again, Stone might have a different view.

But the girlfriend had proved elusive. Whoever she was, she had left no trace, no hint of an identity in the written and electronic chronicles of Rob's life. He had been unusually discreet. He had not talked to Larry or, apparently, any of his other friends about her. The police had come back to Larry twice on the subject, asking him to search his memory for anything that might give them a lead. They may have considered that she did not exist. It was possible that Stone thought *Larry* had been having the affair with Rob. The keys had been left in the wine bar so Rob could let himself in and Larry had returned later. To a violent quarrel.

He had the opportunity; he might have had the weapon – the odd bale hook lying about the place – all they needed now was the motive.

Larry thought again about getting himself a lawyer. But a lawyer might prove expensive – he didn't know if he was entitled to legal aid. More to the point, a lawyer might very well get round to asking questions that hadn't occurred to the police to ask yet.

He should call Meg. But the longer he left it, the more difficult it became. What could he say? How could you explain the complexity of alliances, of loyalties and betrayals, that led you to something like this?

He suddenly remembered the call he'd had last night when he was on the gangway and went down to the cabin for his mobile phone.

Ben was still drawing birds.

Larry looked at them. They all had teeth and mad staring eyes. They were the kind of creatures that would give Larry nightmares, never mind Ben. This was obviously something that would have to be dealt with at some stage. Something to add to his list of worries. But nowhere near the top.

There were three messages on Larry's phone. One from his Auntie Ethel – checking to see how he was and to invite him for Sunday lunch – one from Jud and one from a woman called Jo who said she was a friend of Meg's and would he phone her back.

He phoned Jo first.

She sounded American. He remembered her then. He'd met her at Rob's wedding. She'd taken his tie off and rolled his trousers up as far as his knees. She'd said he looked better that way. Larry had thought she looked just fine as she was, if a little mad.

She wanted to talk to him about a church service for Rob.

'Oh yes?' said Larry guardedly.

He remembered her riding on a carousel they'd hired for the wedding reception. Meg had insisted upon it. It was an old-fashioned one with the usual gilded horses and lots of other creatures, like lions and tigers and giant birds. While Jo was talking Larry pictured her riding on the carousel with Meg riding beside her. Two beautiful women spinning round and round in a blur of animal faces, all bared teeth and glaring eyes and dancing hooves and talons and claws. He'd thought of a movie he'd seen, a French movie called *La Ronde*, directed by Roger Vadim, where the lovers went from one to the other, like swapping rides on the roundabout.

The service was in the church at Highgate, she said. 'We wondered if you'd like to say a few words.'

Larry heard himself saying he wasn't very good at this kind of thing – as if it was a rare social skill he hadn't quite mastered, like after-dinner speaking.

'Well, Meg didn't ask me to put any pressure on you or anything, but I think she'd like you to be there.'

'Oh I'll be there,' Larry assured her. 'I just don't feel ready to say anything, that's all.'

The roundabout went round and about, the eyes of the gallopers wild above the red mouths, the black flaring nostrils. He saw the detached retina in the blood on his kitchen floor and pushed it back – as far back as it would ever go.

He asked her how Meg was – and the girls.

'Well, still pretty devastated,' she said, as if it was a silly question, which it was.

'Give her my love, will you? Tell her I'm thinking of her.'

She said she would. He had a feeling she wanted to say more but changed her mind, or didn't know how to put it.

'I'll see you on Thursday, then,' she said.

Ben had stopped drawing birds and now he was drawing what looked like a Christmas tree with different-coloured balls on it.

Larry thought what it must be like to be six.

Six was when you stopped living in the dream world. Six was when you were told: 'You're too big to be carried.' 'You're old enough to walk on your own.' Six was when you were told: 'You're old enough to know better.'

There was a part of Larry that still wanted to be six. Before they taught you to Know Better – to Feel Guilt.

Rob had managed to resist for longer than most.

'Rob had some difficulty with monogamy,' Larry had told DI Stone. In fact, Rob had no difficulty at all with monogamy. It didn't trouble him in the least. If it ever occurred to him at all, it was as something that other men did, like supporting a crap football team. It was *their* problem.

'So why did you get married?' Larry had once asked him and he'd just shrugged and grinned and said, 'It seemed a good idea at the time. Anyway, *you* can talk.'

In a curious way, despite his philandering, Rob had been quite domesticated – more so than Larry. He was the 'marrying kind'. And with some perspicacity, Rob had recognised that Meg would make the right kind of wife for him: attractive, intelligent, not too demanding, and madly in love with him, at least when they were first married. There might also have been the expectation, never openly acknowledged, that her mother would be more generous with her funds than had proved to be the case, but Larry didn't really think this was a factor. Rob just liked his creature comforts. He was like the tomcat who needed somewhere warm and safe to come back to after he'd been out on the tiles.

Once Larry had turned up unexpectedly at Rob's home – shortly after his own marriage had broken down and he needed to crash for the night – and found him and Meg in their dressing gowns. It was about nine o'clock. There was a log fire, the girls were in bed, they had some classical music on and they'd both been reading novels – Larry noticed that they'd put their books face down to mark the page when he'd disturbed them. It was the perfect domestic scene. Larry was surprised, although he didn't know what else he had expected. He had seen Rob many times before in the role of husband and father. But the apparent harmony of this occasion, the *symmetry* of couple, books, fire, struck Larry as a little bizarre, when just a few evenings before he'd been out on the town with Rob and one of his girlfriends. Perhaps it was the fact that Rob was so clearly at ease in the role of husband and father, so perfectly suited to it. He saw nothing incompatible in combining it with that of the womaniser, even the woman-hater. He saw no reason to change the habits of a lifetime. Sometimes he was back for supper; sometimes he wasn't. It was as simple as that. It was the game of childhood continued. Sometimes you came home for tea, sometimes you went Playing in Duggan's Yard.

Women – especially women who tried to control him, to make him feel guilty, to make him grow up – were like his mother or Larry's aunts. They were there to be outwitted, outplayed; otherwise they'd stop *you* from playing. That's what women did. They couldn't help themselves. They wanted you in *their* backyard, where they could keep an eye on you.

Larry had never challenged this assumption, either as child or adult. But he had never entirely gone along with it, either. He didn't know why this was. Partly it was a question of conscience. He didn't like to upset people. He particularly didn't like to upset women – the aunts had done their job well. But it was also because he wasn't that competitive. Not where women were concerned. He was not a natural polygamist, more of a serial monogamist who overlaps from time to time.

But the one thing Rob and Larry had in common was their fear of women. Rob was afraid they'd suffocate him; Larry was afraid they'd leave him. And in the end it came to the same thing. You had to keep moving, swapping rides on the carousel.

He returned the other calls. He spoke to his Auntie Ethel and confirmed that he and Ben would be round for Sunday lunch. He had to talk to her for about ten minutes, assuring her that he was all right, everything was under control, fighting to keep the irritation out of his voice. Then he rang the number Jud had left.

A woman answered. Jud wasn't in, she said.

Then she said, 'Is that Larry?'

He recognised the voice. It was Amy.

Larry felt a familiar embarrassment. He and Amy had once had what he called 'a bit of a thing' shortly after his break-up with Ruth. He'd met her at a party at Rob and Meg's and ended up taking her home, but although they'd spent the night together Larry hadn't been able to make love. He had told her it was because of Ruth – and it might well have been – but he suspected it was more because Amy was not his type physically. She had a rangy, almost boyish body and he was more inclined to women who were more well-rounded – 'plumpeties' as Ruth called them, unflatteringly. Amy had accepted this without apparent rancour and had phoned him a few days later to ask if he'd mind taking a few publicity photos for her. She was pleased with the results and subsequently he'd recorded a play she was in on a DV camera. They'd never tried to get it together again but Larry always felt there was unfinished business between them and he was never really at ease with her.

Now he said awkwardly, 'I got a message to ring Jud on this number.'

'That's right, he's moved in for a while. Is it about the walks?'

It was Amy who'd got him on the list of approved guides when he gave up being a cameraman. She asked him how it was going and he told her he didn't think he was much cop as a guide but maybe it was the subject matter. 'I mean, the Ripper,' he said, in case she didn't know.

There was a slight pause. Then she said, 'How have you been feeling?'

He took this to mean she knew about the murder.

'OK, considering,' he said.

'Any progress from the police?'

'Not that I know of,' he told her.

She asked if he'd been back to the house since it happened and he told her, no – he was living on his dad's boat at Wapping.

'How's that working out?'

Larry looked out of the windows. He'd wandered up to the wheelhouse with the phone so Ben wouldn't hear too much.

'Some days are better than others,' he said.

There was another small pause. Then she said, 'If you're ever stuck, you could live here for a while.'

Larry thanked her but said he'd be fine.

Amy had an apartment on the top floor of an old Victorian house overlooking the railway line at Peckham. When Larry had been there he had assumed she rented it but Meg had told him she owned the whole house. She had bought it some years back – or at least put down the deposit – with the money she had earned from her one financial success as an actress – a shampoo commercial – and filled it with lodgers. Meg said she was a tyrant of a landlady and that one of the house rules was that the male lodgers were not allowed to pee standing up because they *sprayed* it everywhere and rotted the floorboards. They had to pee sitting down, like a woman. Rob had seen a notice to this effect in the lavatory he had used while he was there but he had assumed it was a joke.

'It's not a joke,' Meg had assured him.

Once he had asked Amy how she would know whether her male visitors peed standing up or sitting down.

'I'd know,' said Amy darkly.

'I didn't know Jud was living with you,' Larry said.

'It's a temporary arrangement.' Larry detected a cool note. He wondered if Jud had any problems with the toilet arrangements. He seemed the kind of man who would and being her brother he might be inclined to put up a fight about it.

It was probably Jud's childhood spraying, Larry reflected, that had alerted Amy to the problem in the first place.

'I'll tell him you called,' she said. 'Or you can ring him on his mobile. I'll give you the number.'

Larry said he had it.

But when she rang off he stood there for a while gazing out over the river and thinking about Amy and Meg and how well they knew each other. It seemed an unlikely friendship to Larry. They didn't seem to have much in common. Then he recalled that Amy was in the same book circle, the one Rob kept joking about.

Larry had told Rob that he hadn't been able to make love to Amy and Rob had said he wasn't surprised.

'She's mad,' he said, as if that would make a difference.

Larry wondered if Rob had ever told Meg about his failure in this regard.

It was all very incestuous.

La Ronde, he thought. Ridiculous.

CHAPTER TEN

The Green Woman and the Wolf Men

ON SUNDAY MORNING JO had a call from Liz to ask if she fancied coming over for a spot of lunch. The invitation was unusual. Outside meetings of the Used Women's Book Club, Jo saw even less of Liz than she did of Amy but recent events had forged a tacit, if unspoken, alliance. Now, Jo guessed, they were about to speak of it.

Liz lived in Balham, nine stops down the Northern Line from London Bridge. When Jo arrived, shortly before one o'clock, Liz was in the front garden wearing overalls and a man's trilby, shovelling a large heap of horse manure into bags. It looked like it had just been dumped there. It was still steaming.

'I've just had a delivery,' Liz said. 'Got to shift it before the neighbours complain.'

'Was it one horse or two?' Jo asked, looking at the size of the heap. She wasn't sure if she should offer to help or not. She had not dressed up for the occasion but not so far down as to be comfortable shovelling shit.

Liz was a garden designer. She ran a company called the Green Woman and employed three full-time assistants. One of them had just dumped the shit straight from the back of a tip-up, she said, and rushed off on another job. Seeing the mystified look on Jo's face, Liz explained that they had an arrangement with a riding stables in Wimbledon. It was cheaper than buying the stuff ready-bagged but you had to take it as it came.

A bit like Liz herself, Jo thought, feeling compelled to hold the bags open while Liz shovelled. Liz was not a large woman but Jo noted the strength in her wrists and forearms and recalled that her ex-husband had once remarked – not intending to flatter – that she had shoulders like an Irish navvy after he'd dug the Regent's Canal.

Liz, Meg said, was an example to them all. (An interesting assessment which Jo was still thinking about, not for what it might tell her about Liz but for what it could almost certainly tell her about Meg.) She had told Jo that when they first met Liz had been penniless, homeless and in the midst of a bitter divorce. Her husband, Desmond, claimed to have lost loads of money on a dot com company and their house had gone – along with everything else they owned – to pay his debts. Shortly after the divorce, however, Liz had discovered he had been having an affair with one of his former work colleagues whom he had since married. They now lived in some considerable affluence which Liz, and most of her friends, were convinced had been purchased at least in part with the money he should have shared with *her*.

But what made Liz really bitter, Meg said, was that 'bloody Des' had not wanted them to have any children – he had even persuaded her, before they were married, to have an abortion. He'd since had two children by his new wife. *And* they had two houses – one in Putney and one in Kent – both with very nice gardens.

It had taken Liz a long time to pick herself up after all of this but at last she seemed to have made it. If you saw her now, Meg said – perhaps a little enviously – so shrewd and tough and energetic, you'd never have known what a wimp she was when she was breaking up with Des. Liz would joke now about serving her time as a Used Woman but Jo reckoned the wounds had gone deep and you didn't have to look very hard to see the scar tissue. She could be quite unfeeling at times and hard on any weakness in others. Sometimes after a few hours with Liz you felt as if you'd been rubbed down with sandpaper.

They filled twelve bags before they were through and Jo helped stack them against the fence. She was bracing herself for the assistant to come back with the next load but thankfully when they were finished Liz led her into the house for a scrub down and a glass of wine.

Lunch was in the oven. It smelled good but Jo knew better than to count on it. She'd had experience of Liz's cooking from when it was Liz's turn to host the Used Women's Book Club. You often came away feeling like you needed a long lie down and a lot of space to yourself. Liz had once served them a dish she called Three-Bean Casserole.

Liz left her sitting in the small conservatory at the back of the house while she went upstairs to change. When she came down she was wearing a tunic shirt with baggy cotton pants and delicate golden sandals. Liz bought all her clothes from charity shops in upmarket south London suburbs like Barnes and Wimbledon where, she said, all the 'rich bitches' took their designer cast-offs. She looked great in whatever she wore. Her skin was the colour of dark oak, her eyes were deep brown pools and she had braided her hair with beads. If Jo made her a character in a fairy-tale it would be a dryad, a nymph of the forest. A nymph who works out. Amy said that Liz looked a lot better since she had given up men. After the defection of Desmond she had messed around for a while with younger men and then confined herself exclusively to female partners. They never seemed to last very long, not long enough for Jo ever to remember their names. Except for the latest whose name was Lurk – not an easy name to forget. She was called Lurk, Liz claimed, because as a schoolgirl the teachers at her south London comprehensive had always accused her of 'lurking about' and the name had stuck. She worked at Kew Gardens, in the temperate-ferns house. Amy said that she and Liz were becoming a number but there was no sign of her today, so perhaps Liz was ready to move on.

She sat down in the wicker chair opposite Jo – across a small wicker table – and topped up their wine glasses.

'So how's the book going?' she asked.

Jo had told her some months ago that she was trying to write a follow up to *Sleeping Beauties* and Liz was constantly monitoring her progress. It was an idea that appealed to Liz because it was about women in literature who had encountered the Wolf.

'Isn't that all of them?' Liz had enquired bitterly.

But the women Jo was writing about were women who had unleashed the Wolf – or the 'bad girl' – inside themselves. The new generation of heroines who fought their way to fame, fortune and self-knowledge. Jo wanted to know whether they were any more use as role models than unreconstructed Good Girls like Jane Eyre or the heroines of *Little Women*. Or even Cinderella.

She told Liz about her current chapter which featured Clarice Starling, the tough but vulnerable FBI agent in *Silence of the Lambs* and its sequel *Hannibal*.

Agent Starling interested Jo because although she didn't take any crap, could shoot better and think better than all the boys in her class, she had the same problem as Jane Eyre in relation to father figures. In *Silence of the Lambs*, Clarice is a Good Girl who believes she serves the forces of Good against Evil. She believes in the essential rightness of authority: in effect, of patriarchy. Her father figure is Crawford, the FBI section chief who shows a special interest in her progress and sends her to meet the Wolf, in the person of Dr Hannibal 'the Cannibal' Lecter – though warning her to stick to the path through the forest and on no account to let him 'get inside your head'. In the next book – *Hannibal* – Clarice starts off as a Good Girl but turns 'bad' when key members of the patriarchy turn against her. Her main father figure fails her and she is 'rescued' by the Wolf – Hannibal. Instead of devouring her, he induces her, under the influence of drugs, to eat the brains of her foremost enemy at the FBI – fried in a *beurre-noisette* with shallots and minced caper berries and served with a garnish of parsley and a single nasturtium blossom on watercress 'to achieve a little height'. Then he re-educates her – again with the help of drugs – releasing her from her bondage to Authority and liberating the 'bad girl' within. The new Clarice freely gives herself to the Wolf and they live happily ever after – in Buenos Aires – where she has her hair dyed silver blonde and they go to the opera and dance tangos and have lots of sex.

Jo quite liked the ending – she thought it was far, far better than the ending in the film (where the Wolf chops off a paw to avoid hurting Clarice and slinks into the night leaving her to continue as the Faithful Servant of Authority) – but it gave her a problem because Clarice was only liberated from her old dependencies by a new father figure in the shape of the Wolf himself. This seemed like copping out to Jo but, then, the writer was a man.

Liz agreed. She thought Hannibal Lecter should have been a woman.

'I wouldn't go so far as that,' Jo said cautiously. She was always cautious about Liz's contributions as literary critic. Liz's suggestion of a title for Jo's new book was *Cunts with Teeth*. (Jo had settled rather less controversially on *Wolf Women*.)

Jo felt that the experience of being used and abused by her husband Desmond had made Liz antagonistic to *all* men, whereas Jo's experience as the wife of Michael Geraghty had only made her antagonistic to Michael Geraghty – and one or two others in whom she recognised the same exploitative characteristics. When Liz launched on one of her swingeing attacks on men in general Jo was often amused, often sympathetic, but sometimes uncomfortable, just as she'd been uncomfortable when Liz had gleefully seized on the title of the Used Women's Book Club as a way of summing up their mutual experience of the married state. Even if you were a victim with teeth, you were still a victim.

'So . . .' Liz leaned back in her wicker chair and gave Jo a look that indicated that, now they'd shovelled enough shit, they could move on to the real purpose of the meeting. 'You get any more out of Meg yet?'

Jo compressed her lips, shaking her head. 'You saw how she was.'

'She's said nothing to you at all?'

'Only that she panicked.'

'She *panicked*? Great. Did she say *why* she panicked?'

'Not really. She wasn't thinking straight.'

'So she dumps us right in it.'

'That's what friends are for,' said Jo, immediately regretting it, feeling like the school prefect. She wondered about telling Liz she had timed the route from Spitalfields to her apartment but it would only have alarmed her more.

'It's asking too much,' Liz said. 'We could go to jail. For a long time.'

This seemed like stating the obvious to Jo.

'Well, we've done it now,' Jo said. 'We just have to stick together.'

She asked the question that had been on her mind all weekend.

'Did you tell Amy?'

Liz shook her head but Jo thought she looked a little shifty.

'Don't worry about Amy,' Liz said. 'It's Meg you should be worried about.'

In the unwritten rules of the Used Women's Book Club – or the rules privately drawn up by Liz – Liz was responsible for Amy and Jo for Meg.

For once Jo felt she'd got the worst of the bargain.

They were both silent for a moment. Then Liz said, 'Why did she stay with him?'

Another black mark against Jo's girl.

'She was determined to make it work,' said Jo defensively. 'She didn't want to be like her mother.'

'Her mother's got a lot going for her if you ask me,' said Liz.

'And then there were the girls,' Jo said. 'Besides, it wasn't as if he beat up on her or anything. It was just the women. Some people don't mind that so much.'

'Meg did.'

Jo looked at her sharply.

'How do you know?'

'Because she told me,' Liz said with some satisfaction.

'When?'

'Recently. A few weeks ago. When you last came here for the book club. Something had happened – I don't know what – but she was really upset. I'm surprised you didn't notice.'

'What did she say?'

'Just that he'd gone too far this time.'

Jo wondered if this was true. It didn't sound like Meg. And why would she confide in Liz and not Jo?

'Did she say who with?'

Liz shook her head. She stood up, picking up her glass of wine.

'Come on, let's eat.'

They ate in the kitchen. A casserole. When Liz took the lid off it looked like lumpy custard. It turned out to be sweetcorn and chickpeas with chunks of carrot and swede. Hearty Stew, Liz called it.

As they began to eat Liz said, 'Women usually kill people they know.'

'Excuse me,' said Jo. She thought for a moment it was a reference to the stew.

'It's a fact. Not that they do a lot of killing compared to men, of course. About a thousand a year in the States – I don't know about England – but when they do, they kill their husbands or their lovers – and occasionally their children.'

'I know,' said Jo.

'I expect the police do, too.'

Jo said nothing. She was staring down at her stew and remembering the convent school she'd been to with Meg in East Anglia.

'It used to be over fifteen hundred a year,' said Liz, 'but the growth of sheltered accommodation and legal remedies for battered women and that kind of thing have brought it right down.' She leaned over the table to fill Jo's glass. 'So you could say the women's movement has saved the lives of around five hundred male bastards every year.'

It was dark when Jo left. She would have caught a cab at London Bridge if there'd been any around but she couldn't be bothered to wait. It wasn't far to walk home – about fifteen minutes along the river – and there were still plenty of people about, ambling along the waterfront. This was the Upper Pool of London dominated by Hay's Wharf – 'London's Larder' as Jo had heard it was called in the days when three-quarters of the city's food imports were stored here. She could still catch a whiff of what it must have smelled like – aided, no doubt, by the new smells from the restaurants and delicatessens in Hay's Galleria – of wood and straw, tea, cheese, coffee and smoked ham. And other things besides.

Jo loved descriptions of the old waterfront. One of her favourites was by Charles Graves, written in the *Sphere* magazine of 1933. (Jo had found it in a later publication: *London's Riverscape, Lost and Found.*)

The first things we see are large boxes of Almeria grapes from Spain. They have already been sold in advance by auction in Pudding Lane. Nearby is the season's first crop of Greek currants: 1,550 tons of them arrived on the 'Ariosto'. There is also the sour smell of sultanas in good time for the Christmas trade. Then there is gum damar used for varnish. It comes from the Malay States in sacks with a green line on them. Nearby is plywood and cases of senna pods from Mombasa. More gum from New Zealand is piled near sacks of African ginger. Barrels of capers (which look like nasturtium seeds) are parked besides them. Baskets of butter beans from Madagascar are cheek by jowl with match-sticks from the Baltic, canned peas from Italy, and glazed tiles from Spain. Apricot pulp in cans and more butter beans confront you a few yards further on ... All this on the ground floor of a single warehouse.

Jo walked along the modern waterfront seeing the cranes and the cargoes and the ships that had brought them here – the *SS Baltallin*, sunk by torpedo in 1941 *with the loss of seven lives*; the *Hontestroom* from Holland *with bulbs, eggs, butter, poultry and Christmas trees*; and from an earlier age the tea clippers of Jardin & Martheson: *Deerhound, Flying Spur* and *Deerfoot*. She saw the men who would have worked here up until the late 1960s: dockers in flat caps and their supervisors in bowlers, ships' officers with gold bands on their sleeves and crew in blue jerseys, London policemen ...

Then she saw the kids. That's what she first thought – kids – four of them, in their mid teens. She only noticed them because they were clowning around, making a nuisance of themselves, pushing each other into the fountain on Hay's Wharf and getting in people's way. Jo walked on, past the *Belfast* and under Tower Bridge and along the riverside restaurants. Soon there were fewer people about and it was less well lit. She paused for a moment and looked back the way she had come – she didn't know why – and saw the kids again. About thirty or forty yards behind her, just sauntering along, doing nothing in particular. They looked less like kids now though. They were kind of hunched into their sweaters, two of them with the hoods up. She suddenly thought of wolves, the wolf pack dogging her heels. She dismissed the thought as neurotic, paranoid, but she knew there was a darker, quieter stretch of waterfront coming up. This was the extension to Butler's Wharf, which was still under development and where the walkway crossed St Saviour's Dock by a narrow footbridge. Then it was really dark for a couple of minutes, winding between old warehouses, until she reached her apartment block.

Jo decided to linger a little outside the Design Museum to let the pack drift by. She leant on the embankment looking out over the river and they passed quite close to her. She watched them out of the corner of her eye until they were out of sight. She felt a little foolish doing this but you heard so many stories these days and she'd become more cautious lately. Jo had never been seriously frightened in London but she was beginning to think there could be a time when she *might* be.

She gave it about five minutes or so before she carried on. But first she slung her purse around her neck by the shoulder strap and buttoned it into her leather jacket out of sight. She looked like she was pregnant but it wouldn't stop her running if she had to. She was glad she was wearing her Timberlands.

She was coming off the footbridge over St Saviour's Dock when she saw them again, heading back towards her. The walkway was very narrow here, running alongside a warehouse conversion, with scaffolding up. She kept in close to the side of the wall, still walking, not looking at them. As they drew level, one of them pushed his pal into her, knocking her back against the wall. There was laughter.

'Oh, for God's sake,' she said, more angry than scared. 'Grow up.'

She kept going, thinking it would have been better to say nothing. She was still angry but the fear was there now and growing. She didn't hear them coming up behind her. The first thing she knew was when the arm was round her neck. She didn't even think about it. It was a reflex, just as she'd been taught in the classes she had attended at the gym. She raised her right foot and stamped sharply down on his instep. One, she said to herself, counting the moves in her head. She heard him yell and the arm was no longer so tight across her neck. She twisted round, grinding her heel into his foot where it joined with the ankle and driving her right elbow into his stomach. Two. Three was where you stepped to one side and chopped him on the back of the neck but Jo decided to give three a miss. He wasn't holding her any more and the path was still open in front of her and she was away.

Jo could run. She'd been the best runner at convent school over the short distances. The hundred metres, two hundred, and the hurdles, they were her specialities. At the inter-school sports the nuns used to stand at the finishing line cheering her on like black crows on the branch of a tree. At longer distances she wasn't so good. She didn't have the staying power. When she went for runs now, jogging along the waterfront, she always finished up with a sprint, lengthening her stride, arms going almost as fast as her legs, feeling the blood pump through her heart. A hundred yards was about her limit now though, at that pace.

It was about two hundred to the apartments.

The walkway made a sharp right angle ahead of her, running back from the river with buildings now on both sides. Jo took it fast, cannoned off the wall, grazing the side of her hand. She didn't even feel it. She had heard their shouts at first, now all she could hear was the slap of trainers on the concrete walkway behind her. She even thought she could hear their breathing.

The walk turned again, to the left this time, and continued along the back of the apartments. There were lights here and CCTV cameras and iron railings with a gate opening into the water gardens. But the gate was locked and the swipe card was in her purse. It sometimes took her half a minute to find it even when she didn't have a pack of muggers breathing down her neck. She reached the gate and hung on to it, twisting round to face them, ready to kick and scream.

But there was no one there.

The walkway stretched back the way she had come, dark and silent and empty. She could have imagined the footsteps or they might have stopped chasing her when they saw the cameras. She didn't care either way. She was trembling now and had trouble swiping her card through the lock. When she reached the main entrance the duty porter was standing there waiting for her. He'd seen her on one of the monitors. She'd come back running before but in a tracksuit, not leather jacket and jeans, and he'd thought something was wrong. She told him what had happened and waited in the lobby while he called the police.

She felt sick now. She couldn't stop shaking. The porter gave her tea from his flask, hot and sweet, and asked her if there was anyone he could ring for her. She said there wasn't and thanked him for the tea. She didn't normally take sugar but she felt her blood probably needed it.

A patrol car arrived within minutes – it was that kind of area. Two of them came in and took details. They kept getting messages on their radios and talking back. They had people checking the riverside walk, they said, but Jo could tell they didn't expect to find anyone. She said that when she'd stamped on his foot she'd felt something give, like chicken bones breaking. They said they'd check the hospitals to see if anyone came in with a broken foot but she could tell they didn't think that would do them much good either. The way they said it, it was like it was a joke. They clearly didn't think a woman like Jo could break a man's foot. They thought she should be in hospital, though – just for a check up, they said. She shook her head. She was fine now, she said. Just a bit shaken, that was all. She would go up to her apartment and have a shower and a stiff drink, maybe not in that order.

They said someone from CID would be in touch with her, probably in the morning. She thanked them and thanked the porter again for his tea and sympathy and took the lift up to her apartment. She felt OK. She even felt quite pleased with herself for the way she'd reacted. She'd been on the Survive the Streets course, every Saturday morning for ten weeks. She was going to write to the instructor and tell him it worked.

When she reached the apartment and closed the door behind her she suddenly burst into tears. She knew it was delayed shock but it didn't help that there was no one else there.

CHAPTER ELEVEN

The Artful Dodger

LARRY HANDED BEN OVER at Clapham Junction early on Sunday evening.

'Did you have a nice time on the boat?' Ruth said, smiling at Ben as her eyes scanned him for cracks. 'Everything all right?'

'Yes,' they both said, exchanging what might have been interpreted as a guilty glance if you were the suspicious sort. Larry said nothing about the birds – it would keep till later – and Ben said nothing about the slip off the gangplank.

He told her about the Christmas tree, though.

'That's nice,' said Ruth. 'Has it got lights?'

'No,' said Ben. 'You don't have lights when it's on the mast.' He sounded superior.

There was a slightly awkward silence. They were in the entrance to the shopping arcade that led to the station and people were hurrying in and out.

'Well, we'd better be going – I'm on a double yellow line,' Ruth said.

Larry handed her the backpack with Ben's overnight things. He hoped she wouldn't notice the absence of Monks.

'Ring me if there's any ... you know ... *developments*,' she said to Larry and kissed him on the cheek.

He wondered if Oscar was in the car, watching them.

He took the train back to Victoria and then, after some hesitation, the tube to Aldgate. The phone call from Jud had been to invite him to a Christmas party for the tour guides at the *Ten Bells*. Larry had thanked him and said he'd try and make it, with no intention of doing so, but now, after parting with Ben, he thought anything was better than an evening by himself on the boat. He told himself it was about time he did a spot of networking. He needed the money.

He regretted the decision as soon as he walked through the door. The pub was packed, mostly with men, all shouting against a background of loud music. Larry felt like he had entered a section of the Underworld in which hundreds of tour guides were condemned to repeat their patter for all eternity in a kind of marathon bullshit competition. He forced his way through the crush in the general direction of the bar. Halfway there he changed his mind and began to retreat towards the door. Then someone he vaguely recognised yelled directly at *him*. A woman appeared, her eyes shining up at him, her lips moving. Larry couldn't hear a word. Who was she? The hostess? Had they met before? His smile felt like a rictus. He was not a party person. How did you get to *be* a party person? Was there a trick or a tactic? Parties were like battlegrounds he'd been pitched into without knowing whose side he was on. World-weary luvvies wheeled around and about him, neighing greetings, trading bon mots like badly aimed blows, their wit withered in the blast of music from the speakers behind the bar. Larry's own attempts at conversation were like skirmishes with unknown opponents identified by a distinguishing feature or function: Bald Head and Ponytail, does Ghosts of the Old City, Ginger Hair and Beard, does London of Charles Dickens, Bow Tie and Eyebrows, does A Walk With Dr Johnson.

Then he saw Jud wedged into a corner of the bar. The Artful Dodger, does pockets.

The connection – which had sprung instantly to mind – puzzled Larry. Why should he think that? He knew little about Jud and nothing to indicate a measure of dishonesty. Perhaps it was in his appearance. He had the face of a street urchin with lanky blond hair and a snub nose that looked as if it had been pressed up against a lot of shop windows and old-young

eyes, wise beyond their years in the ways and wickedness of the world.

He saw Larry looking at him and smirked and made a mocking bow. If he'd worn a beaver hat, Larry thought, he'd have tipped it over one eye.

Larry disengaged himself from the particular crush that had embraced him and pushed his way through to the bar. Jud appeared to have found a small backwater where the currents of sound were less boisterous.

'Wotcher, me old mate,' he said. Perhaps he was *playing* the Artful Dodger: his role for the night.

'Evening,' said Larry warily. There had been no indication, thus far, that Jud considered him an old mate and Larry was not at all sure he wished to enter that category. He sometimes had the impression that Jud was taking the piss – out of Larry, himself, and the world in general.

'Surprised to see *you* here,' said Jud, as if he hadn't invited him personally a mere twenty-four hours ago.

'I thought I'd make the effort,' said Larry.

'You know Stan and Trevor?' He indicated the two men nearest to him at the bar, their backs turned firmly against the throng. They glanced around briefly and nodded a greeting. So far as Larry could remember he had never met either of them.

'I don't think I know anyone here,' he said to Jud.

'You know Amy,' said Jud. Larry followed the direction of his gaze and glimpsed her through the ruck. Or at least the top of her head. She was wearing a kind of Alice band with a peacock feather in it.

'Might have something for you in the New Year,' Jud said. 'But it means dressing up as a pirate.'

Larry took this as a joke.

'Ho, ho,' he said.

'No. *Yo* Ho,' said Jud, leaning closer and raising his voice. 'As in Yo Ho Ho and a bottle of rum. *Ho Ho* is Father Christmas.'

'What?'

'Old Wapping and the Pirates of Execution Dock,' said Jud. 'They used to hang them in chains for three tides . . .'

'I know,' said Larry, 'but why . . .'

'The guides always dress for the part,' said Jud. 'Like Patsy there.'

He jabbed his chin across the room and Jud saw a woman who seemed to be dressed like Bo Peep.

'She doesn't look like a pirate,' Larry said.

'That's because she's Jane Austen,' said Jud.

Larry felt like he was losing it. It was either his ears or his brain or both.

'I'm confused,' he said.

'Patsy does Jane Austen's London,' said Jud. 'But if you do Old Wapping and the Pirates of Execution Dock you dress up as a pirate. It should be right up your street.'

Why should Jud think he liked to dress up as a pirate?

'How come?' he said.

'I heard you were living there at the moment – on your dad's tug at the Old Hermitage.'

'Who told you that?'

'Amy. Why, isn't it true?'

'Yeah, it's true,' said Larry. 'For the time being.' But he wondered how Amy knew. Who had he told who knew Amy? Larry searched his brain but there was too much noise to think straight. He had a feeling it was important but he didn't know why. He saw Amy looking in their direction, a little anxiously, he thought, but when she caught his eye she blew him a kiss.

'So what about it?' Jud said.

'I'll think it over,' said Larry, 'and let you know.'

CHAPTER TWELVE

The Scene of Crime

ON MONDAY MORNING LARRY had two appointments, neither of which he was looking forward to. At ten o'clock he had to report to the police station on Bishopsgate to meet DI Stone and at half-eleven he had to meet Muriel Hoffman at his house in Spitalfields. Larry took his gym kit with him in a sports bag. If he had to go *into* the house he intended to go straight to the gym afterwards for a shower, a work-out, a sauna and another shower.

DI Stone kept him waiting for half an hour before he was ready to see him.

'Sorry to keep you,' he said. 'Sergeant Harris was typing up your new statement and she has trouble using the computer.'

He smiled his peculiar smile. Sergeant Harris said nothing. She gave the statement to Larry to read and sign.

Larry knew it wouldn't be as easy as that, though, and he was right.

'I believe you've arranged to have the house cleaned,' Stone said.

Larry said he hadn't arranged anything yet, except to have it inspected so the cleaners could give him an estimate.

Stone checked his watch.

'Eleven-thirty this morning, I believe.'

He must have spoken to Muriel Hoffman. But had he rung *her* or had she rung *him*? Larry asked if this was a problem.

'No problem,' said Stone, 'but I'd like to have one final look over the place beforehand, if that's all right with you.'

'You mean before they do anything?'

'I mean right now – if you can spare the time.'

Larry felt he'd walked into a trap.

'You want *me* there?' he said.

'It would be a help,' said Stone. 'If you have no objection.'

Stone had prepared for it. There was a police van parked at the corner of Larry's street and, as soon as they arrived, men in yellow plastic jackets started piling out and sealing it off at both ends.

'Let's assume this is when you found the body,' said Stone as they walked up to the front door. 'You're arriving home at, when was it . . . ?'

'2.20 p.m.,' said Sergeant Harris. She had a notepad on a clipboard but she didn't have to look at it.

'2.20 p.m. You've been at the art college. You've come back to tidy the place up before you go and pick up your son from school. Now what are you thinking?'

'What am I *thinking*?'

'Take yourself back. What was going through your mind as you walked up to the door?'

Larry took himself back. He'd had a meeting with his tutor to talk about his project. He was getting a bit behind with it. He intended to catch up over the Christmas holidays. He might have been thinking about this, or he might have been thinking about what he was going to do with Ben over the weekend. Most likely he was wondering did he have enough food in the house. Did he have enough juice? Did he have enough bananas? Ben liked bananas. He was probably thinking, I'll dump the folder, check the fridge and then stock up on bananas and suchlike from the shop down the street. He gave Stone an edited version of this – just the highlights. Sergeant Harris didn't bother writing it down.

'OK, so now open the door,' said Stone.

Larry took out his keys – a Chubb and a Yale. Stone was right behind him with Harris and a police photographer. Larry didn't know why they needed the photographer. They had scores of photographs already. They'd even made a video.

Larry turned the Chubb in the lock and then opened the door with the Yale.

Someone – it must have been the police – had put a strip of plastic sheeting on the floor, presumably so they wouldn't be treading in the blood. They'd done nothing to cover the blood on the walls but at least it was dry now.

'So you see the blood,' Stone said. Larry felt his breath in his ear. 'What's going through your head?'

Larry said nothing.

'You know it's bad. You can see it clearly, all over the walls and on the floor. You know this isn't somebody just cut a finger opening a tin. So what are you thinking?'

'I can't remember. I was probably too stunned to think anything much.'

'But you go in.'

'Yeah.' It came out as a sigh.

'You're not *afraid* to go in?'

'I *had* to go in,' Larry said. 'I had to find out what had happened. He might have needed help.'

'The killer might have been there, too – did you think of that?'

'It might have crossed my mind. I don't remember.'

'So you go in. Off you go.' He gave Larry a slight nudge in the back. Larry took a step into the hall and then stopped. Stone bumped into him.

'Why do you stop?' he said.

'I stepped in the blood.'

There had been blood on the sole of one of Larry's shoes. He'd left a footmark.

'And that's when you saw the eye,' said Stone.

That's when he saw the eye.

'Yes. Just there . . .' He pointed to the foot of the stairs at the far end of the hall.

'And you knew that's what it was – a human eye?'

'Yes.' Larry knew what it was but he couldn't believe it.

He had been through all this with Dent. The only reason he could be going through it again now, with Stone, was that Stone didn't believe him. He wanted to see how *convincing* it looked.

'But you couldn't see *into* the kitchen yet?'

'No.'

'Go on then, in you go.'

Larry felt the hand in the small of his back, again, gently propelling him forward. He took two more steps down the hall until he could see through the open door into the kitchen. Then he stopped again. Stone was right behind him. You couldn't stand side by side in the hall, not comfortably, not without rubbing your shoulder against the wall and you wouldn't want to do that.

'So then you see the body,' said Stone. 'You see the eye and then you see the body. *Then* what do you do?'

'I go back. I back off.'

He felt there was something wrong with his voice. He cleared his throat.

'Right away? You don't go into the kitchen?'

'No. No.' Larry was shaking his head emphatically. He *emphatically* did not go into the kitchen.

'I could see he was dead. You didn't have to look twice.'

The blood had dried here, too, though not as thoroughly as it had in the hall. It looked like a skin had formed on the surface, like paint when it has dried, and that, if you scratched it, it would start to bleed again. The chalk outline of the body resembled a large foetus, curled in its mother's womb, the knees drawn up to the chest, the arms covering the face. On the edge of the pool, near the head, there was something black. For a moment Larry thought it was a piece of decayed flesh or tissue the police had missed but then he saw that it was a fly – a large bluebottle. It took off and circled the room.

It was the wrong season for flies but sometimes they revived in a warm house. Forensics had spent several days here and they must have kept the central heating on. Larry knew he was deliberately thinking of trivia so he wouldn't think of other things. He looked around the walls. There seemed to be blood everywhere, as if it had been *sprayed*.

'Cosy,' Rob had said on his first visit here. 'Intimate.'

Already seeing it as a scene of seduction, those *intimate* little suppers, those post-coital snacks. But with irony, too, noting the cheap kitchen unit and table, the linoleum tiles, the strip lighting . . . Larry didn't have the money to do much about it but he'd done his best with a few tins of paint. He had painted the cupboards blue and the floor terracotta with a large yellow sun in the middle. Rob thought it looked like a slice of ham with a fried egg on top.

'When you said you wanted to be a painter,' Rob had said, 'I didn't think you meant a painter of floors.'

Larry pictured Rob standing here in the centre of the room, near the table, pulling the cork on the bottle of wine. The cork came out, but he did not pour. They had found no wine glass among the broken shards on the floor so the doorbell must have rung before he had found one.

Larry backed a couple of steps down the hall and then turned round. Stone's face was a few inches from his own. Harris and the photographer were still behind him.

Stone turned round too and they all filed out into the street.

Larry shut the door behind him.

'Why did you do that?' said Stone.

'Why did I shut the door?'

'Yes.'

'I suppose to stop anyone seeing in.'

'What about getting out?'

Larry frowned, puzzled.

'The killer,' Stone said. 'If he was still inside.'

'I'm not sure I thought about that,' said Larry.

'If you had,' said Stone, 'you'd have double-locked the door. With the Chubb.'

'I suppose so.'

'But you didn't.'

'No.'

'And then you phoned the police. On your mobile.'

'Yes.'

'And you stay put, outside the door, until they come.'

'That's right.'

Stone seemed to have a problem here. He was stroking his chin.

'You don't think of getting help from any of the neighbours. Or passers-by.' He looked up the narrow street, empty now, with the police at the far end. One of the shopkeepers poked his head out of a door and withdrew it quickly when he saw the detective looking in his direction.

Larry shook his head. 'There was no one around. I don't know the neighbours.'

'That's curious,' Stone said. At first Larry thought he meant it was curious Larry didn't know the neighbours. 'You said in your statement you didn't go any further into the house because you thought the killer, or killers, might still be there. Yet you stand outside the door for several minutes until the police arrive and you don't lock the door or try to get help from the people in the street.'

'I'm not sure that I was thinking it out at all logically,' Larry explained patiently. 'I'm not even sure that I thought about the killer at all. I just wanted to get out of the house as quickly as possible. I expect I was in some shock.'

He meant this to be sarcastic.

'Yet you must have seen things like this before. In Bosnia, in Kosovo. That's where you were, isn't it? Among other places. You must have filmed worse than this.'

'This was different,' Larry told him. 'They weren't my friends.'

'OK. OK.' Stone looked at his watch again. 'Now if you'll just bear with me I'd like to try a little experiment. I want you to come into the house with me again. Sergeant Harris, have you got your spoon?'

Harris rummaged in her shoulder bag and took out a wooden spoon. The kind you used for stirring things in a non-stick saucepan. Mystified, Larry stepped back into the house. Stone followed him, closing the door after him and switching on the light.

'That's right, isn't it?' he said. 'When you came back in the morning the light was still on.'

Larry confirmed that it was. It felt much worse in the house now, with the door closed.

'There was no light outside?'

'No. The bulb had gone. It had been gone some time. I hadn't got round to replacing it.'

Stone pointed to the small spy-hole set into the door.

'But you could see anyone standing outside, even in the dark?'

'I don't know,' said Larry. 'I've never looked.'

'Really?' Stone seemed surprised. 'So – if you heard the doorbell, late at night, you'd open the door without checking to see who it was?'

Larry thought about it. 'Probably,' he said. 'I'm not sure I would now, mind you.'

'No. So, what do you think your friend would have done?'

Larry didn't have to think about it.

'He'd have just opened the door the same as I would.'

'Without looking?'

'Without looking. Especially if he was expecting someone.'

'Well, we couldn't find any prints on it,' Stone conceded. 'But let's say he looked.'

He slid back the brass cover and put his eye up to the hole.

'Peep-oh.' He took his head away. 'You look.'

Through the fish-eye lens Larry had a blurred view of Sergeant

Harris, standing there with her deadpan expression and her clipboard and the photographer behind her.

'You can just about tell if it's a man or a woman,' said Stone. 'And in Sergeant Harris's case not even that.'

Larry looked back at him. He was smirking.

Stone raised his voice a little.

'Sergeant Harris?'

'Yes, sir?' They heard her voice clearly through the door.

'Have you got your spoon ready?'

'Yes, sir.'

Stone took Larry's place by the door.

'All right. Ring the bell.'

He went into a mock karate stance. The bell rang.

'Avon calling,' said Stone. He assumed a normal pose and opened the door. Harris hit him in the neck with the spoon. The photographer took a picture.

'Thank you, Sergeant,' said Stone. 'What was it like for you?'

'Bit awkward, sir. I couldn't get much of a swing.'

'No. Well, you wouldn't. Not with a forehand. Besides, he was hit in the *right* side of the neck, not the left. Try a backhand. And stand with your back to the door. You're looking up and down the street to see if anyone's coming.'

He closed the door again.

This time Harris hit him with a backhand, in the *right* side of the neck.

'Bloody hell, Sergeant,' said Stone. He put his hand to his neck.

'Sorry, sir.'

'I take it that was easier for you.'

'Much better, sir. Much better swing, especially with my back turned.'

Stone looked at the door.

'The only problem is – why is there no blood on the door?'

He turned to Larry.

'If it was a stranger,' he explained, 'the first blow had to be in the doorway – but why is there no blood on the door? When he opened it, it would have been by his right shoulder.' Larry shook his head.

'But say he *knew* the killer,' Stone said. 'Say he let him into the house. Or her. Show me how he'd do it. Give us your bag.'

Larry lifted his sports bag off his shoulder and passed it to Stone and reluctantly took his place at the door.

'Not *hard*, Sergeant,' said Stone. 'Nothing like as hard as you hit *me*, if you don't mind.'

He told Larry to close the door.

'Now you're alone in the house,' said Stone. 'You've just opened a bottle of wine. You hear the doorbell . . .' The bell rang. 'You know who it is. You don't have to look. You open the door . . .'

For a moment Larry was Rob. He didn't even have to think about it. He opened the door towards him with his right hand and took a step back and to the side with an ironic bow and a gesture with his left arm. Sergeant Harris stepped past him. Larry was conscious of the flash of a camera. He closed the door and turned round. Harris was standing much closer than he had anticipated. Her arm swung and Larry felt the edge of the spoon against his neck. Even though he knew it was going to happen, it was a shock.

'Hold it there.' Stone stepped round them and opened the door again and the photographer took another picture. 'Excellent.' He stood behind Larry and put a finger on Larry's neck and then made a line with it to the bloodstain on the wall.

'Exactly right. How did it feel, Sergeant?'

'Comfortable,' said Harris.

'He's expecting her. He sees her in the doorway. He lets her in and closes the door and she's behind him. A backhander to the neck.'

'She?' said Larry.

'Or *he*. If he was *expecting* a man.' He met Larry's eyes directly again. 'Do you think he was expecting a man?'

'No,' said Larry.

'No. Well, of course, it could have been a man he *wasn't* expecting. But he'd have had to know him, wouldn't he, to let him in?'

'If he was hit in the neck like that,' said Larry, 'with a sharp weapon, it would have been lethal.'

'Exactly.'

Stone hadn't got the point.

'But the body was in the kitchen.'

'Yes. And?'

'Well, I'm standing here, with my back to the front door, and Sergeant Harris is standing there with her back to the kitchen. I can't think why I'd want to push past her into the kitchen at this particular time.'

Something like dislike flickered across Stone's expression.

'You don't *know* it's lethal,' he said. 'All you know is that someone has hit you in the neck. You don't know how bad it is. And they're standing there ready to hit you again. What do you do?'

'Well – I suppose I might try to grapple with them.'

'Do it, then. Try to grapple with her. He's going to grapple you, Sergeant, what do you do?'

Larry moved towards Harris. She took a step backwards and hit him again, with a forehand this time, just above the left eye. Larry was standing in the doorway to the kitchen.

'Freeze,' said Stone. 'Action.'

The photographer took another flash.

'Well done, Sergeant, well done,' said Stone. 'Two wounds to the face. One to the right side of the neck, severing the carotid artery. One to the left side of the head, taking out the left retina. And he's falling back into the kitchen where . . . well, where the rest happens. Are we convinced?'

Harris looked down at her feet, saying nothing.

'The blood, Sergeant, look at the blood.' Stone pointed to the wall. He was impatient with her. 'Right-hand side of the neck, right-hand side of the wall. How does it get there if he doesn't let them in the house?'

She looked embarrassed. Larry didn't know if it was for herself or Stone.

'It might have been somebody selling something,' Larry said. He didn't know why he said this. It wasn't a theory he'd considered until now. It was partly because Stone seemed to have all the answers.

Stone looked at him. '*Somebody selling something*. I see. Door-to-door salesman, you mean? Help the homeless. Brushes, dusters, dish cloths, that sort of thing?'

'Something like that. You do get them round here.'

'And then what?'

'Well, just to play devil's advocate . . .'

'Please.'

'Well, it's the kind of thing I might do: you leave the door open and go back to get some money. They follow you and hit you from behind.'

'This has happened to you before then?'

'No, but . . .'

'What did they hit you with – a brush?'

Larry said nothing.

'So that's what you think, is it? You think that's plausible?'

Larry shrugged.

'Well, come on, you knew the chap. Was he the sort to give money to a door-to-door salesman? Are you short of dusters, dish cloths? Sponge to wash the car, perhaps? Would he be thinking that? Bearing in mind he wants to get rid of this chap fairly fast, I imagine, with his bit of totty on the way. Or upstairs in the bedroom waiting for it.'

'I've really no idea,' said Larry coldly. 'I suppose it does seem unlikely.'

'Indeed it does. But, just for the sake of argument, let us

concede that it is not impossible. It is for the homeless after all. "Yes, I'll take a few J-cloths," he says, "and you can throw in a cover for the ironing board." Now, think about this carefully, how *likely* is it that he'd leave this chappie standing there with the door wide open and go back into the kitchen to fetch some money which we are *assuming* he has in his coat pocket? At which point said chappie takes a hook out of his box of tricks and rushes down the hall after him and lets him have one in the back of the neck.'

Larry looked at Sergeant Harris, as if for moral support, but she was looking embarrassed for *him* now. Stone seemed to be waiting for Larry to say something.

'It's not very likely,' Larry admitted.

'Oh well,' said Stone. 'It was worth a try.'

CHAPTER THIRTEEN

The Damage

'WHAT WAS ALL THAT about?' said Muriel Hoffman.

They'd all gone. Stone, Harris, the photographer, the wooden spoon, the whole works, leaving Larry standing with his sports bag outside the closed door of his house. And now here was Muriel Hoffman. With a clipboard. Just like Harris.

'I've no idea,' said Larry.

For a moment he had no idea what *she* was about either. He looked down at her while his brain groped for clues. She was wearing a raincoat in shiny blue PVC and a matching cap with a peak and she had a large bag over her shoulder. Larry recalled their appointment at half-past eleven. She looked smaller than he remembered.

'Bizarre,' he said.

'I beg your pardon.'

'Did you know about this?' he said, not quite accusingly.

'About what?'

Larry waved his hand vaguely in the direction of the departed police van.

'The performance. The re-enactment.'

She let her eyes slide from right to left as if looking for help if he turned violent.

'Sorry? What are we talking about?'

'The police. Didn't you talk to them and say we were meeting here?'

'Oh, the police. Yes, they said they wanted to have another look round before I did anything. Why? Is anything the matter?'

'I don't know.' Larry looked up at the house and then down at her. She smiled at him reassuringly. 'Do you know a guy called Stone?' he asked her. 'DI Stone?'

'Well, not personally or anything. Only through contacts. He's from the Yard.'

'The Yard?'

'As in Scotland Yard. They've brought him in to help out.'

Larry wondered who Muriel Hoffman's contacts were. Sergeant Harris, for instance? He had an idea that she knew a lot more about the City of London police and this particular inquiry than she might be prepared to let on.

'They call him No Stone,' she said.

'Nostone?'

'As in No Stone Unturned. He's a bit weird. Well, shall we go in?'

It wasn't so bad second time round. Larry stood at the foot of the stairs while she peered into the kitchen and took photographs with a Polaroid camera and made notes on her pad. She made sure she didn't brush her coat against the walls but otherwise she seemed completely unfazed. He supposed she'd seen it all before. When she'd finished he led her up to the bathroom.

'What made them think he was in here?' she wanted to know.

'They found some flecks of blood – on the floor and the shower curtain.'

There was no blood on the floor now and no shower curtain – it had been taken away by forensics.

'So they think he took a shower?' she said.

'There'd have been a lot of blood.'

'Were you missing any clothing?' It was like having Stone back again. How many times did he have to go through this? He sighed, thinking no wonder he avoided his friends.

'No, but I think there's a towel missing. I can't be sure. I don't really keep track of them. But I think so.'

'So – what do you want us to do in here?'

'Well, I'd like the whole room cleaned – floor, tiles, bath . . . cleaned *and* disinfected.'

'Naturally. We always disinfect.' She made a note.

'And the drains. And you said you could get some other work done, more major work.'

'Such as?'

'A new shower unit?' He'd worry about how to pay for it later. He still hadn't checked his insurance.

'That's not a problem. Just choose the one you want.'

As they left she paused on the landing and glanced up the stairs to the attic.

'Your studio?'

Had he told her about his studio? Clearly somebody had. He nodded.

'Can I look?'

'Go ahead.'

He followed her up the stairs.

'This is wonderful,' she said.

Privately, Larry thought so, too. It was the best part of the whole house for him. The other rooms were a bit poky. In the attic there was more sense of space and light. He'd had a large dormer window set in the roof and stripped the floorboards and painted the floors a very pale yellow. He looked around it as she did, seeing it as a stranger might. He had a trestle table for his paints – up against the only wall that didn't slope – and his easel next to it, empty at the moment. There was a big white porcelain sink in one corner with a wooden draining board. It was quite comfortably messy and it smelled pleasantly to Larry of linseed oil and turpentine.

'Did you do these?' She was looking at the charcoals propped against the sloping walls.

'Yes,' he said.

'Demons?' she said. She looked at him archly. 'Is that what you do – demons? Are they your thing?'

In the clear light of the studio he saw that her face was slightly freckled and there was a glint of red in the strands of hair that escaped from under her cap. He could imagine her as a child, suddenly, one of the brats who used to play round the docks, freckled and ginger and cheeky. There were gangs of girls he and Rob feared, though they affected not to, and repeated dark rumours of what they did with you, if they caught you.

'At the moment,' Larry said.

She looked back at them.

'They're gargoyles, aren't they?'

'Gargoyles – or grotesques.'

'What's the difference?'

'A gargoyle is the mouth of a drain. A grotesque isn't.'

'You must have been in a lot of churches.'

'They're outside the churches. That's the point.'

'What point?'

'The demons stay outside. They can't get in.'

'Oh.'

She knelt down to look more closely at one of them. A fly with a human face and a tiny skull on each of its wings.

'What's this one – if it's got a name?'

'That's Beelzebub. Lord of Lies.'

She looked up at him.

'You know a lot about demons, do you?'

'The police think I'm a Satanist,' he told her.

'Is that what they said?'

'Not in so many words but I could tell they were thinking it, some of them.'

'But you're not?'

'Of course not.'

'You just like painting demons?'

'It was something I had to get out of my system,' he said. 'Before I did something else.'

'And have you?'

'I was beginning to,' he said.

When they were back on the street he closed the front door, again, and locked it.

She asked him if he fancied a coffee.

'I was going to the gym,' he told her. He indicated the sports bag.

'That's funny, so was I. I brought my swimsuit.' She raised a shoulder to show him *her* bag. No, he thought, this cannot be.

Pleasant as she was, Muriel Hoffman belonged to that compartment of Larry's brain reserved for Death. He was not sure that he wanted her intruding into the compartment where the gym and the pool belonged. Once they started moving around, you never knew where you were. On the other hand, it would be interesting to see her in a swimsuit.

'OK,' he said. 'It's not far to walk.'

This is not wise, he thought.

She wore a brown bikini, a little darker than her suntan. Ruth had always considered it tacky for a woman to wear a bikini in an indoor swimming pool. Larry found it erotic. Muriel Hoffman looked terrific in hers. Larry had always had a thing about small women with large breasts. It probably went back to his childhood – seeing Barbara Windsor in the *Carry On* films, the nearest thing he could get, in those days, to soft porn.

They had the pool to themselves, this time of the morning. Larry gave her lots of space and for a while they swam up and down in opposite lanes without any acknowledgement. But when Larry decided he'd had enough and hauled himself out, she swam over to where he was standing and sat at the edge of the pool, dangling her feet in the water. Larry deliberately avoided looking down at her. He gazed out over the water with a stoic expression – like an explorer, he thought, who's not at all sure where he is heading.

She pulled her cap off her head so her hair fell down over her wet shoulders and in the same action looked up at him.

'You look fed up,' she said.

'I'm just thoughtful,' he told her. 'It's been a difficult morning.'

She reached out her hand for him to help her up.

'Come on,' she said. 'I'll buy you lunch.'

Well, that was it then, he was hooked. He'd never been very good at struggling.

They had lunch at a wine bar and restaurant called the Grapeshot on the approach road to Tower Bridge just a short walk from Dead Man's Hole. It was Larry's choice. Although he would always tell himself that it was Muriel Hoffman who had picked *him* up – and not the other way round – he knew he could have chosen somewhere that was not quite so close to the *Lady Jane*.

Over lunch he talked about his former life as a television cameraman. He talked about the documentaries he'd shot for Rob and the places they'd shot them. Iraq and Afghanistan, the Balkans and the Congo.

'Do you always do wars?' she asked him. Just as she'd asked if he always did demons and he said no but they tended to crop up fairly regularly.

'And you always worked with Rob?'

'No. Not always.' He thought about it, wondering if he wanted to get into this.

'He was the producer,' he said. 'And I was the cameraman. He came up with the work – and I shot it.'

It was the game of childhood continued. At his most cynical, or self-critical, Larry felt they had simply found new places to trespass, a different mischief to make for themselves. But he did not want to say this to Muriel Hoffman.

'And you were happy with that?'

'More or less. Maybe I'd have liked to do other things instead but ...' He shrugged as if it hadn't mattered. 'They didn't happen.'

He changed the subject. He told her about being an art student and how strange it was to be twenty years older than most of the other students.

'I bet they fancy you something rotten,' she said.

He pretended to consider but had no more desire to talk of this than she did. 'Not so I've noticed,' he said.

'And the nude models? Do you paint nudes? I've always fancied being an artist's model,' she said.

He wasn't sure how they moved from this to the *Lady Jane* but it seemed like a natural progression at the time.

'I'd love to see it,' she said.

The tide was in and they could step easily from the waterfront to the bridge of barges. Larry took her hand on the way over. The birds did not seem to bother her and he did not mention the rats. He made her go ahead of him across the gangway, steadying her with his hand on her hip.

A little later she said, 'I've never done this on a *tugboat* before.'

They'd had two bottles of red wine with their lunch and Larry was adrift, cast off from any lingering ties between sea and shore, action and consequence. In some dim, dulled region of his wits, he knew this was reckless and that sooner or later there would be rocks. He could hear the bell from the warning buoy, distantly tolling.

Women said men were led by their pricks but it wasn't quite as straightforward as that. There was the erotic pleasure of seeing a woman naked, revealed. It was as much cerebral as genital. The best of his time with Muriel Hoffman, he would reflect later, was the thrill of anticipation on the way back from the restaurant when he knew that failing a sudden hurricane or a tidal wave he was going to see her nude. He was going to see those wonderful breasts fully exposed. And after that there was the moment when she removed her bra and he did. Nothing much had changed since adolescence.

'I don't usually mix business with pleasure,' she told him afterwards when they were lying together on his bunk. He had known for some moments that this was what she was going to say.

He said nothing for a while. He lay sideways on to her with his back pressed against the bulkhead, feeling the cold of the river through the wooden panelling. His eyes were closed and his mouth half open against her hair.

Then, opening his eyes, he asked her, 'Did it ever cross your mind that *I* might have killed him?'

She moved her head away to look at his face, frowning as if it was a preposterous suggestion. But then she changed her mind and she let her head fall back. 'Briefly,' she said. 'But I could tell you didn't.'

'How?'

'You're not the type.'

'You know the type?'

She didn't answer but she looked at him again, thoughtfully now. 'You could be, I suppose, physically . . .'

'And mentally?'

'No,' she said firmly. 'Your eyes are too nice.'

'So I couldn't have killed him because I have nice eyes.' His tone veered on the sardonic but he was pleased.

'Not only that. You have a nice mouth, too.'

She lifted her chin to kiss it. He wondered what he was going to do with her now. If he had any choice in the matter. Usually he let the woman make the choice unless it became too inconvenient.

He was so tired. He'd hardly slept all weekend.

'Would you like a cup of tea?' he asked her.

'I'll make it.' She rolled off the bunk and stood up.

He protested. 'You won't be able to find anything.'

'It's hardly big enough to hide anything – and I'm used to

strange places.' She left him to make what he would of that. He watched her move across the cabin towards the galley. He had the familiar, slightly sinking feeling of being taken over.

When he woke up it was dark and he was alone.

He reached for the light cord.

She'd left a note on the shelf by the bunk.

'You fell asleep. I'll let you know the damage! Love M.'

The damage? This alarmed him for a moment until he realised she meant the estimate for the cleaning.

Oh my God, he thought, what have I done?

He was aware of having crossed some kind of moral line. Worse, far worse, than Playing in Duggan's Yard.

It was absolutely no comfort to know that Rob would almost certainly have approved.

CHAPTER FOURTEEN

Prayers for the Dead

ON THE DAY OF Rob's memorial service, the four members of the Used Women's Book Club met at Meg's house and drove together, in Meg's car, to the church in Highgate where it was to be held. They all wore black. Black suits, black shoes and stockings, black coats and black hats. Amy even wore a black veil. It was Jo's private opinion that the veil was well over the top. Amy also wore the highest heels of the four women. Jo did not say anything but she could see that Liz was having to bite her tongue.

The two girls were still with Meg's mother, who was taking them directly to the church. Rob's parents were driving up from Sussex. It was largely on their account that it was to be a religious ceremony. Meg would have preferred it to be humanist but she did not want to upset them. Rob, she said, would not have given a toss either way.

Many of his friends and work colleagues would be there and several of them would be saying a few words of tribute. Jo had told Meg that his closest friend, Larry, had declined. Meg had made no comment.

The drive to the church took them along the side of Highgate Cemetery where Meg said that Rob would have liked to be buried. He liked to walk there, she said, reading the inscriptions on the gravestones. This was so at variance with Jo's own image and impressions of Rob, she wondered if Meg had already begun to rewrite the history of her marriage. On the other hand, she knew that, in the privacy of their relationships, men and women did sometimes say the most unlikely things to each other. Michael Geraghty had once assured Jo, with tears in his eyes, that he went to church to light a candle to his dead mother every Mothering Sunday. Complete bollocks of course – she'd never known him go near a church on Mothering Sunday or any other time of the year – but he did not simply want *Jo* to believe it; he wanted to believe it of *himself*. And it was entirely possible, she conceded, that if he had been once – the year she died, perhaps – and that if he ever got up in time to get to the church before the pubs opened he might very well go again.

Jo thought it highly unlikely that Rob would be buried in Highgate Cemetery. If and when the police got round to releasing his body, he would probably be buried near the village in Sussex where his father and mother now lived. Or in the graveyard of the church in Bermondsey where his father had been vicar all the time Rob was growing up. And then they would have to go through this all over again, with a body this time.

Jo was in that kind of mood. Dog in the manger. It was, she knew, a form of defence, a shield for her conflicting emotions. She was braced for her conversation with Rob's daughters – and his parents.

She wondered if the police would be there.

Looking at her friends as they sat in the car on their way to the church, Jo wished they had chosen to dress down a bit, to look a bit more drab. Black is not a drab colour. Black is a glamorous colour. They should look less glamorous, she thought. They looked as if they were putting on a show.

They had been here before, dressed like this, on a Used Women's Book Club outing. That had been a show. Liz had arranged it. Dress Funereal, she had written on the formal invitations. They had come to visit the graves of a number of writers who were buried at Highgate Cemetery. At each grave they had read out a passage from one of the writer's books, more than a little tongue in cheek, it had to be said. Jo had read at the grave of Mrs Henry Wood who had written the

Victorian melodrama *East Lynne* famous for the line: 'Dead! – and never called me mother.' They had become a little less frivolous when Liz conducted them to the grave of Lizzie Siddal who had been the model and then the wife of the pre-Raphaelite painter Dante Gabriel Rossetti and had subsequently become a painter and a poet in her own right. Afflicted by melancholy and addicted to laudanum, she had taken an overdose and died at the age of thirty-two, her talents largely unrecognised. Siddal was one of Liz's icons and a perfect example, in her view, of the Used Woman. Jo considered this a little unfair on Dante Gabriel Rossetti who had encouraged Siddal to paint and to write at a time when it was difficult for a woman to do anything on her own account. But it was Liz's contention that she would have done a lot better if he had left her alone.

'He couldn't even leave her alone when she was *dead*,' Liz had said.

When Lizzie Siddal died – in what Liz darkly described as 'very suspicious circumstances' – Dante Gabriel Rossetti, apparently heartbroken, had taken a manuscript of poems that he had written especially for her and laid them beside her in the coffin. Seven years later he had begun to regret this impulsive and romantic gesture. His friend Swinburne had won recognition as a poet and although Rossetti was a painter, he wanted to show the world that, whatever Swinburne did, he could do better. Unfortunately his best poems were buried with Lizzie Siddal. Through friends in high places Rossetti secured permission to exhume the body and remove the manuscript.

So on a cold, dank evening in October 1869, by the light of several lanterns and a small bonfire, the 'ghastly business', as Rossetti called it, was done. He was too sensitive to be there himself. The coffin was opened and the manuscript peeled away from what was left of poor Lizzie's face, disinfected, dried and conveyed to the waiting painter-poet who, after shedding a few manly tears, sent it straight round to his publisher. The publicity over its macabre recovery helped make it an immediate bestseller.

Even by the standards of outrageous male behaviour, this – the Used Women had agreed – was exceptional. If Dante Gabriel Rossetti had been buried in the family plot they would have danced on his grave in their black high heels but he had chosen to be buried somewhere in Kent and they had to be content with reading one of Siddal's poems aloud over *her* grave.

> *A silence falls upon my heart*
> *And hushes all its pain.*
> *I stretch my hands in the long grass*
> *And fall to sleep again,*
> *There to lie empty of all love*
> *Like beaten corn of grain.*

As Liz had remarked in her final moving epitaph: 'I know he was a bastard but sometimes you do feel like giving her a good kicking and telling her to butch up a bit.'

Liz had not been asked to speak at Rob's service. Nor had Jo or Amy. It was probably better, they had agreed, for Meg to leave it to his colleagues in television, who were good at that kind of thing. Meg had chosen the music, though. A few of Rob's favourite tunes.

There was quite a crowd waiting outside the church when they arrived. Rob was not a celebrity by any means but he'd had something of a reputation as a film-maker. An obituary in the *Guardian* had said he was cut off in his prime – an unfortunate choice of expression, Liz had remarked at the time, given the nature and extent of his injuries. Most of the people here must have worked with him, Jo figured, for he'd had few friends outside his career. She thought she recognised one or two faces of people she had seen on television. When she climbed out of the car she thought everyone was staring at them but they quickly looked away. She thought she heard a collective male sigh but it might have been in her imagination. She wished, once again, that they had not looked quite so distinctive. They appeared altogether too bold, she thought, even brash. They should look like the four Prayers for Pardon: *Lame, pale, wrinkled things with eyes cast down.*

She had the uncomfortable feeling that she was attending some fringe production that Geraghty had written, knowing that when it was over she would probably have to lie through her teeth to avoid giving offence. *We are here for Meg*, she told herself firmly. But it might have been easier if she had liked him more.

When they were inside the church Meg joined up with the girls and the other members of her family on the front pew and Jo sat with Liz and Amy on the pew behind. Watching Meg with an arm around each of the girls Jo felt the tears coming. It would not be so difficult then.

When they came out Jo found herself standing alone for a moment in the churchyard. A chill wind had blown up while they were inside, swirling the dead leaves about, threatening rain or sleet. She had to hold on to her hat. She wanted to be gone now but Meg was doing the rounds, thanking people for coming. A few of them would be returning to the house; not many, Jo hoped. She planned to stay in the kitchen, making sandwiches.

She felt a hand on her arm and turned to find Larry there.

She knew it was Larry, a moment before he told her. Probably from the pictures she'd seen, though he'd had a beard in those and he didn't have one now. He looked younger than she had expected, though she knew he must be Rob's age. He was dressed less formally than most of the men at the funeral, in a thick padded jacket that just avoided being an anorak. At least it was black. For some reason she felt embarrassed. Perhaps it was being seen in all the gear. She felt silly holding on to the hat, like a lady at a garden party, but she couldn't let go of it in case it blew away. Then she would feel sillier.

What do you say at memorials for the dead?

'We met at the wedding,' she said.

Not that.

'You were all in red,' he said. 'A red dress and a red hat.'

'*Was* I? Good God, it must have been fifteen years ago.'

She was stunned that he could remember what she was wearing at the time – and then felt at once embarrassed and pleased. She sensed that he was only embarrassed.

They said nothing for a moment and then they both spoke together.

'Go on,' he said.

But then Rob's parents came over. They looked so old and frail. How could Rob have been born to people so old? How could he have died before them? Over the years she had known them, meeting them no more than once a year, sometimes less, Jo had seen the father age more than the mother had. She had looked older to begin with but she had kind of plateaued out at seventy and he had caught up and then overtaken her. Now he walked with a stick and she held on to him. But Jo did not know if it was to support him or to stop *herself* from falling over. She started to say something but to her surprise Larry stepped forward and hugged them. First he hugged *her*, and then he hugged *him*. He did it very gently but Jo could almost hear the snapping of bones. Rob's father looked surprised too. Meg had told Jo that, in all the years she had known him, Rob had never once hugged or kissed his father. He would touch cheeks with his mother very lightly when they first met on a visit and then again when they left but Meg knew he did not like it. She thought Rob's mother knew it, too.

She was holding on to Larry's hand and leaning her head forward to say something. The words meant nothing to Jo – some fragment of the past – but she saw the white parchment skin of her hand with its dark-brown freckles and blue veins and how it trembled in Larry's as if it was supporting her whole being, like a hand clinging to the edge of a cliff. Jo murmured something inadequate and moved away.

And now another man was at her side. Tall, dark and balding, wearing a black overcoat. For a moment Jo thought he was one of the undertakers, until she remembered there wasn't a body, and then he said, 'Miss Connor? DI Stone, City of London police.'

Jo could not recall seeing him before, either at Meg's house or at the police station on Bishopsgate where she had gone to sign her statement. She heard him telling her he had recently taken charge of the case and would appreciate going over a few small details with her. She wondered how he had known who she was.

'What – *now*?' she asked.

His smile was condescending. 'Now is probably not the best time for you,' he said. 'Perhaps we could call on you some time tomorrow.'

'What exactly is it about?' she asked him.

'Oh, just one or two things we're finding a little confusing,' he said.

But she saw he was no longer looking at her and following the direction of his gaze she spotted Larry standing with Meg, a little apart from Rob's parents. Meg was doing the talking and although Jo could not hear what she was saying, or see her face, she sensed an anger in her body language. Larry's head was bowed, as if in contrition. She's giving him a bollocking, Jo thought, but what about?

'I have to go,' she said to Stone and started towards them to break it up but Meg was already moving away in the direction of the cars.

'Ten o'clock, then,' Stone's voice reached after her. 'We know where you live.'

It seemed an odd time to make a joke.

'What were you talking to Larry about?' Jo asked Meg as she drove them back to the house. She tried to keep her voice light.

'Nothing,' Meg said, keeping her eyes on the road. 'Nothing worth talking about.'

But there was bitterness in her voice and for once Jo wasn't going to let her bring the curtains down.

'It was about lending Rob his house,' she said. 'Wasn't it?'

Meg said nothing. Jo sensed the discomfort from Liz and Amy on the back seat behind her but she couldn't let it go now.

'It can't have been easy for him,' she said. 'What was he supposed to say?'

'Go and shag the bitch somewhere else,' Liz muttered as if to herself.

Jo turned round in her seat. 'For heaven's sake,' she said, 'they're old friends.'

'They're *men*,' Liz said and Jo was shocked by the look on her face.

'We'd do the same for each other, wouldn't we?' Jo appealed to them.

But no one answered her.

Jo was surprised to find Larry at the house. He was standing by himself in the kitchen, studying the bits and pieces on the noticeboard like a schoolboy waiting to see the headmistress.

'Can I get you a drink,' she said, 'or anything?'

But he didn't want anything.

'Rob's parents asked me to come,' he said, as if he had to apologise for being there. 'But I don't know what to say to them.'

She didn't know what to say to *him*.

'I'm sorry Meg was giving you a hard time,' she said. Probably not that. Fools rush in, she thought.

'She's not really angry with you,' she continued desperately. 'It's him.'

'Is it?' He nodded to himself a few times, not looking at her.

She saw the pictures on the wall, of him and Rob together, smiling in the sun.

'I hope . . .' she began but she didn't know what she hoped.

'What?' He looked at her now but she just shook her head. It was something about them all staying friends, him and Meg, him and her . . . but she couldn't possibly say that.

Not knowing what else to say she asked him where he was staying.

'I take it you're not . . . ?'

'No,' he said, shaking his head. 'Not yet. I'm living on a boat. On the river.'

'Great,' she said brightly, and, when there was no response, 'Bit cold, though, I suppose, at this time of the year.'

She was really beginning to dislike herself. She couldn't imagine what *he* must think of her, but she knew she would give it her full consideration in a little while. She would chew over every word, like broken glass.

'It would be all right,' he said, 'if it wasn't for the seagulls.'

She tried to reach for it, but it was too far out of court.

'Noisy,' she said, 'are they?'

'My son's frightened of them,' he explained.

He had a *son*? She seemed to recall Meg saying something about this at some point or other but she couldn't remember the details. Only that he lived alone.

'He's only there at weekends,' Larry was saying, 'but I'm going to have to find somewhere else if I want to see him over Christmas.'

'It's that bad?' How old was this kid? she wondered.

'It seems to be some kind of a phobia. He'll probably grow out of it.'

She had not thought until now how much of a victim *he* was. He'd not only lost his best friend, he'd practically lost his home. She hesitated for just a second, then she said, 'I'm going away for Christmas. Why don't you use my place?'

'Oh, that's very kind of you,' he began, 'but I couldn't possibly.'

'Why not? It's completely empty from the 19th of December to the 3rd of January.' It seemed such a good idea now that she'd thought of it. 'And I'd really feel so much better if someone was there. You'd be like a caretaker.'

She could see he was thinking about it.

'Seriously, it really would be doing me a great favour,' she pressed him. 'Why don't you come over and take a look at it? It's on the river. Where's your boat?'

'Wapping,' he said doubtfully.

'Wapping. But that's practically opposite.' She was amazed at the coincidence. 'You'll probably be able to keep an eye on it from the window.'

'I don't know what to say.'

He seemed genuinely affected.

'Come over tomorrow evening,' Jo told him. 'Say, six o'clock? And I can show you around.'

'OK.' He still seemed doubtful but at least he was smiling. 'That's great. Thank you.' But then he glanced over her shoulder and his smile faltered. Jo looked round and saw Meg watching them from the kitchen doorway but she turned away before Jo could read the expression on her face.

'I'd better be going,' Larry said.

Jo gave him a sympathetic smile but he wouldn't meet her eyes. 'Tomorrow at six, then.'

He nodded but she wondered if he'd come.

Later, when he'd gone, she sought out Meg.

'I didn't know Larry had a little boy,' she said.

'Didn't you?' Her manner was distant.

'What's he like?'

'Oh . . . quite edible. As you'd expect.'

As you'd expect. Jo didn't get it at first.

'Why,' she said, 'is his mother beautiful?'

But Meg had seen someone who was just leaving and she moved across the room to say goodbye.

CHAPTER FIFTEEN

Dog Days

JO STOOD IN THE window of her apartment gazing out over the river. She was looking for Larry's boat but all she could see that was floating were the police launches at Wapping Pier. They were a reminder – had she needed one – of the imminent arrival of Inspector Stone. Which would have taken the shine out of anyone's day – she considered – if it had possessed anything remotely resembling a shine in the first place.

A thick layer of cloud grouched over the city like a golem, grudging it the few hours of daylight the season had to offer. It recalled an earlier London, the London of her childhood imagining (based on a leather-bound collection of Dickens in her school library with its grim illustrations of slums and long rows of chimney pots and railway arches and the dark river running through). A city flecked with soot or smothered in a filthy brew of smoke and fog.

Jo had ways of dealing with days like this. She dosed them with St John's wort and cleared their membranes with essential oils. If she was working at home she scruffed around in a tracksuit and thick woollen socks. She played music and spread all her notes out on the floor and poured herself a dry sherry, sometimes two. If it was one of her days at college she wore bright colours. She bought flowers for her office and lit joss sticks. She did yoga. She put out more flags and banged gongs. And if all else failed she took herself off to the wine bar for lunch and got pleasantly pissed.

That's how you dealt with days like that, you kept them out of your head.

Stone brought the weather in with him: an oppression of clouds, a chill wind with rain in it. Jo had the impression that this was something he knew and enjoyed.

He arrived a few minutes after ten with a woman detective he introduced as Sergeant Harris who looked like she had a bad cold. If she'd been one of Jo's students, Jo would have told her to go home and take a Lemsip. As it was she made them both coffee and braced herself for Germs.

'You're an American citizen, I believe,' said Stone, gazing round the room as if it showed in the decor.

Jo told him she had married a British citizen and that she had a British passport. She did not say that Michael Geraghty was a Republican from Northern Ireland and that their divorce was imminent but she wondered if he knew anyway.

'And you like living in London?'

It felt like a threat of deportation.

'There's good days and bad,' she said.

He asked if they could tape the conversation and Jo could think of no legitimate reason to object but it bothered her all the same. Jo was schizophrenic in her attitude to officialdom. She had enough of the American in her to demand her rights and stamp her feet; enough of the Middle European to shuffle obediently from room to room, presenting the right documents, bowing her head, answering their idiot questions . . . On her mother's side of the family she was the product of generations of Bohemian peasants, cowed by officialdom, who always did what they were told. Bullied by Habsburgs, Nazis, Communists . . . Kafka's victims, ever fearful of the file with their name on it, even if it was buried under a million other files. One day it would surface. One day they would find you out . . .

'So, tell me,' Stone began, 'how well do you know Lawrence Hunter?'

It was not a question Jo had anticipated and for a moment she was stumped.

'Oh, *Larry*,' she said, when it clicked. 'Oh, hardly at all. I mean, I knew *of* him, of course, through Meg, but I've only met him once or twice.'

'And what do you know of him?'

'Only that he was a friend of Rob's – his best friend, I think. He was a TV cameraman until quite recently but he quit to go to art school . . . That's about all really.'

He's divorced, he has a child – a boy – whom Meg says is 'quite edible'. I suspect Meg thinks that Larry is quite edible, too. Possibly I am beginning to think the same. Why else have I invited him to move into my apartment – or is it purely an act of charity?

'So you've never been to his house in Spitalfields?'

'No. Of course not,' she said. 'I didn't even know he *had* a house in Spitalfields until recently.'

'So I take it you didn't know the victim was in the habit of using it – for his . . . private purposes?'

She supposed he was being delicate but 'private purposes' sounded rather more sinister than straightforward adultery. It conjured up images of a whip and chains.

'Of course not,' she said again. 'Why should I?'

'It might be something the victim's wife had mentioned to you.'

'Well, she didn't. I'm pretty sure she didn't know either – until your people told her.'

'No?' He pretended to consider this as if it was just within the bounds of possibility. 'Well, let's go back to the night of the murder, shall we?'

'If we must,' she said, 'but I've been through all this before.'

She wondered if this was a technique they had – to make people go over everything two or three times to see if they changed their story or slipped up on the detail. She was conscious of the red light on the recorder and imagined them replaying it back at the precinct with the rest of the team, analysing her words, comparing notes.

'Yes, you had a meeting, I believe, to talk about books.'

He said it as a non-believer might say to read the Bible or to consort with demons.

'We take it in turns to be the host,' she said, 'and it was my turn.'

'The Used Women's Book Club,' he said with slow deliberation, as if marvelling that anyone could come up with something so exotic – or absurd.

'It's a joke,' she said. '*Used* as in second-hand.'

'I'm sorry, I don't get it. Is that funny?' He looked at the sergeant as if she might know but the sergeant was blowing her nose on a tissue.

'I guess not,' said Jo.

But she was wondering who had told him the name. There was no reason why they shouldn't but it worried Jo, just as it had worried her when they had arrived together at the memorial service, all four of them, dressed in their glad rags, graves for the visiting of.

'And in what order did they arrive?'

'First Liz, then Meg and then Amy.' She worried that it sounded too pat but she had already given this information to his colleagues and might be expected to remember.

'And all within a few minutes of half-past seven?'

'That's right.'

'And how did you let them in?'

She didn't quite roll her eyes.

'How did I let them in? They rang the bell and I opened the door.'

'From up here, in the apartment?'

'Ye-es.'

'So they'd have crossed the lobby and come straight up to the second floor by the lift – as we just did?'

'I guess.' She shrugged, wondering what he was driving at. 'Unless they wanted to walk up the stairs.'

'But they'd have still had to cross the lobby?'

'Sure.' The night porter, she thought. Of course. The police were bound to have talked to the night porter. But what had he told them?

She felt the blood rush to her face. It was an affliction she had, not only when she felt guilty, but when she thought people *assumed* her to be guilty. It had got her into a lot of trouble in the past.

'And they were here until about 11 p.m. and then they all left together?'

'Yes. Liz had her car and she gave the other two a ride to the nearest subway.'

He seemed to be mulling this over.

'Well, the thing that puzzles me is this: you say all three women arrived around half-past seven that evening and left at around eleven. But the night porter can't remember seeing a single one of them – either arriving or leaving.'

Jo was relieved but tried not to show it. For a moment she had thought the night porter might have remembered something else.

'Perhaps he didn't notice them.'

'Seems unlikely, don't you think? Three women as striking as they are.'

'Perhaps he was reading a book,' she said.

She could see he took it badly.

'Anyway,' she added hastily, 'won't you have a record of them – arriving *and* leaving – on the security cameras?'

He looked at her in a way she remembered certain teachers would look at her at school, when she was being too clever by half.

'The ones at the front are on a three-hour loop,' he said. 'And they don't keep the tapes. Didn't you know that?'

'No,' she said. 'I have no idea how they work.'

'OK. Leaving that aside for the moment, tell me – why did Mr Reynolds call you two days before he died?'

She stared at him.

'Rob? Call *me*?'

'We have a record of the calls made on his mobile phone. One of them was to this number.'

'Are you sure? Two days before . . .' She floundered through the mess of truth and lies in her head and clutched at a memory. 'But of course . . .' This time she did not hide the relief. 'It was Meg.'

'Meg?' He looked at the sergeant.

'The wife,' said the sergeant.

'I know she's the wife, Sergeant,' he said, 'but why should she . . .' He turned back to Jo, sighing and shaking his head. 'So you're saying *she* phoned you – on her husband's mobile?'

'No. She was *here*. She'd been to the Tate Modern, just along the river, and she just dropped by. She had to call Rob but the battery had gone on her mobile phone so she rang him from here and left a message and he called her back.'

'She'd been to the Tate? Two days before the murder?'

'Yes. Why? Is that so surprising?'

'It is, rather. Considering she was there on the night it happened – so she tells us – before she came here. To a late viewing, between six and seven o'clock in the evening.' He was watching her as if for cracks in the façade and she could feel them showing. 'You didn't know that?'

She shook her head.

'And now you're telling us she was there only two days previously?'

'Well, that's what she told *me*. Is there any reason why she shouldn't have?'

'Well, I suppose if you've got plenty of time on your hands . . .'

'She works part time as a speech therapist in a hospital . . .' Jo let a little ice creep into her voice. 'And she has two young children but I believe she does find time to go to art galleries, even twice in one week. *And* read the occasional book.'

The smile again. He put her in mind of a rather sinister clown. You splash him with water at your peril. Forget ice.

'So – Mr Reynolds phoned here to speak to his wife. You didn't speak to him yourself?'

Now *he's* floundering, she thought, with satisfaction.

'No. I mean, I might have taken the call but I'd have passed it straight on to Meg.'

'So you weren't what you might call *close*, then, you and the victim? Not exactly "matey".'

Jo shook her head, trying to keep her temper, aware that he was probably trying to make her lose it, if only for the satisfaction it would give him.

'And what about your other friends – the other "used women" – Miss Roper and Miss Gerard – was he "matey" with *them*?'

'No.' She shrugged, wondering if he was simply being offensive or trying to catch her out with something.

'So you can think of no reason why he might have phoned them in the week before the murder?'

It was a shock but she tried to hide it.

'No, none at all. Why? *Did* he?'

'He did. On several occasions.'

'Well, I'm sorry,' she said. 'I've really no idea. You'll have to ask them.'

'We *have* asked them. In one case, I'm told, it was to discuss something to do with his garden. In the other, some work for the BBC. A voice-over, I believe the expression is.'

He made both explanations sound equally unlikely.

'Well, then . . .' Jo said. 'Why did you ask me?'

'I thought you might have some theories of your own, that's all.'

'I don't understand.'

'Well, let me put this to you: the victim had something of a reputation as a womaniser. And his wife's friends – those I've seen, anyway – appear to be the kind of women he might be attracted to.'

'You can't be serious.'

'You don't think so?'

'All *four* of us?'

'The Used Women's Book Club,' he said, again with the same slow deliberation but as if this time he had finally got the joke.

'No . . .' She shook her head. 'That is not . . . That is totally and completely insane.'

'Is it?' He considered her. 'You may not have known, of course, until recently . . .'

'And when we found out – that he was screwing all four of us – we marched round to Larry's house, having somehow discovered he was there, and took turns to slice him up with a meat hook or whatever it was. Is that what you think? You must know some very weird women.'

Stone inclined his head in polite acknowledgement.

'It goes with the job,' he said.

When they had left, Jo spent the rest of the morning going over the conversation in her head, trying to recall exactly what she had said and thinking of better ways of saying it. She wanted to call Meg, or Liz, or even Amy, but she was paranoid enough to suppose that the phones were tapped. Stone had that effect on her.

In the afternoon she had to go out for a couple of hours. The college term had ended but once a week she did voluntary work at one of the local schools in Southwark, helping children who were having difficulty with their reading. They were mostly the children of parents for whom English was a second language, schools-speak for immigrants and asylum-seekers, who could use a bit of individual tuition. Jo would spend a quarter of an hour with each of them, listening to them read from the story books they had been given, each marked with a little coloured tag that indicated the reading level the child had reached. There were children from Bosnia and Kosovo and Afghanistan and Somalia who had fled from wars and persecution and the stories were about English children called Biff and Chip who dealt with crises like going for a family outing when the car broke down. The children would read slowly, their brows furrowed in concentration, stumbling over the words. All Jo did was listen to them and help them with words they found particularly difficult. Although she practically knew the stories by heart – and found them achingly boring – she never felt the work was a chore and it was a lot more rewarding at times than trying to get some of her older students enthused about English literature. But today she felt she was going through the motions, automatically correcting their mistakes while her mind grappled with problems of her own, and she felt the children sensed it and made more mistakes than usual.

She got back to the flat a little after four and ran a bath. She added a generous measure of bath foam and then, from a collection of essential oils, a few drops of geranium and orange blossom. She expected the purists would tell her that whatever was in the bath foam cancelled out whatever healing properties the oils possessed but Jo liked the bubbles. There were too many instances in life when she had been deprived of bubbles for the sake of righteousness and she was damned if it was going to happen when she had a bath. She also lit two jasmine-scented candles and placed them at the end where the taps were so the hot wax wouldn't drip on her shoulders. Jo had been brought up in a shower culture but she was a woman who loved ritual and you could not make much of a ritual out of a shower. You certainly could not light candles.

When she had completed these preparations to her satisfaction she took off her clothes, switched off the light, and lowered herself into the water, letting the combined scents of geranium, orange blossom, jasmine and whatever was in the bath foam fight over her body and do wonderful things for her mind. She could feel Stone trying to get back in there but she resolutely kept him out.

One of the stories that had been read to Jo as a child was about the Drohung – a kind of goblin that lived in the forests of her mother's homeland on the Czech–German border. The

Drohung was consumed by a hatred of humanity. Or rather, it hated the love that humans had for each other; it hated families and friendships and communities and it lived only to destroy them. If you were unfortunate enough to run into the Drohung, it planted a terrible thought in your head – it might be about a member of your family or a friend or a neighbour – and the thought would grow and grow until it took you over completely and you did all the damage yourself.

Stone was like the Drohung and she had to keep him out of her head.

At six o'clock Larry came to look over the flat. She had discarded the tracksuit for an expensive knitted top in peacock blue and a pair of creamy chinos and as soon as she saw him she felt overdressed, over *formal*. He wore the same black weatherproof he had worn at the church in Highgate over jeans and a sweater. She felt like a hostess, or worse, a realtor hoping to make a sale. To compensate she became brisk to the point of rudeness. Then – when she realised what she was doing and to compensate for *that* – she showed him how everything worked in great detail. The central heating, the oven – even the *kettle*.

She was sure he'd leave as soon as the tour was over and that would be that – the end of a very bad day.

Fortunately, after the business with the kettle, she calmed down and offered him a glass of wine. When they'd drunk the best part of the bottle she asked him if he'd like to stay for supper.

'I was just going to make a pasta,' she said, wondering if she *had* any pasta.

But he took her out instead. To thank her, he said, for the loan of the flat.

He took her to a little Italian in one of the side streets near Tower Bridge. The waiters obviously knew him.

'We come here a lot,' he said. 'We like the paper tablecloths.'

'Yes,' she said, feeling them for the quality. 'They're very nice. Very ... *white*.'

'You can bring your crayons,' he said, 'and draw on them.'

'Fun,' she said. Then she said, 'Who's we?'

'Me and Ben. My son.'

'Of course,' she said.

So they talked about Ben for a bit and then they talked about Larry – and why he had given up being a cameraman to go to art school. But whatever they talked about she always felt they were making an effort *not* to talk about the murder. It was as if they were edging around it, skirting the dark pool. But it was always there, no matter where the conversation took them, waiting to draw them in.

Even when he asked her where she came from in America.

'I've never really lived in America,' she said. 'I kind of visit there from time to time.'

'But you *are* American?'

'Oh yes, but my dad was in the US Air Force and we moved around a lot. From base to base. I was born in Germany and then we moved to England, to East Anglia.'

'And that's where you met Meg?'

'Yes. She went to the same school. A convent school near Cambridge. She's my oldest friend.'

'Rob called you her guardian angel,' he said.

'Among other things, I imagine.'

One of them she knew about was Sister Jo.

'He probably felt threatened,' Larry said. 'He always seemed to feel people were either for him or against him. They couldn't be neutral.'

'And I was for Meg.'

'I guess.' He looked at her and she thought suddenly of one of the lost boys in Peter Pan. So did that make her Wendy? She hardened her heart. She had never liked Wendy.

'I know she thinks I kind of ... *colluded* with him,' he said.

And didn't you? she thought. But she said, 'You mean by letting him use your house?'

For his own private purposes, as Stone had put it.

'I found it very difficult to say no.' He realised what he'd said and smiled, shaking his head. She thought he was thinking of the sexual ambiguity but it was something else. 'That's what my aunts used to say when we were kids and we got into some kind of trouble. Trespassing or something. They always thought it was Rob's fault. That he led me on. "Larry finds it very difficult to say no," they'd say. And it was true. If I'd said no, or even implied a measure of . . . disapproval, he'd have taken it as a rejection, a rebuke – a moral judgement. He'd have thought I'd gone over to the other side. The enemy.'

'Meaning Meg.'

'No, I wasn't meaning Meg.' He sounded defensive. 'I was thinking more of his father – on this occasion.'

'His *father*?' Makes a change, she thought. They usually blame the mother.

'He was the one who made the moral judgements – in those days.'

Jo remembered Rob's father at the memorial service. 'He looked very surprised when you hugged him,' she said.

'I know. It surprised me too. But I felt . . . I don't know what I felt, maybe I was doing it for Rob.'

She didn't understand. He was hugging him for *Rob*?

'I don't know what was going through my mind, to tell the truth. I just felt like reaching out to him – and Rob never could, poor bastard, his dad would never let him. He was a tight-arsed old sod, his dad – the Rev, we called him. You know, man of God, socialist, did a lot for the community . . . People said he was a good man. But he was a bloody awful father. And an even worse husband, I should think. He was the kind of bloke who couldn't handle emotion, you know, and hated any display of it.'

She thought of her own father. And her husband. But Geraghty wasn't afraid to show emotion. He revelled in it. It was another bottle he could get drunk on.

'I mean, my dad wasn't much better,' he was saying, 'but Rob's was kind of . . . I don't know. I mean, my dad, he'd fight with you, you know, he'd box with you, or he'd wrestle, it was his way of hugging – then he'd draw back, you could feel him drawing away . . . but Rob's dad – he was like, *Don't touch.*' He raised his arms as if in surrender, or like the priest at the Eucharist . . . 'It was like he had the pulpit in front of him, he carried it around with him like a barricade. And he was a bully, a control freak. Rob *loved* his mother. I know Meg thought he hated her but he loved her. He just wasn't allowed to show it. She was always wanting to touch Rob. All she wanted was for Rob to give her a hug, give her a kiss. Say, "I love you, Mum." But he'd have lost face with his father. You'd see Rob wondering what to do. In the end he chose his father. And he never really forgave himself for it.'

This was so close to Jo's own behaviour as a child it brought the claws out.

'So screwing all these women made him feel better about that?'

'Well . . .'

'Or d'you think every time he fucked one he thought, That's for you, Dad?'

'Well, I think he got quite a lot of pleasure out of it, too. But he liked the element of trespass. And *that* was getting back at his father. Or *anyone* who tried to make some kind of moral judgement.'

'He *used* them,' Jo said. She surprised herself with the way it came out, the venom of it. He looked startled.

'He used Meg,' she said, 'and he used *them*. Whoever they were, whatever the reason. He used them as a prop for his ego, and that's about the extent of it. I'm sorry. He was your friend. But . . .' She shrugged. 'There you go.'

He looked down at the tablecloth. Bring on the crayons, she thought. She had not wanted the evening to go like this.

'Let's talk about something else,' she said.

'OK.' He nodded to himself a few times but it was clear nothing else presented itself to him.

'Tell me about being an art student,' she said.

So he told her about being an art student and she told him about being an expert on fairy-tales and all things considered it could have turned out a lot worse.

It was after eleven when they left the restaurant. The moon was full, the sky clear. She felt the chill in the air and hugged her coat a little tighter to her shoulders.

'I'll walk you home,' Larry said.

She was glad of the offer but a little perturbed when he set off in the direction of the river. She told him that the last time she had walked home this way she had come close to being mugged. She kept her voice casual, as if remarking on the weather, but he stopped and looked at her with concern.

'What happened?'

'I ran away,' she said.

'We could take a cab . . .' But his expression was doubtful. They both knew it was not far enough for a cab.

'It's all right,' she said, 'but if it happens again don't hang around for me. I'll be streets ahead of you.'

She saw him glance down to see what she was wearing on her feet – trainers, as it happened – and as they walked on he took her hand. She figured that if it made him feel any better it was all right with her.

When they reached the river he pointed out the mooring where he had his boat. It was much closer to Tower Bridge than Wapping Pier and she wouldn't have been able to see it from her apartment. It looked bleak. More like a breakers' yard than a mooring. She thought of Peter Grimes, alone on his mud flats, a poem she disliked but whose opening lines had lodged perversely in her memory.

Thus by himself compell'd to live each day,
To wait for certain hours the tide's delay.

The tide was running high, the moon tethered in its flood. She asked if he'd had any more thoughts about moving back into his house and he told her he was going to get it cleaned up first and then decide.

'There's a firm that specialises in cleaning up after dead people,' he said.

It was difficult to know what to say to that.

'Is it expensive?' she asked.

He told her he was waiting for the estimate. She could not believe they were having this conversation, walking hand in hand in the moonlight by the river.

'Couldn't you get some friends to help you?'

He was shaking his head.

'I couldn't ask anyone to do that.'

'Is it that bad?'

'It's that bad,' he said.

When they reached the front of the apartments he was unexpectedly formal, kissing her on the cheek and leaving quickly. She had thought – with the hand-holding and everything – that there might be more. She had wondered about asking him in. She knew as she waited for the elevator that she would spend the best part of the weekend wondering how she could contrive to see him again before she went away.

CHAPTER SIXTEEN

Fear of Birds

ONCE, WHEN LARRY HAD felt disillusioned with his work as a TV cameraman and had not yet decided to become a painter, he had considered the possibility of running a small hotel in Cuba. It was never a serious prospect – he could never have left Ben for a start – but running a small hotel in Cuba had, for a time, become a kind of private code for running away, changing his life, making a new start.

He had even made a list of the pros and cons. In the For column he had written: *Sunshine, Growth of Tourism.* In the Against he had written: *Chaos after Castro? Return of Mafia? Protection Rackets. No Contacts. No Spanish.* And finally: *Hurricanes.*

In some ways, he felt he could have done a similar list for falling in love. They would not have been the same words but there would have been the same disparity between For and Against. And the same sense that, in the end, it made not a blind bit of difference. Sometimes you just couldn't resist the sunshine.

When it came to falling in love with Jo, Larry did not have to make a list. He knew exactly why it was not a good idea – why it was, in fact, a very bad idea. But for most of his short journey back to his refuge on Hermitage Wharf all he could think of was how good it felt.

Larry liked falling in love. Rob used to say he liked it so much, he did it as much as possible. Larry would have denied that he was so undiscriminating – or such a philanderer – but he accepted that the process of falling in love was more pleasurable for him, or certainly less problematical, than *being* in love.

He had once read that in Japan there was an annual ritual of watching the cherry trees bloom. He imagined that you sat in the garden, or on the roof terrace, or wherever you had your cherry tree, with a bottle of sake to hand, and you waited for that moment when the buds opened. Then you went away. You did not hang around to watch them fade. That would be sad. The problem with falling in love was that you were expected to hang around afterwards. There was supposed to be some kind of fruition. And fruition, in Larry's view, was perilously close to decay.

But he would not dwell on this now. That would be to spoil the moment. He thought instead about their evening together – or at least the last hour when they managed to avoid the subject that haunted them both. Halfway across Tower Bridge he realised he felt better than he had at any time since the murder, perhaps since a lot earlier than that. He felt almost euphoric. For no particular reason – certainly not because he was in a hurry – he started to run. He jogged most of the way back to the Hermitage.

Then, as he approached the mooring, his mood changed again and he slowed to a walk. He did not want to go back to the tug. It was not the first time he had felt such reluctance but tonight it was combined with a deep sense of apprehension. He paused at the top of the steps that led down to the water, puzzled by this. He had come back many times late at night and had never worried about it. But now he was oppressed with a distinct sense of menace – more than that – of malevolence. He glanced over his shoulder but there was nothing there to alarm him. Then out across the barges to the mooring. It looked much the same as it always did. The *Lady Jane* was obscured by the huts on the jetty but he could see the little Christmas tree he had lashed to her masthead. It was some comfort but not much. He stepped cautiously down the stairs and on to the first of the barges. From somewhere in the darkness of the hold came the squeak of a rat.

Nothing abnormal in that . . . but then he realised there were no birds. Perhaps that was it. But *why* were there no birds?

The gangplank was in its usual hiding place. Still, he moved like a cat burglar across the deck of the jetty, placing his feet with care, his ears strained for any unfamiliar sound. He used the pencil torch on his key ring to examine the padlock on the door of the wheelhouse but could see no sign that it had been tampered with. When he was inside, he stood in the dark of the wheelhouse looking back towards the waterfront. Everything was reassuringly, almost mockingly normal: the modern globe lighting along the Free Trade Wharf, the new luxury apartment blocks along the Hermitage. They even had a Christmas tree on top of the giant crane, with fairy lights.

His nervousness surprised him. And now he was trembling. Shaking and sweating as if he had a fever. This had happened before and he recognised it for shock, long delayed. He waited for it to pass and when it did he began to grieve. He sat in the darkened wheelhouse, gazing out over the water, mourning his dead friend as he had not mourned when he found his corpse or at any time since.

Next morning he called Ruth. He told her there was a possibility of borrowing someone's flat over Christmas but that they were a little apprehensive about turning a child loose on the place and he thought it might help if they met Ben in person.

'I wouldn't count on it,' Ruth said. 'He's a bit hyper at the moment.'

'The thing is – it has to be this weekend,' Larry told her. 'They're leaving for the States on Monday.'

The anonymous 'they', the ambiguous, perfidious, sexless 'they'.

Larry felt like an adulterer.

'So when did you want him?' she said.

'I'll call you back,' said Larry.

Then he phoned Jo.

'I was just thinking that you ought to meet Ben before we move in,' he said. 'Make sure he's not going to wreck the place.'

'I'm sure he won't – but I'd love to meet him,' she said. 'Why don't you come for Sunday lunch?'

'Are you sure?' he said. 'You're not too busy packing?'

She said she was sure.

He phoned Ruth back and told her Sunday would be good. It was only when he rang off that he realised he hadn't arranged a location for the hand-over. He'd have to go to the house, Ruth and *Oscar's* house. Larry was considering this and wondering whether to call her back, for a third time, when the phone rang. He answered thinking it was Ruth – and that she had just had the same thought – but it wasn't Ruth, it was Muriel Hoffman.

'Oh hi,' he said.

She came straight to the point.

'I was wondering what you were doing this evening,' she said.

Larry was doing nothing that evening. He had a sudden graphic image of what he *could* be doing with Muriel Hoffman.

'I have to pick up my kid,' he said, as if it was a chore.

'Oh.' A small pause. 'And Sunday?'

'I've got him till Monday.' And then rushing to fill the silence ... to *forestall* the silence: 'But look, why don't we meet one evening next week ... ?'

He left it that he'd ring her on Monday. He sat there for a moment with the phone still in his hand, thinking about it.

Jo was wearing a black dress. Not quite the little black number of Larry's fantasies but sufficiently close to it to tease his imagination. Her long, slightly frizzy hair was tied back with a ribbon and she wore shoes with a heel and a strap across the ankle. Ben appeared tongue-tied and Larry thought he knew how he felt. He was impressed with her efforts to make the kid feel at home. Ben had been unusually subdued on the way over.

Larry thought he might be worrying about something. He had explained the situation to him.

'She's an American lady and we're going to look after her flat while she goes home for Christmas.'

'But not on Christmas Day?'

'No. On Christmas Day you'll be at your mum's.'

'So Father Christmas will know where I am.'

'Exactly.' It seemed as good a reason as any.

'But how will Father Christmas know where *you* are?'

'I will let his people know,' said Larry, with what he considered to be an impressive flash of inspiration, 'on the internet.'

This had seemed to reassure Ben somewhat but he was still not quite his usual self. Certainly not hyper. Ruth would have warned him to be on his best behaviour, of course. Perhaps she had told him that Daddy needed somewhere to stay over Christmas. Larry had a feeling that he had become the lame duck of the family, the one you had to look out for, because he wasn't very good at looking out for himself. Not in the domestic sense. Soon he would be 'Poor Daddy', if he wasn't already.

Jo left them in the living room while she saw to the lunch. She had found Ben a book to read, an illustrated edition of Grimms' Fairy Tales. He sat on the sofa and turned the pages while Larry made a tour of the room with a glass of wine in his hand. He hadn't taken much in on his first visit, apart from things like how to control the heating and dispose of the rubbish and a vague impression of the decor. Muted shades of yellow and grey. Bolder colours in the curtains. Modern furniture. Lots of books. Now he noted details. A glass vase filled with white lilies. Lots of candlesticks with large creamy white candles. A single painting on the only wall where there were no bookshelves – of a city in the snow. Larry thought it might be Prague. There was something about the room he couldn't quite define and then he thought, with surprise, *It's religious*. Not in any formal, old-fashioned, overstated way. There were no icons, no crucifix, no sticks of burning incense. But there was a kind of harmony that he associated with a religious retreat – or a health sanctuary. It was like a room you waited in before you were admitted.

He cruised the bookshelves reading titles at random – too many, too generic to tell you anything about the reader. One wall seemed to be reserved for novels, the other for factual books and reference works. A title among the latter caught his eye – *Women Who Kill* – and he slid it out and turned it over to read the quotes on the back cover:

> *. . . women whose lives have taken them to the edge . . .*
> *. . . revolutionary in what it suggests about women and control, women and empowerment . . .*
> *. . . a murderess is only an ordinary woman in a temper . . .*

Larry looked for more on the same subject. Instead he found a whole section on Jack the Ripper – four, no, five volumes. Why was Jo interested in Jack the Ripper? But then he thought, They might not be hers; her husband might have left them here. It was strange – and disconcerting – to imagine her with a husband, to think of him living here, sharing her space, her bed. He imagined them curled on the sofa together, or sitting as he had seen Rob and Meg that time, reading their books, in their own separate worlds but somehow together.

Another title caught his eye: *Presumptuous Girls* – a history of the heroine in literature. He opened it at random and a sheet of paper fell out. He was about to put it back, unread, when he saw that it was a poem, handwritten with several crossings out. His attention was caught by the title. 'A girl could die waiting.' So he read it.

> Well, it's been a while now
> And she's still kipping.
> No prince has come
> Hacking through the thickets

> With his trusty cutting edge.
> Only reminders for bills unpaid,
> Only circulars for a new takeaway –
> A free lager with every pizza delivered.
> Only the notice from the council
> Warning that untrimmed hedges
> Are a nuisance to the neighbors.
> A girl could die waiting.

Larry wondered if it was Jo's writing. The words seemed kind of *staggered*. Some sloped one way and some another. Others were upright. Some joined, some not. Larry thought, oddly enough, of old gravestones that had sunk at different levels and angles. Then he noticed the American spelling of the word *neighbours*. So it probably was Jo. He turned the page over and there was another. This one was called 'An Ode to Celibacy'.

> Celibacy is no bad thing,
> She murmured,
> In the hundredth year of sleep.
> While assorted princes
> Considered the advanced state
> Of the undergrowth
> And decided
> To give it a miss.

Larry heard a noise from the kitchen and slipped the page back in the book guiltily, feeling like an intruder.

'Lunch is ready,' Jo called.

Larry had brought one bottle of wine with him and Jo provided another. Larry drank most of it. By the end of the meal – with Ben in the other room watching a video – he was sufficiently relaxed to tell her about his recent, unscheduled meeting with Oscar.

'I don't usually pick Ben up from the house,' he said, 'but this time I did.'

She nodded understandingly but he could see she didn't get it.

'It's the first time I've seen him since we split up,' he explained. 'Five years ago.'

She dropped her jaw theatrically. But he could see it was a real shock.

Larry felt some further explanation was called for.

'I didn't want to get too chummy,' he said.

'Well, I think you probably succeeded in that.'

'OK, I mean, this is irrational, right, but while I accepted what happened between me and Ruth – I mean, that we'd got problems and they were more to do with me than her and that it probably wouldn't have worked anyway . . .'

She watched him patiently, waiting.

'I didn't feel I had to accept *his* part in it. I didn't want him in my life then and I didn't want him in it afterwards.'

'So how did it go this morning? Between the two of you.'

'Oh we were perfectly amiable. You know, like people are. I think that's the real reason I avoided him all these years. I didn't *want* to be amiable. It felt . . . false. I mean, quite apart from what happened, he's not someone I would have wanted as my friend.'

'But he's Ben's stepfather.'

'I know. I know.'

'So what did you talk about?'

'Birds. *Fear* of birds.'

She looked puzzled for a moment and then she said, 'Oh yes. Ben.'

'Apparently Oscar was walking with him in the country one weekend – they'd gone to see his parents – and he was attacked by a bird of prey. A marsh harrier.'

'Ben was?'

'Yes. He was running ahead and this bird suddenly dived on

him. Maybe he'd gone too near its nest or something. Anyway, Ben was huddled up on the ground and the bird kept diving at him.'

'What was Oscar doing?'

'Well, he ran up, of course, and scared it away.'

'And do you blame Oscar for this?'

'No. As a matter of fact I blame myself. I think Ben has always been afraid of birds, ever since he was a baby. I just hadn't noticed it so much before. I think he's frightened of butterflies, too. And moths and bats. Anything that flutters. And I think it's because of a toy I bought him when he was about six months old – a plastic bird that you wound up by the tail so it flapped its wings. I think it fell into his cot one day and scared the shit out of him.'

'So, you're not even going to let Oscar give him any complexes. It's got to be you.'

'I'll have to think about that,' he said.

'Why did you and your husband split up?' he asked her.

She raised her eyebrows slightly. 'You know about him?'

'Not really. I think Rob said something once, or Meg, when I was round there . . .'

'And what did they say?'

'God, I can't remember. Nothing much. He's an actor, isn't he?'

'He would rather think of himself as a playwright. Is that all they said?'

'They might have said he was a bit of a lad. Liked his wine.'

'And his women.'

'I don't think they said that. I don't remember it, anyway.'

'I suppose he and Rob had that in common.'

There was an edge to her voice and he was about to change the subject when she continued, still with some bitterness but more thoughtfully. 'I didn't see it for a while. That's probably why I found it hard to forgive myself. Finding myself in the same position as Meg was. Only we didn't have any children so I didn't have to put up with it.'

There was something he wanted to say but he didn't know how to put it without sounding corny or obvious. He thought of an analogy.

'Did you ever see the film *Trop belle pour toi*? She shook her head. 'Gerard Depardieu plays this provincial car dealer with a beautiful wife. Nice house, money, everything. But he starts to fancy his secretary. She's plain, dumpy . . . wears this awful anorak. But he has this incredibly torrid affair with her. There's no explanation for it – except that his wife is too beautiful for him.'

'Well, thank you – but so far as I know, Michael didn't go for plain women, or women in anoraks . . .' She reflected a moment. 'Though I guess he'd be none too fussy about the anoraks – but with him it was actresses. Young actresses. The younger the better.'

'How old was he?'

'Forty when we met. Forty-three when we split up.'

'And it had been going on for some time?'

'I would think so. I don't think marrying me interrupted the flow, as it were. Not for very long, anyway. You can never really tell with an actor. And that's what he was, basically, an actor who writes. He spent all his time with other actors – and actresses. How do you know what's going on with them? It's like a man who breeds budgies. He's out there in the aviary making kissing noises, teaching them to say, "Who's a pretty boy, then?" How do you know when he starts fucking them?'

Larry declined to express an opinion. Instead he asked, 'So how *did* you know?'

'Oh . . . the usual things. He'd come in late at night and go straight into the shower, or he'd ring up and say he was on the other side of town and he was going to doss down on someone's couch. You'd go to a party with him, or a performance, and you'd catch them looking at you, kind of reproachful or smug

– or sorry for you, like they'd be nice to you. There's nothing worse than an actress being nice to you, let me say. Or they'd phone up and ask for "Michael" in that way they had. I felt like his mother. "He's out playing," I'd say. Of course he'd never admit it. Still won't.'

The phone rang in another room and she went to answer it. It was not a long conversation but when she came back she looked thoughtful.

'They've found the mugger,' she said.

He didn't know what she meant at first.

'One of the guys who tried to mug me the other night. I stepped on his foot. They put a check out on the hospitals and they think they've found someone. He turned up for an X-ray and he had a fracture. They want to fix up an identity parade. I told them it would have to wait till I get back from Boston.'

Larry needed a moment to take this in.

'You broke his foot?'

'He had me by the back of the neck,' she said, as if he had accused her of excessive violence. She saw the way he was looking at her. 'What's the matter?'

But he couldn't tell her. He wasn't sure if he knew himself.

CHAPTER SEVENTEEN

Secrets and Lies

ON MONDAY, JO CALLED round at Meg's to say goodbye before she left for Boston. They sat in Meg's kitchen drinking coffee. There were things Jo needed to say to her but she didn't know how to start. They talked inconsequentially for a while about Jo's family. Meg knew Jo's mum and dad from when they were all in East Anglia together and she had been over to Boston one summer while they were at university and met the rest of the family. Jo's Irish uncles, Meg called them.

'I wish you were coming with me,' Jo told her.

'So do I,' said Meg.

She reached over the table and held Jo's hand.

That was as good as it got. Jo should have left then, she thought later.

Instead she said, 'There's something I have to tell you.'

'Go on,' said Meg, but she let go of her hand and Jo felt the shutters come down.

Jo told her about Stone's visit.

'Why did you tell him you went to the Tate?' she said.

Meg didn't answer at first. *Take your time*, Jo thought, *think about it*. She wondered if Meg would tell her the truth at last. But finally she said, 'They knew I left here before five o'clock. They'd talked to the girls and I didn't want them to lie for me. I had to say I went *somewhere* before I got to your place.'

'But why the Tate?' Jo persisted.

'Because I'd just been there to see the Andy Warhol exhibition. So if they asked me anything about it I'd know what to say.'

'It didn't occur to you that they might find out you'd been there two days previously?'

Meg looked concerned.

'How could they?'

'Because I told them.'

Meg stared at her in disbelief.

Jo felt exasperated. 'Meg, how was I supposed to know what *you'd* told them if you didn't tell *me*?'

'But why did you have to tell them anything?'

Jo told her about the police checking Rob's calls.

'Oh Christ.' Meg put her face in her hands.

'It could be worse.' Jo took pity on her. 'I told him you were an art freak. You often went to the Tate twice in one week.'

Meg took her hands away from her face but Jo saw that she had lost what little colour she had.

'Sergeant Harris phoned me this morning,' she said. 'She wanted to know when I last went there and I said I couldn't remember. I said it must have been over a year ago.'

'Oh no.'

'I wondered why she wanted to know.'

Jo recalled something Larry had said about Stone's investigative technique. He just flails around with a wooden spoon seeing what he can hit. Well, now he'd hit something.

'Meg, I'm sorry,' she said, 'but if we're going to tell a pack of lies we have to tell the *same* lies. You should have told me.'

'I just didn't see how they could possibly find out about the first trip.'

'You must have known they'd check Rob's calls.'

'Yes but . . . I forgot he phoned me at your flat. I'm sorry. I should have said I'd gone shopping or something.'

Now, Jo urged her silently. *Tell me*. But Meg just sat there chewing her thumb, saying nothing.

'I don't suppose you know why he phoned Liz and Amy,' Jo said finally.

'When?'

'The same day. Or sometime that week, anyway.'

She told Meg what Stone had told her.

'It's possible,' Meg conceded. 'He's used Amy for a voice-over before.'

'And the gardening?'

'Well, we did talk about getting something done with the garden. Anyway, why else would he call Liz?'

'I don't know,' Jo said. She didn't want to tell Meg about Stone's theory.

'What a mess,' Meg said.

'Yes.'

She waited, but it was clear Meg wasn't going to say any more. There had been a time when there had been no secrets between them. Or so Jo had thought. Now she wasn't so sure. People had always said Meg could be tricky. That she wasn't as guileless as she appeared.

She decided to tell Meg about letting Larry have her flat over Christmas.

'Why?' Meg's voice was unexpectedly sharp, like the look that went with it.

'I feel sorry for him,' Jo said. 'Living on that boat.'

Meg shook her head, her lips a thin line of censure.

'You shouldn't be so hard on him,' Jo said. 'He's grieving, too.'

Meg said nothing.

'It's because you can't be angry with Rob,' Jo said.

'Thank you, doctor.'

'Well, it's true, isn't it?'

'What makes you think I'm angry with Rob?'

'Oh Meg.'

'No.' Meg was shaking her head almost fiercely. 'You always thought I minded more than I did.'

'You're telling me you didn't *mind*?'

'Don't lay your own hang-ups on *me*,' Meg said. 'It's you who *minded*.'

This was true. Jo had minded. There were times she had hated Rob for what he was doing to Meg. Not just for cheating on her but for making her his creature, his handmaiden, his hostess. A decorative asset, a provider of the luxuries and the laurels he considered appropriate to his station in life. A cook, a waitress, an interior decorator, a *doll* who would dress up nicely for him – and undress – who would put out for him whenever he wanted it and look the other way when he wanted it from somebody else.

Jo was aware that she had found it hard to forgive Meg for accepting this. It always made Jo uneasy to think of a woman as being a victim. A part of her felt that if there was no legal or financial reason for it, a woman did not *have* to be a victim. She could choose *not* to be. She was aware that this was regarded in some quarters as naïve – Liz, in particular, had expressed herself forcibly on the subject – and Jo acknowledged that it was difficult at times, even for the most independent of women. She knew that Meg had felt trapped – by her insecurities, her concern for her daughters, her desire to give them the kind of childhood security she felt *she* had been denied. 'When they're older . . .' Meg would say. 'When they've finished school . . .' 'When they're through their A levels . . .' But in the meantime she had put up with it.

Jo had often wished that Meg would leave him. She came close. This was the time they went on vacation together, just the two of them, so that Meg could think things over. They had rented a small villa in the hills above Amalfi in southern Italy. It was early April, out of season. Jo had loved that holiday. It was one of her best times. During the day they hardly spoke, they read books. Over the fortnight Jo had read over eight books – the six she had brought with her and two of Meg's. Sometimes, in the afternoon, Jo would come into the kitchen and cut herself a piece of bread and cheese, or fill a small bowl with olives. She would pour herself a glass of wine from a bottle that was already open and carry it out to whichever part of the garden she had colonised for the day. Sometimes at night she would wake up and continue reading the book she had been reading during the day, perhaps for a couple of hours or more. It was paradise. She felt a kind of peace she had never felt with any man.

They met for meals, which they took turns to prepare, and in the evening they would sometimes dress up and go out for dinner – to Amalfi on the coast or Ravello in the hills. The waiters fussed over them but also left them their own space, which was unusual. Two women on their own, one blonde, one brunette, both considered beautiful, at least by waiters. This was when they talked, usually about the books they were reading, but sometimes about *real* people. Sometimes about Rob. This was before Jo had met Michael Geraghty. Before she knew how easy it was to slip into a role you despised in yourself and how hard it was to slip out of it. She had thought Meg was brave to do what she was doing, to burst the bubble of security that she knew was so important to her, but she didn't really understand why it was so difficult.

Within a week of returning to England, Meg and Rob were together again. After that, Rob's attitude to Jo had more of an edge to it, a more active, rather than passive dislike, and even Meg had been reserved for a while, perhaps recalling some of the things she had said during their vacation together and regretting them – or feeling ashamed that she had reneged on them.

'It's not even about me or Rob,' Meg was saying. 'It's about you and Michael.'

Briefly, Jo wondered if this was true. But she had felt these things before she had met Michael. If anything marrying Michael Geraghty had given her more understanding of Meg's position – her plight.

'You can never accept being in any position of . . . *dependence*,' Meg insisted. 'In any sense, emotional or otherwise. It's like you think you have to lose something by it. But not everyone's like you, Jo. Some people *like* being used.'

Jo thought of reminding Meg of the things she *didn't* like, or had *said* she didn't like, in the past, but she bit her tongue.

'Anyway,' Meg continued, 'it's not as clear-cut as you like to think. You think Rob used *me*, but *he* was the one being used. I *used* him to give me all the things my mother didn't have, or didn't want and wouldn't give anyone else. He could see that and he had to break loose from time to time. He didn't really want any of the things I wanted – the house, the kids, the holidays, the PTA meetings, for Christ's sake, that I used to drag him to – he wanted to live on the edge. I wanted security and he hated it.'

There was probably some truth in that, Jo reflected. Certainly he had liked to live dangerously, with his job and with his women. But it did not excuse his behaviour. And Meg *knew* that. She knew how *angry* it had made her. Why was she so determined to rewrite history? Jo was as ashamed of the question as she was afraid of the answer.

CHAPTER EIGHTEEN

Dolls and Demons

LARRY ARRANGED TO MEET Muriel Hoffman at five o'clock on Monday evening in a wine bar round the back of St James's Square. It was where he and Rob used to meet sometimes when they needed to talk quietly about something – usually a job, sometimes a woman. Larry arrived about ten minutes early and passed the time sketching in the small pad he often carried about with him, while in his mind he sketched the broad outlines of the conversation he planned to have. In his mind, it went OK.

Muriel arrived as late as he had been early. She wore a black leather coat, belted at the waist, with a trimming of fur at the collar, black leather boots and a fur hat. Larry had never thought of Muriel as an animal rights activist and was not disillusioned. He could not help but imagine her in just the boots and the hat. The conviction that this fantasy was probably not unattainable, given the right circumstances, rekindled an inner debate that had been raging, off and on, for the past twenty-four hours, reaching a peak at around 3 a.m. that morning.

The speaker for the motion, *Why you should continue fucking Muriel Hoffman*, argued thus:

You will enjoy it.

You will not enjoy telling her you have to stop.

There is no reason *to* stop, outside of some insane Judeo-Catholic guilt complex.

You are not Jewish nor are you Catholic. Nor is there any reason for you to feel guilty.

Despite what you appear to think, there is no unwritten

universal law that says if you stop fucking Muriel Hoffman you get to fuck Josephine Connor.

And finally, but most seductively: If you must stop, why not wait until after Christmas?

Now, seeing her in her black leathers and furs, an additional thought occurred: *Why not wait until after tonight?*

The speaker against the motion had just one point to make. He made it over and over again.

You will not feel good about it in the morning.

Larry ordered her a white wine from the bar and another beer for himself.

Cheers, he said.

Cheers, she said. He thought she seemed a little tense, her eyes over-bright in their regard, as if they'd been wax-polished to hide the bits she didn't want you to see. Her face was shining too. He thought she looked like a little china doll.

'I've brought you the estimate,' she said. She took a long white envelope out of her handbag and laid it on the table between them.

'Ah,' he said. He looked at it but did not pick it up. After a moment he said, 'Muriel, I've been thinking things over and I've come to a decision.'

This was not the opening he had sketched out. He sounded like the chairman of the board.

'About the house?'

'Not just that.' Why was he putting them both through this? A letter, a message on the answer machine, a Strip-o-gram – *anything* would have been better than this. Cowardice in the battle of the sexes is not to be despised.

'I'm not very good at casual sex,' he said.

Inside his brain he felt something shift. After a lifetime of quiet desperation, a cluster of brain cells finally gave up the struggle and abandoned ship.

'Oh,' she said. Fractionally, before she looked down, he saw the wax sheen fade from her eyes. 'And you think I am?'

'No, not at all. Of course not.' In fact it was the suspicion that, despite appearances to the contrary, she was *not* very good at casual sex – at least, in the emotional sense – that had been troubling him.

'That's why I think we have to stop,' he said gently.

She looked away, towards the bar, saying nothing.

'The timing is all wrong.' He kept his voice gentle. 'I haven't really got over my divorce and now, after what happened at the house . . .'

With cold deliberation and some force she threw the wine in his face.

Then she stood up.

'What a pathetic little prick you are.'

Larry blinked the wine out of his eyes but made no attempt to wipe his face. 'I'm sorry,' he said.

She stood over him and he thought for a moment she might do something with the glass. Then she said, 'Not as sorry as you're going to be.'

When she'd gone the barman came over with a towel.

'At least it wasn't red,' he said.

'Sorry about that,' said Larry.

'Happens all the time,' said the barman. 'Must be something about the place.'

The envelope was still on the table. Larry picked it up and put it in his pocket. He sat there for a while, not wanting to leave until he was sure he wouldn't run into her on the street.

First thing in the morning he went to the Army and Navy stores in Victoria. He bought a pair of heavy-duty overalls, rubber gloves and boots and a white PVC helmet with a Perspex screen like they wore in movies for cleaning up after a nuclear disaster or after the aliens have landed. He found all the cleaning stuff he needed at B & Q – and a tin of brilliant white emulsion. He went a bit overboard on the disinfectant.

There was a bad moment when he opened the front door. He

headed straight for the bathroom and had to sit down on the bath for a moment until his stomach settled. It was much worse being there by himself. Even Stone would have been a comfort. He put Muriel Hoffman out of his mind but for one ridiculous moment he had a vision of her waiting for him in the darkened house. He could feel the sweat cooling on his forehead.

After a few moments he switched on the boiler and while he was waiting for the water to heat up he changed into his decontamination suit. Then he prowled round all the rooms in the house to make sure they were empty. The fly was watching him from the kitchen ceiling. He left all the curtains drawn and switched the lights on.

He started in the kitchen and worked his way back through the hall to the front door. After the first few minutes, it wasn't too bad. There was even a kind of satisfaction in it, a sense of purification. First he washed down all the walls and surfaces. Then he used a trowel to scrape the dried blood off the floor before getting to work with a scrubbing brush. He finished off with a mop soaked in disinfectant. He used about twenty buckets of water, emptying them down the drain in the backyard. Anything that was lying around – plates, saucepans, cutlery, even the kettle and the electric toaster – he threw in a large plastic bag to leave out for the dustmen. He scraped off the bloodstained wallpaper in the hall, relined it and painted it over with two coats of the emulsion.

The shower was the worst part. The police thought the killer had used it to wash the blood off himself. Larry turned on the water and used the showerhead to sluice everything down. The water heater had been on for some time now and he turned the temperature up to maximum so it was like a steam bath in there. Then he scrubbed the whole area with disinfectant. He kept the water running so long it was almost cold by the time he stepped under it himself. Stripped of his protective clothing he felt particularly vulnerable. In his imagination he saw the blood bubbling back up through the drain, spreading out across the shower tray towards his feet. He knew now, if he had not known before, that he would never live in the house again.

When he'd finished in the shower Larry packed a suitcase and a rucksack with some clothes and other stuff that he'd been in too much of a hurry to take with him after the murder. He thought of taking his paints and easel but they were too much to carry without paying for a cab and he thought Jo might not appreciate the smell of oils and turpentine in the flat. He would miss the studio more than anything else about the house. He spent some time just standing there, looking around the empty room and out through the window to the rooftops and the sky.

As an afterthought, before he left, he selected two of the demons to take with him: Farfarello, the scandalmonger, because he liked the expression on his face – or rather he liked the way he'd *captured* the expression – and Asmodeus, the demon of matrimonial misery who slew the seven husbands of Sara on their wedding night. Larry did not know why he chose Asmodeus and did not like to think about it too much.

Instead, as he set out for Jacob's Island with his bulging rucksack and his suitcase and his demons, he thought about where he was going to live next and how he was going to pay for it.

One of the police officers – the one who had given him Muriel Hoffman's card – had told him it could take a couple of years to sell a house where there'd been a murder unless you were prepared to take a lot less than the market price. He didn't need a calculator to work out where that would leave him.

He'd bought the house with the money Ruth had raised to buy him out of the place she now shared with Oscar and he'd sold his car and his camera equipment – Digibeta, lenses, lights, the lot – for a little over £40,000. Just about enough, he'd reckoned, to put him through art school. But not if he had to rent a flat as well as keeping up the payments on his mortgage. So either he had to live permanently on the boat, or cut down drastically on his living expenses, or get a job – something he could combine with the art degree.

He could try freelancing for one of the news networks but you had to be willing to work whenever they needed you – if you turned them down more than a couple of times they stopped calling – and most weekdays were out because of his art course and every other weekend because of Ben.

He decided to ring Jud and remind him about the Pirates of Execution Dock. He'd learn to cope with the costume. It might have been a joke anyway. Jud reckoned himself as a bit of a joker.

He knew from Jud's tone of voice that he'd picked a wrong time. Not that there was ever a right time with Jud. He always answered the phone as if you might be his agent, or a casting director about to offer him a part, and when you weren't, you had the feeling he took it personally. Larry had to remind him of their last conversation.

'We've stopped doing Wapping,' Jud said, as if it was something Larry should have known. 'The committee decided to drop it. Not enough interest.'

'Well, what about Guy Fawkes?' Larry said. He'd been pushing to do Guy Fawkes for a while. He'd made a film with Rob about the conspiracy and he reckoned he knew enough about it to spin out a tour in the streets around Westminster.

'Look, Larry, you know, I gotta tell you, forget Guy Fawkes. Guy Fawkes is not on the A list. Guy Fawkes is not even on the D list. In fact we got more people like you on the *waiting* list to do Guy Fawkes than we got on the goddamn tours.'

Jud had a talent for impersonation. This was his Hollywood producer. Larry felt like telling him he should be on the stage but decided against it.

Instead he said, 'Well, if anything comes up . . .' In fifteen years as a cameraman Larry had never had to ask for work. Now he was begging for scraps from an out-of-work actor. But Jud was telling him to hang on a minute. Larry could hear music in the background. After a moment, he came back on again. 'Amy wants to talk to you,' he said. 'She's pissed.'

Larry heard Amy's voice. She sounded a little husky, presumably with drink. 'Take no notice, darling, we're only on the second bottle. Now listen, I've just had a recall for this job at the Gate . . .'

'That's how bad it is . . .' Larry heard Jud's voice again. 'We celebrate recalls.'

'Where are you?' Larry asked. He could barely hear them. He imagined they were in some wine bar.

Now it was Amy again: 'The thing is, if I get it, I'll have to give up the walk for a couple of months. How d'you fancy taking it on?'

Amy's walk was Bloomsbury London. Virginia Woolf and her set. Not exactly Larry's territory. He pointed this out.

'You could pick it up in a week,' Amy assured him. 'Get a couple of books out the library. I'll walk you round the course. Piece of piss, darlin'.'

This from a woman who usually talked as if the study of Virginia Woolf was her life's work. He heard Jud's voice again. 'And I can give you an interesting link with Jack the Ripper.'

'I'll let you know if I get the part,' Amy said. 'How's things, anyway? Still on the boat?'

Larry said he was, for the time being. He thought it wiser not to mention Jo's flat. She might get the wrong idea.

Larry spent the next couple of days doing Christmas shopping. He was supposed to be spending Christmas Day with his dad and Auntie Ethel in Bermondsey. On Boxing Day he was picking Ben up. He had him until the 3rd of January while Ruth and Oscar were off on a skiing holiday. That meant Larry would see more of Ben over the holidays than Ruth would but he missed not seeing him in the build-up to Christmas Day itself. Ben was the perfect age for Christmas. He got so excited about it all. But mostly about Santa Claus. Once Santa Claus had come and gone that was it really, end of party, the rest was just going home with the balloon. He'd been to the grotto at Selfridges, he'd told Larry on the phone. Ruth and Oscar had taken him.

Larry went there himself, while he was out shopping. He didn't go *into* the grotto but he spent some time hanging around looking at it from the outside and watching the children go in with their parents. He bought a cuddly lion that might go some way to replacing the missing Monks and a load of decorations for Jo's flat so it would be more festive when Ben came to stay. He even picked up another Christmas tree. *Bought* it, this time, from a street stall in Bermondsey. Norwegian spruce, guaranteed non-drop, guvnor, yours for a tenner. It occurred to Larry that he could have sold Christmas trees himself. It was more his territory than Bloomsbury London.

Larry had heard of Virginia Woolf, of course, though he had not read any of her novels and knew very little about the author. He was aware that she was some kind of feminist icon but not precisely *why* she had achieved that status. He knew that she stood for something but not precisely *what*. When he got back to Jo's flat he checked her bookshelves. She had five novels by Virginia Woolf and two biographies of her. Larry selected the thinner of these two and riffled through the pages, reluctant to start on something that he felt would require considerable effort on his part with no certainty of reward. A plain white postcard had been inserted in the pages – he assumed as a bookmark. But there was some writing on it. A list of names and dates.

Tabard Aug 6,
Nichols Aug 30,
Chapman Sept 8,
Stride Sept 30,
Eddowes Sept 30,
Kelly Nov 9.

They were startlingly familiar. The six suspected victims of the

Ripper and the dates they had died. But why? And what were they doing in a book of Jo's on Virginia Woolf?

Larry began to read the page where the card had been placed but was interrupted by the ringing of his mobile phone. It was Sergeant Harris. Something had come up, she said. She wanted to know if he'd mind dropping in at the station some time in the morning. She sounded as if she had a cold.

'And the DI wants to know if you keep a diary,' she said.

Larry said he did. Not that he kept much in it. Ben's school holidays, the weekends he had him over, a few birthdays . . .

'Can you bring it along with you?' Harris said.

CHAPTER NINETEEN

The Hooker

THE SCREEN SHOWED THE concourse of Liverpool Street Station: a wide shot looking down towards the platforms. Larry picked out the figure a moment before Stone pointed it out to him – dark coat, dark hat and boots – walking among the crowd in the direction of the camera. The brim of the hat covered her forehead and the bottom of her face was lost in a collar or scarf. When she reached the bottom of the screen the operator pressed 'pause' to freeze the frame. Larry leaned forward for a closer look.

'Have you tried to enhance it?' he asked them.

The operator gave him a look that said, *Another fucking expert*.

'The lens was covered in shit,' he said. 'The tape has been recycled half a million times and you can't see much more than her schnozz anyway.'

There was a grim satisfaction in his voice, as if he had seen it all before and said the same thing and been proved right, yet again.

'But does she remind you of anyone?' Stone pressed Larry. 'Anyone who springs to mind. Anyone who wears clothes like that.'

Larry asked them to wind it back and play it from the top so he could watch her moving across the concourse again. He was aware that Stone was watching *him* and not the picture.

'No,' he said. 'I'm sorry.'

'Put the other tape in,' Stone told the operator, but his voice was weary.

The other tape was worse. It was a view down Bishopsgate towards the river. It was dark and it was raining and the lens was even filthier than the one in the station concourse. You could just make out the figure in black crossing the road from right to left with a group of other people at the traffic lights.

The time code told him it was six minutes past seven.

'No shots of her going the other way?' he asked Stone.

'No. She must have taken a different route.'

'What makes you so sure it was her?'

Stone was silent for a moment. Then he said, 'I'd like you to think back to the night of Friday, November the 3rd – three weeks before the murder – and tell me what you were doing.'

'God, that's asking a lot,' Larry protested.

'Which is why I asked you to bring your diary. Did you?'

Larry took it out of his pocket and flipped through it without much hope that it would tell him anything. He didn't really keep a diary. Most of the pages were blank.

'Just think back,' Stone urged him. 'Could you have been away that weekend? Could it have been one of the nights you lent your house to Rob?'

What had happened that weekend – and why was Stone so interested in it? The 3rd to the 5th. It was Guy Fawkes Night on the 5th. *Remember, remember the 5th of November . . .* The only thing he did remember was that it wasn't one of the weekends Ben had been with him. Larry had been upset about it at the time because . . . because? The fog lifted.

'I met Rob after work for a drink.' In the same bar he'd met Muriel Hoffman. 'He invited me to a bonfire party on the Saturday night with Ben – my son – only . . . he was already going to one with his mother.'

And Oscar, of course.

But Stone wasn't interested in Saturday night or in Larry's domestic life, not that part of it, anyway. 'How long were you with him?' he wanted to know.

'About an hour or so, I suppose. Time it took to have a couple of rounds.'

'And then what?'

'Then he went home and I went to the pictures.'

'You didn't give him the keys to your house?'

'No.'

'You're absolutely sure about that?'

'Absolutely.'

'OK. So what time did you get back from the pictures?'

'About eleven o'clock, maybe a bit later.'

'And when you got back, was there anything unusual about the place? Any sign that someone had been there in your absence?'

'No.' He was irritated now. 'Look – why don't you tell me what all this is about and I might be able to help?'

Stone glanced over at Sergeant Harris who was taking the usual notes. He rubbed the side of his nose again with the knuckle of his index finger. 'On Friday, November the 3rd,' he said, 'shortly after 8 p.m., a man was attacked on Plumber's Street, Whitechapel, by a woman with a knife. At least that's what he said when he was first questioned about it. Now he says it was more like a hook.'

Larry stared at him for a moment.

'Oh shit,' he said.

'I expect that's what *he* said at the time.'

'Who is this guy?'

'It doesn't matter. A big guy.'

'And she just attacked him – just like that – in the middle of the street?'

'I suspect it might not have been unprovoked. He's got form. My guess is he probably tried to mug her. His story is he was trying to chat her up.'

'How long have you known about this?'

It made a change to be interrogating Stone. He clearly didn't like it.

'I personally heard about it yesterday,' he said. From his tone of voice Larry gathered that he was not best pleased about this, either. 'It's a different manor and the Met have been a bit slow passing it on. However, he's not the most reliable of witnesses. It was only when they questioned him a second time that he mentioned the hook. And he wasn't able to give much of a description. Except that she was wearing a dark coat and hat and was about five foot five. But then he's well over six foot himself so you can't even rely on that.'

'He didn't see her face at all?'

'He says not. I expect he ran at her from behind and she turned round and whacked him one. After which he clearly wasn't taking any notes.'

'But he got away.'

'Ran like fuck. Minus half an ear and a pinkie.'

'So what the hell is this woman doing walking around with a hook?'

'There are a number of theories. The sergeant here thinks she could have been playing Captain Hook in *Peter Pan* and was rehearsing for the fight scene.' Larry glanced at Harris but her face was the usual blank wall, devoid of expression. Stone's foil.

'It's possible that it is a prosthesis, mind you,' Stone continued, 'and that she has it in place of a missing hand, but I'm told they fit you up with something a bit more sophisticated these days and not quite so lethal. The victim says she had it concealed inside her coat but, as I say, he wasn't too clear on the details of the encounter. A hook isn't the easiest of weapons to carry around with you. Or to use to slice someone up, for that matter – it tends to get caught up on bone and sinew – but perhaps it has a sentimental attraction. Perhaps her father was a docker, like yours. Perhaps she's a hooker and chose it as an appropriate form of protection. Or perhaps she was heading for your place and he got in her way.'

Larry wondered if he was serious.

'Why on earth would she be heading for my place?' he said.

'Well, it's only a five-minute walk and she *was* going in the right direction. And she *did* turn up there three weeks later with the same nasty little toy. *And* wearing the same outfit judging from what we've just seen. Unless there's two of them. Maybe there's more than two. Maybe there's a whole gang of them, dressed in black. Perhaps it's a cult. Like the Ninja. Ninja Hookers of the East End. What do *you* think?'

He looked at Larry as if he really wanted to know.

'I think that's an awful lot of conjecture,' Larry said. It was a politer word than the one that had sprung to mind but Stone looked as if he might still take offence.

'Well, we don't seem to have an awful lot of anything else at the moment,' he said.

He looked at his watch and Larry took this as a prelude to dismissal but then, unexpectedly, Stone said, 'Fancy a pint?'

In his private list of Embarrassing Social Situations, going to the pub with DI Stone would not have occurred to Larry as even a remote possibility. Had it done so it might not have been as high up the list as, say, going to the pub with Oscar or running into Muriel Hoffman at a party, but it would probably have made it into the top twenty. It was gratifying to think that Stone's sudden affability indicated that he no longer considered Larry to be a suspect, but he imagined there must be an ulterior motive: something Stone wished to talk to him about outside the formal confines of the police station. There was. Stone wished to talk to him about women.

He began by asking Larry if *he* had any theories.

'I thought it was someone's husband,' Larry said, 'until now.'

'And now?'

'It's still hard to get my head round it,' Larry said. 'That it was a woman.'

'Why's that?'

'Just not the kind of thing they do, is it? Judging from the crime figures.'

'You make a study of the crime figures, do you?' Stone enquired.

Larry had to admit that he didn't but that it was widely known that women committed far fewer crimes of violence than men. Stone put his beer down and leaned across the table.

'Has it ever occurred to you that this might be because they're not *reported*?'

Larry admitted that it hadn't. He thought of making some joke about this but a look at Stone's face suggested that this might not be wise. There was a fanatic gleam in his eye.

'Has it ever occurred to you that men might be *ashamed* to report it?'

'I imagine there might be a few cases of that, yes.'

Stone leaned back and studied him thoughtfully.

'Have you ever been frightened by a woman?'

Larry considered. 'No – I can't say I have.'

'Then you're a liar – or you're a fool. I don't know what's worse. You've been married haven't you?'

'Ye-es.'

'Well, I don't know what terms you're on now but you want to ask her some day did she ever feel like sticking a knife in you.'

Larry wondered if Stone was married, or ever had been. He might have asked him if he could have got a word in edgeways but Stone was in full flood.

'A man will lash out if it gets too much for him. A woman – it builds up inside. Years of frustration. Impotent rage. They feel they've been *used*, they feel they've been *wronged*. They don't know what to do about it. It builds up and it builds up until one day ... Snap. Don't tell me you've never split with a woman and not worried what she'd do if she had half a chance and thought she could get away with it. Don't tell me you haven't opened the door at night and wondered if she isn't going to come at you with a machete. Why are you living on a boat?'

Larry didn't follow.

'Why are you living on a boat with six feet of water between you and the pier and a gangplank you pull up at night?'

'Well, it isn't because I'm worried about opening the door and getting a hook in my neck,' Larry said. He wondered how Stone knew he pulled the gangplank up at night.

'Isn't it? Really? Well, you're the only man in my experience who isn't. Deep down.'

Larry shook his head. 'You must meet some very fucked up men,' he said.

'Oh I do, I do. Some very fucked up women, too. And I expect you do, if you dropped the pc act and started being honest about it.'

'Well, I can tell you I don't know any woman who is capable of doing something like this,' Larry assured him. Or at least he hoped he didn't.

'Really? Well, that is reassuring. How very fortunate for you.'

'So what's your theory?' Larry asked him.

'My theory? I don't have theories. I look at the evidence.'

Now who's fooling himself? Larry thought.

Stone appeared to be considering. Then he said, 'One possibility that has been discussed, however, is that we have a random female killer.'

'A *what*?'

'A random female killer. A woman who is not bothered who her victim is, so long as it's a man.'

'But it wasn't random.'

'Wasn't it?'

'You mean she just *randomly* knocked on doors until she found a man and it happened to be Rob?'

'I'm not saying she hadn't met him before. I'm saying she might not have known him very well. It might have been a one-off. A pick-up. A chance meeting in a bar – so far as he was concerned anyway. They arranged to meet again – at your place – and she came prepared.'

'But – why? For what possible motive?'

'Revenge. Retribution. Maybe for something that was done to *her*, as an individual, maybe for something she thinks men have been doing to women for years. A female Jack the Ripper. Jill the Ripper. Jill the *Hooker*. Nice line for the tabloids, that, don't you think?'

It struck Larry that there might be method in this particular madness. A female Jack the Ripper on the loose in Whitechapel and Spitalfields would make more than a nice line. Even the suggestion would raise Stone's profile considerably.

'So you've ruled out a more personal motive,' he said.

'I've not ruled anything out.'

No Stone Unturned, Larry thought.

'However – we've interviewed every woman your mate had, or was rumoured to have had, in the past two years, including his wife, and they were either with someone else at the time or out of London. I'm not saying I'm entirely convinced but I've reached the point when I'm ready to consider other options.'

'How many random female killers have there been in this country?' Larry asked him.

'None,' Stone said. 'None that spring to mind. A few in the States, though.'

'So this would be the first?'

'The first that's been *detected*.'

He finished his pint but made no move to leave. It was Larry's round.

'There's something I'd like to ask you,' he said when he came back with the drinks: a pint for Stone, half for himself.

'You can't get a policeman drunk, you know,' Stone said archly. 'There's a law against it.'

Larry smiled politely.

'Rob's watch – that was smashed. I was wondering if you couldn't move the hands at all.'

'You think the killer moved them?'

'I wondered if it was possible.'

Stone seemed to consider. Then he said, 'You could move the minute hand. But the hour hand was embedded in the clock face.'

'So you could tell from that – that it was a quarter-past seven?'

'Thereabouts. Given that it might have moved with the blow. We'd never go by the watch alone.'

'But the pathologist could never pin it down to the minute.'

'Not to the minute, no.'

Larry drank some of his beer. Stone was watching him thoughtfully.

'What's the problem?'

'No problem. I just thought it might affect some of the alibis you've been checking, that's all. But if you've already thought of that . . .'

'You think it was personal, don't you?'

'Of course I think it was personal. At least I did, until you came up with all this random killer stuff.'

'There is another theory,' Stone said, as if he was thinking out loud. 'If it *was* personal.'

'What's that?'

'That she might have been after *you*.'

After Stone had left, Larry hung around outside the pub for a few minutes by himself, running through the conversation in his head. People were coming out of the offices all along Bishopsgate, heading for lunch, and he remembered that Ruth worked just a few minutes' walk from Liverpool Street Station.

He phoned her on his mobile on the off-chance that she was free. It wasn't the first time he'd proposed lunch since the end of their marriage but it was a rare enough event for her to sound surprised. She said it could be arranged. She probably thought he wanted to talk about Ben.

Ruth no longer worked with Oscar – they'd decided it wasn't a good idea once they were married – and she had taken a job as a fund-raiser for Shelter. They met in a wine bar in Hoxton Square, a bit noisy for Larry's liking but probably enough to ensure some privacy. There was a long table with people wearing party hats, having their office Christmas lunch.

He told Ruth about the woman with the hook and what Stone had said about her.

'He thinks she might have been on her way to see me,' he said, 'and then she tried again on the 21st and found Rob there instead.'

'But what makes him think she was coming to see *you*?'

'I don't know. He probably just wanted to see how I'd react.'

'And he thinks she mistook Rob for you?'

'That's the theory. He says it wouldn't be the first time someone killed the wrong person.'

'But you don't look anything like Rob.'

'I don't know,' Larry demurred. 'We're about the same height, same colouring. She might not have noticed until after the first blow.'

'But he must have some reason for thinking this – some woman you know . . .'

Larry was already shaking his head. 'No. I can honestly say there's no woman I know who wants to kill me. Not then.'

'Not *then*? How many have there been since?'

'None. I don't know why I said that.' He had been thinking of Muriel Hoffman but he didn't want to tell Ruth that; he didn't want to tell her anything about Muriel Hoffman. *Not as sorry as you're going to be*, he thought. But that didn't mean she was planning to kill him.

Ruth was looking at him strangely. 'But you're obviously worried about it.'

'Nah, not really,' he said. 'It's just Stone fucking with my head. You've never wanted to stick a knife in me, have you?'

'Not a knife, no.'

'Seriously, have you never felt angry – more than angry?' What had Stone said . . . 'Blind rage, frustrated, impotent anger?'

'I wish you'd asked me that when we were married,' she said.

'I take it that's a Yes.'

'No, Larry, that's a joke. Look, the only time I could imagine sticking a knife or anything else in someone is if they hit me. But even then I doubt it – I'd be too squeamish. I'd probably just wait until they were asleep and empty a tube of Superglue over their balls.'

'Superglue?' he said. He had to ask. 'Did you ever . . .'

'Only once. The thought of you sitting in casualty with a duvet glued to your balls was very tempting but I resisted.'

'What had I done?'

'It doesn't matter. Actually, I think it was something you hadn't done. But I never thought there was the slightest danger of you ever hitting me. I don't suppose you've ever hit any woman, have you?'

He shook his head. 'I've hurt them, though,' he said. 'I've made them hate me.'

She was frowning at him now. 'There's something you're not telling me, isn't there? Something you've done.'

'I haven't done anything.'

It was like being with Stone. Or being a kid again, carpeted by the aunts.

'Well, I don't know what you're worried about then. You don't usually worry about being hurt. Not physically. You took all kinds of risks when you were working, just to take a few pictures, and it never seemed to bother you.'

'That was different. You're out in the open – most of the time. You can see what's coming at you. And you've got all this adrenalin pumping around. You're not in your own home, relaxed, opening the door to some woman you've invited for supper, with a meal on the stove and a bottle of wine in the fridge. You haven't got your back turned pulling the cork out of the bottle. You're not asleep in bed with someone lying next to you. You're not *vulnerable* in the same way.'

'Ah. I see. Well, I know what you feel about being vulnerable. But, whatever you've heard to the contrary, women do not usually kill people, no matter how much you provoke them.'

'Why *is* that?'

'Oh Larry, *books* have been written about this. I don't know. Because they're not naturally aggressive, because they don't normally *want* to hurt people, because they're afraid of what men might do back to them . . .'

'You don't think this is changing?'

'I think men are *afraid* it's changing. But that's a different matter. That's more to do with them than us.'

'You think we're scared?'

'I think *some* men are scared, yes. They've been using women for so long they're scared women are going to get their own back, now they're in a position to do so. It's one of the reasons they hate women bosses.'

'Rob hated women bosses,' Larry reflected.

'You don't say? Well . . .' She sighed. 'I remember once hearing you and Rob talking about some woman – someone at the BBC I think it was – she was in some position of power over you and Rob was taking the piss out of her. It reminded me of two little boys I'd seen on a beach once, poking sticks at a jellyfish. Rob had the stick and you were grinning at him, the way you did. Not quite approving but not wanting to say anything that indicated you *didn't* approve.'

'Why a jellyfish?' Larry said.

'I'm sorry?'

'Why did it make you think of a jellyfish?'

'Well, it was the boys I was thinking of, rather than the jellyfish. I mean the jellyfish was just lying there.'

'But it could have stung them, couldn't it?'

'If they'd been stupid enough to step on it, yes.'

'Exactly,' he said.

'Let me get this straight. You think you *deserve* to be stung, yes? You think you've been behaving in such a way that women have every *right* to sting you. Or rip your throat open with a hook.'

'Don't they?'

'Possibly. But being a superior life form, unlike a jellyfish, they usually manage to find other ways of expressing themselves than through physical violence.'

'As yet,' Larry said.

'Excuse me?'

'When I did the Ripper tour I used to talk about retribution,' Larry said. He tried to recall exactly how he had put it.

Their throats slit, their bodies ripped open from crutch to breast, their womanhood extracted and ritually displayed. The ultimate expression of man as predator; woman as prey. And he gets away with it. That is the final obscenity. He is never caught. His identity never satisfactorily revealed. There is no Retribution. No Avenging Angel. As yet.

'You think this is the Avenging Angel?' Ruth said. 'And Rob happened to be the first man she picked on – successfully anyway – and you might be the next.'

'It might have crossed my mind,' he said.

'Hang on a minute – you think *you* might have put the idea into her head, don't you? You think she might have been on one of your tours and thought, Now that's a good idea. I'll start with the guide.'

He thought about it. 'Crazy, isn't it?'

'Yes,' she said. 'It is a bit.'

When Ruth had left for work Larry walked slowly back towards Spitalfields. He stood outside his house and checked the time, then set off, briskly now, back towards Bishopsgate. He waited six minutes for a cab at the rank outside the station and the journey to Jo's apartment took another twelve. Just over twenty minutes, then, from door to door. A car would have been even quicker.

When he reached Jo's apartment he found the biography of Virginia Woolf and opened it at the page marked by the postcard. It read:

Virginia's mother firmly believed in the Victorian social order, including the complete subjugation of servant to master, wife to husband, child to parent. Only the dominant male could protect the nation and the family from the nameless horrors of her imagining. In return for this feudal 'protection', the help-less female had an obligation to conform to male expectations, indulge male whims and tantrums and suffer a degree of male aggression. This was combined with a hopeless ignorance of the extremes to which this aggression had gone in her own household. From childhood to adolescence Virginia and her sisters were prey to the predatory sexual instincts of the young, and not so young, males of the family.

Virginia's two half-brothers, George and Gerald, undoubt-edly took their cue from their older cousin, Jem, who was in his early twenties when he made a series of what can only be described as 'raids' on the Stephen home. The immediate object of his abuse was Virginia's elder sister, Stella, but the younger girls endured a reign of terror by the man Virginia would later describe as a 'tormented bull'.

J.K. 'Jem' Stephen is the dark shadow in Virginia's child-hood. He was a scholar of Eton and Cambridge and had been appointed tutor to Queen Victoria's grandson, the Duke of Clarence. However, in 1886 he was struck on the head by the piston of a beam engine, used by the Victorians to pump water, and thenceforth his behaviour became increasingly erratic. He was given to alternate fits of depression and excitement, sometimes culminating in violence. Judging from his poetry he had also developed a dangerous hatred of women, combined with fantasies of rape and murder.

One of these poems was quoted in its entirety. It was called 'A Thought'.

> *If all the harm that women have done*
> *Were put into a bundle and rolled into one,*
> *Earth would not hold it,*
> *The sky could not enfold it,*
> *It could not be lighted nor warmed by the sun;*
> *Such masses of evil*
> *Would puzzle the devil*
> *And keep him in fuel while Time's whiles run.*
> *But if all the harm that's been done by men*
> *Were doubled and doubled and doubled again,*
> *And melted and fused into vapour and then*
> *Were squared and raised to the power of ten,*
> *There wouldn't be nearly enough, not near,*
> *To keep a small girl for the tenth of a year.*

As an expression of misogyny it seemed more pathetic to Larry than dangerous, but he found it disturbing for all kind of reasons. Not least the thoughts that were lurking in his own head.

CHAPTER TWENTY

Fathers and Sons

HE WOKE UP ON Christmas morning with the phone ringing. He knew who it would be.

'Happy Christmas, Daddy, thank you for my lion.'

Larry had left the cuddly toy with Ruth to give him in his stocking, keeping other presents back for when he came to stay on Boxing Day. They had agreed on the line that although Santa Claus *delivered* all of Ben's presents – by the traditional reindeer – they were *purchased* by Ben's family. Thus far, Ruth and Larry had maintained a united front on this and most other aspects of the Father Christmas myth. Larry was not so sure whether they stood together on the Baby Jesus front. Ruth was more conventionally religious than Larry. She had christened Ben into the Church of England about a year after they had split up and although she didn't take him to church every Sunday she certainly talked to him about religion. Larry had been taken aback sometimes by the extent of his knowledge, though it could be a little erratic at times and sometimes disturbingly so. Once, when he was three or four, he had presented Larry with a painting that he explained was the baby Jesus nailed to a cross. Larry hoped it did not presage his own darker imaginings.

Ben was reeling off an extensive list of the presents he had opened already. Larry groped for his watch on the chest of drawers next to the bed. Just after eight o'clock. He heard a voice in the background and then Ben's polite enquiry.

'What did Father Christmas bring *you*, Daddy?'

'I don't know,' Larry said. He had stacked a few presents

under the Christmas tree. 'I'm waiting until you come round before I open them.'

'I'm coming round tomorrow, aren't I?'

'You are,' Larry assured him.

'Mummy wants to talk to you.'

Ruth's voice, sounding sleepy: 'He wanted to ring you earlier but I managed to restrain him until now.'

'Thank you for that. Merry Christmas.'

'And to you. Happy Christmas.'

'And give my best wishes to Oscar,' Larry said, with embarrassed formality. He almost felt the shock down the line.

'I will. Thank you.'

He'd be turning up for Christmas dinner next, he thought, like old Scrooge at his nephew Fred's. Less of a Scrooge, perhaps, more of a tamed Banquo, the wounds no longer bleeding, the scar tissue discreetly concealed beneath his paper party hat.

Since their divorce Larry had spent Christmas in various places but never with his own family. Twice with the family of a girlfriend. Once up a mountain, skiing. Once in Africa, working. And last year at Rob and Meg's.

It was the first Christmas they had spent at their own home – instead of going to Rob's parents – and they had invited a number of friends around. There had been a faint but discernible atmosphere as if they had quarrelled just before everyone arrived. It had got worse. Over dinner Rob had made a number of cutting remarks. 'My wife,' he insisted on calling her, as if it was a joke. *You'll have to ask my wife that . . . My wife thinks so and so . . .* Later, pretending to be more drunk than he was, Rob had thrown his arm around Larry and said that they had to stick together. Larry, knowing him of old, sensed the appeal behind the jest. Perhaps, in his cups, Rob had seen the exchange of glances, detected that seismic shifting of loyalties.

Later still, he had apologised to Larry and told him he was in a mood because he had seen the current girlfriend at a Christmas party the night before with another man. She was wearing a dress, he said, that made her look naked. Although Rob played a kind of game with his women, he didn't like other men joining in. For the time he had them, he needed it to be exclusive.

Larry wondered what Meg was doing at the moment. He wondered how the girls were coping. He felt he should phone them but he knew he would not.

Just on eleven Larry headed down to Bermondsey for lunch. The two aunts took turns to do Christmas lunch and this year it was Auntie Ethel's turn. Larry knew she would appreciate a hand with it and she wouldn't get much help from his dad.

Larry's dad was making an effort to be cheerful – or a little less of an old misery than usual – but it didn't stretch to helping Auntie Ethel in the kitchen.

Larry watched him unwrapping the present he'd brought him – a bottle of malt whisky and a scarf – forcing his voice and features into a measure of appreciation. Larry knew the only real present that would have brought a genuine smile to his face would have been Ben, if Larry had brought him. He loved Ben, you only had to watch them together to know it. Larry didn't feel jealous – on the contrary, he was glad of it – but it did make him wonder if his dad had been like that with him when *he* was young – or whether he had always been so distant, so miserly with his affections.

Looking at him now Larry thought how old he looked. He was only what . . . sixty-three. But he looked at least seventy. He'd aged a lot in the last couple of years, since he'd given up working the tugs. He had the face of a man who felt that life had not treated him kindly or fairly.

There were some who thought Larry's dad had a fair bit of savings stashed away but Larry wasn't one of them. The *Lady Jane* had never really paid off for him as an investment. She'd been laid up at the Hermitage more often than not and the only bit of work she ever did was towing rubbish barges. Larry reckoned the boat had probably cost him more than it had earned over the years.

On the other hand, he'd never heard his dad complain about money – it was about the only thing he *didn't* complain about. He didn't seem to need much. There was the rent on the council flat, the upkeep of his old Volvo. He had a flutter on the horses now and then but otherwise his only recreational activity was walking the dog – and the odd couple of pints down the Old Justice. (The portrait of Hanging Judge Jeffreys on the pub sign sometimes reminded Larry of his dad.) He liked his football – he followed West Ham like most of the men in the area – but he did his supporting from the armchair these days, watching them on Sky. There'd been the occasional 'girlfriend' over the years – though not for some time now. Larry didn't know if he'd had a sex life since his mum left home and he didn't want to. He kept a tight rein on his emotions. He wasn't a very *giving* man, as the aunts would say. Even with Ben, with whom he was more giving than most, you'd see him drawing back all the time. It was almost as if he was afraid to tempt Fate. If he showed Fate a chink in his armour, Fate would be in there, striking a mortal blow. Naturally, Larry thought this went back to the fact that his wife had left him, but the tendency might have been there all along. It might even have been *why* she left him – or one of the reasons. The fear of *giving* too much and leaving yourself open to hurt. It was something Larry knew he had in himself and it worried him. He fought against it, even to the extent of *inviting* hurt. But it might be that in casting off the armour all he was saying was, 'Here I am, I'm wide open, go ahead and hit me. But you won't hurt me. I *can't* be hurt.'

'No news about the murder, I suppose,' Auntie Ethel said as he stood by her at the kitchen sink, peeling potatoes.

'Not really,' said Larry, not wanting to talk about it.

'I wish they'd hurry up and catch them,' she said.

She used the plural, Larry suspected, not because she thought there was more than one person involved but rather because it was comfortingly vague. It prevented her from putting a face or a form, or a sex, to the killer. Sometimes Larry wondered if she thought *he'd* done it. Not that she'd blame him if he had, of course. It would be Rob's fault, as usual.

She worried about Larry – even before the murder. She watched him all the time, worrying that he'd go the same way as his father. It worried her even more than the thought of him turning out like his mother.

Auntie Ethel was a *giving* person. She'd once been engaged – to a supervisor down the docks – but there'd been an accident. He'd been hitching a ride on the back of a locomotive on the dock railway and fallen off under the wheels of the tender. She didn't seem interested in other men after that. But Larry was amazed she'd stayed with his father. Partly it was her nature – she needed to be needed, to have someone to look after – but there must have been other men, less trying, more appreciative, than his dad. His Auntie May had told Larry it was because of *him*. She couldn't bear to leave him with his dad and she could never have taken him away. Larry didn't want to believe this. He thought that there was a part of Auntie Ethel that didn't *want* a man, not as a sexual partner. She valued her independence too much. She had a good job – she was a sales manager at the John Lewis store in Oxford Street. Like all the staff she was called a partner of the firm, not an employee, and she was proud of that – the firm was her extended family – but she'd be coming up for retirement in a couple of years and Larry wondered what would happen to her after that. He didn't like to think of her stuck at home all the time with his dad. He knew he should talk to her about this – but he didn't know how to begin.

Larry loved his Auntie Ethel but he had no *affinity* with her. He couldn't discuss anything with her – not seriously. If he ever tried, it was like sinking into a bog. Serious subjects worried her, whether personal or impersonal. She did not like to think about them. She did not read books, or even newspapers. She did not like watching the television news – because of the violence. She had not wanted him to be a cameraman but she had not wanted him to give it up either, not to become a painter. Shades of his mother, she must have thought, the demon seed. She was a cautious, even timid person. She was frightened of change and of things she did not understand. Larry's father called her a birdbrain. Larry would never think of her as that but he thought it was unfortunate that, on top of his real mother's desertion, he had a surrogate mother he loved but could not readily respect.

All through his life, his father had shared jokes with him about Auntie Ethel. Teasing sort of jokes about her inability to understand things and how they worked – from politics to an electric plug. It was a kind of male bonding between them, like supporting West Ham. They were not unusual in this. It happened between a lot of fathers and sons – Rob and his father had called his mother 'Twit' – but it was a nagging concern to Larry. It had concerned Ruth more, when she had observed it. 'You think women are all stupid, really, don't you?' she'd said. 'Deep down, you think we're all barking.'

Then, answering her own question, she'd said, 'I suppose we must be to put up with you lot.'

Ruth reckoned that most women she knew ended up *servicing* men. They picked up the socks from the floor, they filled up the washing machine, they did the shopping on the way home from work, they noticed when supplies were running low, they gave comfort and support whenever it was needed – they did all the things that mothers did for their sons *and* they provided sex more or less on demand. They had to be barking.

In fact Larry did not think women were stupid *or* barking. But they puzzled him sometimes. What was it that made his Auntie Ethel look after his dad all these years? Habit? Did she ever feel it was worthwhile, that she got something back? And why did a beautiful, intelligent woman like Meg put up with what she had to put up with from Rob?

Love, of course. There was always that – and a certain amount of conditioning.

Larry finished the spuds and started on the carrots.

'I'll manage them,' said Auntie Ethel, taking the peeler off him. 'You go and talk to your dad.'

He was saved by the bell. Auntie May and Uncle Ron had arrived. Larry busied himself taking coats, pouring drinks. He felt like he'd shed twenty years or more and was still the spotty schoolboy, being extra polite, watching his manners. Certainly Auntie May treated him as if he was about thirteen. She was a big, bustling woman with a loud laugh and an easy manner that fooled nobody. She had a sharp eye for failure. Larry saw the way she looked round the room – and so, he was sure, did Auntie Ethel – making a swift assessment. Weighing it all up, noting the way it had aged and become shabbier with use. Like the three of them. They didn't exactly dread a visit from Auntie May – she didn't scare them *that much* – but they were braced for it. A visit from Auntie May was like taking some kind of test that they knew they were doomed to fail. All three felt that she had long ago made her own private inventory of the nature and content of their lives and found them wanting.

She'd been very supportive of Larry when he was at school but she'd never had much confidence in his progress to maturity. It was as if she was continually expecting him to slip back into adolescence. The break-up of his marriage, followed by his decision to become an art student, only confirmed what she already knew. And now the murder. Like Auntie Ethel she'd be inclined to blame Rob – but Larry had to share some of the responsibility: he'd *gone along with it*.

Auntie May had lived with them for most of Larry's schooldays because she was looking for a man who was prepared to better himself. It had taken her until she was thirty-three to find one. The man Larry now knew as Uncle Ron. He was a carpet salesman when they met. Now he owned a carpet store – a carpet *warehouse*, in fact – the biggest in Deptford.

Larry remained puzzled by Uncle Ron. He was two years younger than Auntie May, mild-mannered and self-effacing, almost to the point of invisibility. His only physical distinction was a small goatee that he kept neatly trimmed. His passions, besides carpets, were cricket, real ale and collecting books about great railway journeys. Larry suspected that, far from wanting to better himself, he'd have been quite content to sell carpets for someone else for the rest of his life – saving up, perhaps, for the great railway journey he meant to go on himself one day – until he met Auntie May.

Auntie May was the driving force of the relationship and the business. It was almost as if – perhaps lacking the confidence or the skill or the means to better *herself* – she had found her vehicle in Uncle Ron, her means of propulsion to a higher plane, a better life – the life she wanted. She had no children and didn't seem to regret it. Uncle Ron and the business were her children – and to some extent Larry. They were all she had ever wanted from life.

But what about Uncle Ron, Larry wondered sometimes, what did *he* want? It keeps you on your toes selling carpets, he'd told Larry once – a little whimsically, a little nostalgically, perhaps for the good old days when he was on the road. Larry imagined that inside Uncle Ron there was quite another kind of carpet salesman – an Arab or an Armenian, perhaps – who sold exotic rugs. Rugs from Kabul and Samarkand, Kashmir and Iran. Rugs that had travelled hundreds of miles on the back of a camel. Larry sometimes imagined him on a train travelling across Patagonia, or the Hindu Kush, in a shapeless linen suit and a Panama hat, the Peter Ustinov of carpet salesmen.

But he was Ron Bullen of Bermondsey and he'd married Auntie May. He was the reliable family car, low-mileage, low-maintenance, one lady owner, perfectly tuned, would cruise all day at fifty, never been revved up at the traffic lights, never left wheel marks on the tarmac, would never race a blonde in a red sports car along the Corniche.

Larry was glad that Auntie May had got what she wanted but it depressed him slightly.

Rob's theory, of course, was that women were attracted to the wildness in men but had a compulsion to tame it out of them. (*That old chestnut*, as Ruth called it, who had no time for Rob or his theories, and in truth it was hard to imagine Auntie May ever yearning for the feral or Uncle Ron howling at the moon.) It was atavistic, Rob had insisted. They didn't want to share their cave with the human equivalent of a cave bear but they'd rather have him on the inside pissing out, than on the outside pissing in. So he had to be house-trained, the same as all the other animals: the dogs and horses, the beasts of burden. They had to be broken in. Unbroken, they were dangerous.

Larry had never openly agreed with Rob when he expressed these views. Mostly, he agreed with Ruth. But it bothered him that the only male role models in his family were Uncle Ron and his dad, one of them a willing slave and the other a miserable old bastard.

He felt better after a pint. Two pints, in fact, of the home brew Uncle Ron had brought, followed by the best part of the claret he had brought himself. Auntie Ethel didn't drink, Auntie May never had more than a glass or, by her own admission, she became 'silly', and the two older men stuck to beer. There were crackers and party hats, turkey and roast potatoes with sprouts and mashed turnips, a rich, dark gravy made from the giblets and Christmas pudding to follow.

No one talked about the murder. Larry imagined they must have made a pact not to. The aunts would have been on the phone together. It was in the air, though, the sense of recent bereavement. Uncle Ron was more thoughtful, Auntie May more careful with Larry than usual. She gave him more turkey than anybody else, more Christmas pudding. He was still the little boy whose mummy had left him.

Towards the end of lunch Larry began to sneeze and snuffle a bit from his allergy – was it the dog hairs or his family? He insisted on helping the aunts to wash the dishes while the two men settled down in front of the television. He was wondering how he was going to endure the next few hours before he could decently take himself off to bed. He was glad when Auntie Ethel suggested he might like to come out with her to let the dog 'do his business'. The fresh air might help clear his sinuses, she said. Dog hairs were no problem in fresh air.

They strolled along the Bermondsey Wall down towards Rotherhithe and stood for a while in the small public gardens next to the Mayflower Inn overlooking the river. There was a sharp wind blowing in from the North Sea, whipping the tide into frothy little waves and driving rags of cloud upriver towards the City. Just down the embankment from where they stood, a man and a small boy were trying to fly a kite – a Christmas present probably – but it was too windy. As Larry watched it took off suddenly and he thought they'd made it but then it twisted in a sudden loop and plunged swiftly into the river. He watched them haul it in and walk away with it dripping. He imagined them going home to a fire and a hot drink and the boy's mother.

'When my mother left,' he said, 'was there a man involved?'

He was smiling, to take the sting out of it, but she looked stunned. She looked as if he had hit her.

'What a funny question to ask,' she said.

'Is it?'

'I mean, now, after all these years.'

'I've thought about it before,' he said, 'but people didn't seem to want to talk about it.'

'It's not that we didn't want to . . .' She looked upset but he hardened his heart.

'So – was there?'

'I don't think there was. Your father never said there was.'

Larry's expression showed her what he thought of that.

'So there was no warning? Nothing leading up to it? She just took off and left? Didn't tell you how unhappy she was?'

'She didn't talk to me like that. Or your Auntie May. She was different from us. She kept herself to herself.'

'Did she have a temper?'

'What a question to ask.'

'Well, it's not difficult. Did she ever get angry? Did she and Dad row? Was there any violence?'

'Your father would never have raised a finger to her. There was never any violence from the men in our family.'

'What about the women?'

She looked at him as if he was barking.

'Honestly, Larry, fancy coming up with all of this now.'

'*Did* she hit him?'

'No, of course not. Not that I knew of. Honestly, how am *I* supposed to know? What does anyone know about what a husband and wife get up to in the privacy of their own home? She had a bit of a temperament, I suppose. She spoke her mind.'

'Except when she was thinking of leaving.' He smiled, but it was like the smile on the face of DI Stone. It had nothing to do with humour.

'Well, she kept a lot bottled up, too. Like your father does. Like you do.'

Frustrated rage. Impotent anger.

'I don't know why you should worry your head about all this now,' she said again.

Both of the aunts were uncomfortable with anything that came under the heading of 'family problems'. They liked to think there weren't any. That their own golden childhood had continued for ever, with not a cloud on the horizon, the magic years of the late 1940s and early 1950s – as they perceived them through the rosy glow of hindsight. The men back from the war, things coming back in the shops. Ships still on the river and nothing bombing them. Holidays in Southend, a normal, happy family – Mum, Dad and the kids. This was the way it should be. Anything that diverged from it had to be relentlessly dragged back into line – like Larry when he strayed. And if you couldn't drag it back into line, it was best forgotten. Better still, it had never happened. 'Pair of ostriches,' his dad used to say about them, 'burying their heads in the sand.' As if he didn't.

'You never tried to get in touch with her family or anything?' Larry persisted.

'Her family had disowned her, or she'd disowned them, one or the other.'

'So she just disappeared – into thin air?'

She sighed. The wind had streaked tears across her cheeks but he thought it was probably from the cold.

'I told you, we heard she'd gone abroad.' Abroad could be anywhere for his Auntie Ethel – Calais or Buenos Aires. There was a finality about it, wherever it was. On his own trips abroad Larry had sometimes wondered if he'd run into her one day – but would they recognise each other?

'I didn't like your mother. I have to admit. Your Auntie May was closer to her than I was. But I will say this for her, once she'd made her mind up that would have been it, she'd have been off and never looked back. She'd have thought it was better that way. Better for everyone concerned. Her, your dad – and you.'

'So I should be grateful for that.'

'Yes, you probably should,' she said.

He got back home at ten o'clock. He was glad, finally, to be alone.

There had been no messages on the voicemail of his mobile phone and there were no messages on the answer machine at Jo's. This was hardly surprising as Jo's friends knew she was away and Larry's friends didn't know he was here but he was disappointed all the same. He had been wondering, vaguely, if Jo would ring. There was no reason at all why she should but he'd had a feeling – not as strong as a hope – that she *might*. Just to see how he was getting on.

He was confused in his feelings about Jo. He had been cruising along in his usual way, watching the cherry buds open, enjoying the moment, and then something else had happened. It had started with the story about the mugging. He'd started thinking about *her* and who she *was*; and not about *himself* or what she felt about *him*. He had fallen in love with a woman because she had broken a man's foot.

He put on the Christmas tree lights to cheer the place up a bit. He'd decorated it fairly simply – almost starkly – but on top of the tree he'd placed a glass angel. The angel was for Ben, he told himself, and maybe for Jo. Larry himself did not believe in angels, except when he was worried about Ben and then he liked to think there might be something looking after him that might have a bit more clout than the average absentee father.

He reached for the TV guide to see if there was a half-decent movie he could watch. There was an old Spaghetti Western he'd seen before but wouldn't mind seeing again – given the alternatives on the other channels – and it was only ten minutes in. He switched on the TV for the background noise and went into the kitchen to fix himself a beer and a sandwich.

The Virginia Woolf books were stacked up on the table where he'd first looked at them. He had read some more of the biography and started a couple of the novels without progressing beyond the first twenty pages or so. This disappointed him. He felt it was evidence of a failing in himself, an inability fully to appreciate the subtleties of the female mind that had been apparent to him for some time now – and to most of the women he knew for somewhat longer. He knew from the part of the biography he had read that in her writing Virginia Woolf had challenged a particularly male perception – a way of looking at things that emphasises the external, rather than the internal, the *act* rather than the thought behind it. Larry's own literary tastes reflected this. He needed something to *happen* in a book and it was no good if it happened entirely in the mind.

Larry's main subject at university had been film studies. Then and since, he tended to see the film before he read the book – and to find the book, on the whole, a bit *wordy*. A bit slow in getting to the point. Usually he read novels on his way somewhere, or late at night when he came back to a hotel room. He preferred reading books about wars or espionage – books in which something *happened*. He liked plenty of detail between the happenings – but detail of a particularly masculine nature. The names of aircraft and tanks and guns, for instance, and an exact description of their capabilities.

Larry knew this was reprehensible but he had found excuses for himself in his former occupation. Shooting film, especially on the move, did not allow of too much introspection.

Larry had believed that this would change when he took up painting but his inability to read Virginia Woolf with any degree of pleasure – or even pain – made it depressingly evident how far he had to go. Perhaps, he thought hopefully, the fault lay with Virginia Woolf.

She was not, as even her biographer had acknowledged, an easy read. *Though she rewards persistence*, he had added – discouragingly in Larry's view, as if describing a woman who achieves orgasm after several hours of imaginative and sustained effort. He thought now that, instead of returning to the living room to watch the rest of the Clint Eastwood movie, he should try a few more pages of *To the Lighthouse*.

It was never more than a thought.

He did open it, though, to look again at the signature inside the front cover. *Josephine Connor, April 1984.* That must have been while she was still at school or in her first year at university. She wrote her name inside all her books, with the date she had bought them. Larry was prepared to think of this as 'cute' rather than 'anal'. However, it indicated a certain pride in possession, or possessiveness, at least where books were concerned, that warned him she might not approve of his reading them in the kitchen, with a ham-and-mustard sandwich and a bottle of beer. Even as this occurred to him, he noticed that he had left a greasy print in the bottom corner of the page. As he wiped it he had a strange feeling of being watched and looking up guiltily he encountered the malignant gaze of the two demons he had brought back from his house. They were stood, side by side, on the tiled surface of the kitchen unit. Larry had copied these two, not from gargoyles on a church roof, as he had informed Muriel Hoffman, but from a medieval *grimoire*, a book of demons, in the British Library. Although their expressions were *meant* to be mocking – and malign – and he was gratified at his ability to achieve this, Larry found their present scrutiny disturbing. He felt *personally* mocked. As if they knew something *he* didn't.

He was distracted – startled, in fact – by the sound of the phone ringing in the other room. He hurried to answer it, thinking it might be Ben, still awake, still excited – or Ruth, more likely, to say he had been rushed to hospital with a turkey bone in his throat and was in the operating theatre, or had just at that moment died under the surgeon's knife. But it was neither of them. It was Jo.

'Just phoned to say Happy Christmas,' she said, 'and to see how you're getting on.'

'Oh, fine,' he said. Then, after slightly too long a gap, 'And to you.'

He was aware that his voice sounded surprised, even a little put out. Though he had fantasised about her calling him all day, he was disconcerted by the reality. He imagined that she could see him, alone, friendless, a social outcast on Christmas Day . . . That she could glimpse through the half-open door into the kitchen and the bottle of beer and the half-eaten sandwich and the pile of books and *To the Lighthouse* still damp from the J-cloth. He reached for the remote to turn down the volume on the TV.

'I just wanted to make sure everything was all right,' she said. She sounded discouraged. 'You've managed to find everything OK and the place hasn't burned down or anything?'

'Everything's fine,' he said.

'Oh well, I hope I didn't interrupt anything.'

'Only a Clint Eastwood movie,' he told her.

'I'm sorry. I better let you get back to it.'

Something – a small rocket from outer space, a boot from a passing angel on its way to save a child from choking to death on a turkey bone – snapped him out of it and he said, 'I've seen it before. How was Christmas?'

'We're still in the middle of it, kind of. It's only a quarter to six over here. We've just been for a walk. By the sea.'

They began talking more easily about the kind of Christmas they'd had and it was all right, it passed for conversation, it was even a little better than that. She told him that on Christmas Eve her mother had cooked them a traditional Bohemian Christmas dinner of carp in aspic that everybody but her mother had found utterly revolting and that today they'd had an *American* Christmas dinner of roast goose and all the trimmings cooked by one of her Boston Irish aunts.

'That's the thing about my family,' she said. 'Everything has to be a statement.'

'Where are you now?' he asked her.

'In my room. I've brought the phone up so they won't hear me.'

He tried to imagine the room she was in. He almost asked her to describe it for him but decided this was a little premature. Their conversation was warm but careful, as if they were both aware of the lines that were drawn and were wary of crossing them. But they had crossed the big one already – she had phoned him – and they were both aware of what it meant.

They talked for about twenty minutes before she made a self-conscious remark about the cost and her father's likely reaction to it.

'Well, thank you for ringing,' he said.

She eased back a step.

'Well, I was just thinking how much I miss my little apartment. I'm glad you're there to keep it company.'

He could think of nothing to say to that. He watched Clint Eastwood silently slaying a bar full of gunslingers. Then she made another leap forward, into the dark.

'I wish I was there now.'

And surprisingly he caught her.

'*I* wish you were here now.'

There was a beat when he thought he could hear her breathing. Certainly, it was not coming from the television.

Then she said, 'I wonder if I could come back a bit early.'

He told her that would be wonderful.

'If I could get a flight. I could try.'

Then, as if she might have misunderstood him, 'If it wouldn't inconvenience you . . . I mean, you wouldn't have to move out or anything . . .'

'It wouldn't inconvenience me at all,' he said.

CHAPTER TWENTY-ONE

Kuratko the Terrible

JO WAS IN TWO minds about being picked up from the airport. On the one hand, it was nice to be met. On the other, she would have preferred not to be met at seven in the morning at the age of thirty-seven after a night flight across the Atlantic by someone with whom she was contemplating a romance.

And is that what I am doing – she asked herself as she assessed the damage in the mirror of the washroom in the baggage hall at Heathrow and assembled the tools of repair – *contemplating a romance?*

It was an odd expression to find in her mental vocabulary. She turned it over in her mind, like a long-forgotten book, suddenly discovered on her shelves. Where did *that* come from, she would wonder, as if it had not been there all the time, as if it had been planted there, mischievously, by person or persons unknown. But she knew where this came from. It had been bought in adolescence and would be with her always: the dream of stately courtship, long walks in country gardens, balustrades and terraces in the dark, Chinese lanterns and candlelit suppers, the lightning glance across a crowded ballroom . . . Darcy, Mr Knightley and the glowing spectre of the Earl of Rule . . .

Instead of which, within two hours, less if the traffic was thin, she'd be having sex in her apartment with a man who was still, in most essentials, a complete stranger to her.

The image had its attractions, but at the same time she could not help thinking that there seemed to be something a little *forced* about it. Something for which an eight-hour flight was not the best of preparations, neither aesthetically nor athletically. Something for which the word 'romance' was not at all appropriate.

She cleaned her teeth with the toothbrush and the small tube of toothpaste that had been given her in the travel kit.

They had not even kissed properly. Should she fall into his arms, her face upturned, her mouth parted expectantly? *My darling, she breathed . . .*

She had read once – in a newspaper – of a couple, reunited at Heathrow, who had pulled each other's pants down and made love on the floor of the moving walkway. A small crowd had run alongside to watch. While Jo could not imagine herself in such a position – she would be too busy worrying, for one thing, about what she would do when they reached the end – she could appreciate that there was something to be said for it. It avoided all that tension on the drive home, all that small talk, all that wondering how to start . . .

She studied her face in the mirror. It stared back at her with apprehension. She read the words in the bubble. *Are you absolutely sure you know what you are doing here? Are you sure you remember how to do it?*

She was aware that the long and painful break-up with Michael Geraghty had done nothing for her self-confidence. The fourteen months of celibacy she had endured since – a celibacy that she had not yet fully explained to herself – was not exactly conducive to relaxed sex – if and when it ever resumed. And then there was the business of sharing the apartment. He would have his things in the bathroom, his clothes in the wardrobe in the spare room . . . It would be as if they were living together already. Panic.

The eyes narrowed, the jaw stiffened. A different image appeared, which she recognised and privately captioned 'The Schoolmarm'. This, too, had its accompanying bubble and the words read: *Just paint your face, dear, and fucking get on with it.*

Grimly, determinedly, like her immigrant forebears, she began to repair what she could repair and make the best of what she could not.

She looked for him as she came out of the baggage hall, not quite expecting him to be there (Geraghty, if he turned up at all, would invariably be a good half an hour late). But he was.

He stood among a group of men bearing cardboard signs with the name of the person they had been sent to meet. He looked as if he'd forgotten his sign and was a bit perplexed about what to do without it. She was suddenly, distractingly, reminded of a scene in *Far From the Madding Crowd* where out-of-work farm hands stand in the marketplace waiting for the farmers to pick them out for employment. Of course, she thought. He was like Gabriel Oak, needing a job as much as any of them but trying to pretend he didn't. She stopped the trolley in front of him.

'Hi,' she said.

He kissed her, almost chastely, on the cheek and took her trolley. She fell into step beside him. She felt like a little girl now, being met by her big brother.

It felt colder outside than it had been in Boston even but she didn't see the snow until they were in the car, driving into London. She had a vague idea now that the pilot had told them as they were approaching London but she hadn't been paying attention. It was piled up on both sides of the motorway and spread, more prettily, across every patch of open land.

'Snow,' she said.

'It started on Boxing Day,' he told her. 'Ben's over the moon but I was worried you wouldn't be able to get back.'

This was encouraging. She put her hand on his knee and he picked it up and kissed it.

'Where *is* Ben?' she said.

'I left him at my dad's.'

This was probably a good sign, too, but she wished she didn't feel so tense about it.

'We made a snowman,' he said. 'Oh, and I've got a Christmas tree. I hope you don't mind.'

'Of course I don't mind.'

She hoped he would not feel like a trespasser. But a part of her was braced for signs of trespass.

They were not immediately apparent, apart from the tree – and a vase of fresh flowers on the table. Chrysanthemums, not her favourite, but still . . .

'Nice,' she said. Meaning the tree, the flowers, everything.

She walked over to the window with its view of the frozen water gardens. There was the snowman.

'Big,' she said.

Her vocabulary seemed to have shrunk to that of a three-year-old. Hi. Snow. Nice. Big.

She stood at the window, waiting. If I don't turn round, she thought, it will be all right. He will put his arms round me and we will kiss and it will be downhill all the way.

He said, 'I should get over to my dad's. I made Ben a sled and I said I'd take him up to Hampstead Heath.'

'Uh huh.' That kind of downhill.

'I thought you might like a bit of time to yourself,' he said. 'Get yourself sorted out . . . have a nap . . .'

A part of her appreciated this. It was thoughtful of him to give her the space. But the rest of her just wanted to get it over with. She almost said this. Instead she walked up to him and kissed him. That was good. That really worked. There was a moment, then, when she thought he'd stay but he didn't. He stood back from her regarding her for a moment and then reached out and with the back of one finger drew a line down the side of her jaw from the bottom of her ear to the point of her chin, like an incision with a surgeon's knife. Though his expression was warm, even loving, it made her shiver.

'I'll see you soon,' he said.

When he'd gone she mooched around the flat. Apart from the Christmas tree and the flowers it looked exactly as she had left it. There was not a single dirty dish in the kitchen. She examined the surfaces. Spotless. She looked into the bathroom. There was nothing of his there. Nothing of the kid's. No toothbrushes, nothing. She knew that if there had been wet towels on the floor, a scum of shaving cream and hairs in the washbasin, she'd have been annoyed, threatened – instantly recalling the dark days of Geraghty when she would return, after just a few days' absence, to scenes of unspeakable, almost creative, squalor. Each time it had happened she had felt like a refugee returning to the homeland after a long period of enemy occupation, fighting the wails of anguish that welled from within, the almost overwhelming compulsion to burst into tears. But the total lack of encroachment was vaguely disturbing. He'd left the door to the spare room open and she poked her head round. Two single beds, neatly made. A cuddly toy on one of them. That was something at least. *They had been here, then.* She didn't like to go in but before she turned away she noticed the books on the bedside table. Saw the name on the spine.

She had to go in then, to look at the titles. *To the Lighthouse* and *The Voyage Out*.

This was ridiculous. She ticked off a mental list:

Met at airport – on time
Immaculate state of apartment
Flowers
Snowman
Reads Virginia Woolf!!!

She checked the fridge. Shit, it was full. And no half-eaten bananas, not a single half-empty tin of baked beans. She had to sit down.

After a while she ran a bath.

Lavender, pine, clary sage. A squirt of bubbles.

She sank into a hot spring on a hill in Provence. Warmth. Peace. A treacherous content.

Early days.

Make the best of them, dear, the Schoolmarm said. They can only get worse.

She was in a forest, picking mushrooms with her mother. There was snow on the ground but the mushrooms were growing through it, which for some reason did not surprise Jo, though she knew that the mushrooms of the forest grew only in summer and the fall. Jo was a little girl but her mother was the age she was now, so she seemed more like Jo's grandmother, the grandmother she had never seen, from the old country.

Walking in the woods and picking mushrooms was one of her mother's rituals from the old country, like serving carp in cold jelly on Christmas Eve. When Jo was a little girl in Germany she had often accompanied her mother on these walks. Her mother would carry an umbrella and Jo would carry the basket for the mushrooms. If it got too heavy for her they swapped. Sometimes her mother told her stories. It was probably on one of those walks in the woods around Wiesbaden that Jo had first heard the story of the Drohung. She could remember being scared sometimes but not enough to spoil her pleasure in the walk. In fact, her mother's stories, scary or not, were an essential part of the pleasure.

Jo's mother had been born in Czechoslovakia in 1935. Her people were members of the ethnic German minority who were forced to flee the country ten years later, 'because of the Communists', she said. Jo's mother did not speak much of her childhood, or the years of adolescence firstly in refugee camps and then in tenement blocks in various German cities, wherever her mother could find work. Her father had been conscripted into the German Army in 1942, she said, and had never come back. She told a tale of watching him from their cottage window as he marched off into the snow in his grey German greatcoat and his coal-scuttle helmet but it was probably imagined. It did not seem as real to Jo as the folk-tales.

The folk tales of Middle Europe were the only memories of childhood that her mother seemed to cherish, or to enjoy sharing with her own children – Jo and her two brothers. Jo's image of her mother's *Heimat*, late into her own adolescence, was of dark forests filled with witches and wolves, goblins and assorted gremlins. Most of the creatures in her mother's fairy-tales seemed to be evilly inclined and the people in them were never quite who they appeared to be. They could change their shape – or their nature – at any time. Jo was most fascinated – and most frightened – of the people who turned into monsters and did terrible things and couldn't remember anything about them afterwards. This seemed to be a feature of the Bohemian fairy-tales, or at least of the ones her mother told her. She couldn't recall any frogs that changed into handsome princes.

Jo's mother had long since stopped telling her fairy-tales, of course, but she still took her to pick mushrooms.

They were not so easy to find in Boston. It usually involved a long car ride inland, or up the coast towards Cape Ann. The best, she insisted, came from the woods and fields around Danvers, which had once been the village of Old Salem where the witches came from. Jo thought this was more because her mother liked the story than because of the quality of its mushrooms. Jo was the only member of her family she took with her on these jaunts and Jo enjoyed them. It was the only time she really felt close to her mother.

The thing she enjoyed most was when her mother saw an Italian waiter in the woods. If she did she would shout at him and wave her umbrella. Jo's mother was on the lookout for Italian waiters because she said they picked the mushrooms to sell in their restaurants *at an enormous profit*. This touched a rare sense of communalism in Jo's mother – though it would have been unwise to point this out to her – that held that mushrooms were the property of the people and must not be appropriated by profiteers. Why she applied this principle to mushrooms and not to any other commodity – like water, coal, iron or electricity

– was something that would always puzzle Jo as she grew older. Just as it puzzled her that her mother, who on most occasions wouldn't say boo to a goose – much less Jo's father – was prepared to wave and shout at total strangers in the woods on the grounds that they were Italian waiters after stealing the people's mushrooms.

Jo's mother seemed to know the Italian waiters by sight, though she had never, so far as Jo knew, visited their restaurants. She could differentiate them from other mushroom pickers, just as she could differentiate between mushrooms you could eat and mushrooms that could kill.

Jo learned a great deal about mushrooms from her mother. She knew all the names and their particular qualities. The nutty chanterelles with their creamy gills which grow in the pine forests in midsummer. The oyster mushroom which grows in clusters on decaying tree trunks and which her mother would dip in egg before frying in butter. The sulphur mushroom which grows on rotten logs and looks like orange-and-yellow rosettes and which you have to catch young before the insects get there and lay their eggs. And the morels which Jo liked best but were found only rarely – in old apple orchards or after a forest fire, under the dead ash.

Jo learned to spot the killers, too. The death cap, or death angel, jack-o'-lantern, *Boletus satana*, or Satan's mushroom, the fly amanita and many others. Jo loved to find the killers, even more than the ones you could eat, though from when she was little her mother had warned her never, ever to touch them (and never to tell her father she even *knew* about them). If you ate them, her mother said, you would have terrible stomach ache with violent vomiting and diarrhoea. Then your blood would turn black. Your liver and kidneys would turn into mush. Your muscles would be paralysed. And finally you would fall into a coma and die.

Jo loved her mother's stories of the killer mushrooms and what they did to you as much as the fairy-tales. She was particularly fascinated by the cunning little killers that posed as harmless or edible mushrooms – like the false morels and the puffballs and the shaggy caps. Her favourite was the shaggy cap which poisons you if you drink alcohol within five days of eating it. Jo thought this was a terribly clever thing for it to do.

As she grew older she would wonder, sometimes, if her mother would like to feed one to her father one day, so she could watch him die in terrible agony a day or two later, just after she'd poured him a glass of his favourite Irish whiskey. (And that this was the real reason her mother didn't want Jo to tell him anything about them.)

Jo knew from reading *Women Who Kill* that the traditional way for women to kill men who used, abused or otherwise displeased them was by poisoning – and that poisoning by mushrooms was one of the methods they particularly favoured.

The reason that Jo thought her mother might like to poison her father some day was that Jo's father was a bully. He had bullied Jo's mother for as long as Jo could remember. He bullied and humiliated her in public – and in private . . . Jo didn't really know what he did to her in private but she would not have been surprised if he hit her. Jo hated her father for the way he treated her mother and despised her mother for letting him get away with it. But not as much as she despised herself for all the years she had been Daddy's girl.

For most of her childhood Jo had been her father's pet, the favourite of his three children. She had played up to his likes and dislikes, partly because she was afraid of him, partly because she wanted his affection and approbation. She had even taken his part against her mother. She had sided with the strong against the weak and would spend the rest of her life trying to atone for it. In her adolescence she had turned against him in a big way, leaving him hurt and bewildered, but mostly angry. She had once overheard him telling one of her brothers that she was a schizo. It did not bother her particularly. By then she did not care what he thought of her.

In later life he had mellowed somewhat. He seemed to have grown fonder of Jo's mother, or perhaps he just felt more dependent. He bullied her less, mocked her more. On her rare visits home Jo did not consider this much of an improvement. Maybe her mother did, it was hard to tell. She never knew what her mother thought about her father. Maybe she was biding her time until she found the perfect mushroom, the shaggy cap that could not be resisted.

Jo did not pick the mushrooms in her dream. She merely noted their shape with interest. Somebody else was picking them, though, beside her mother. She could see him through the trees. Her mother began to shout and to wave her umbrella but Jo saw that it was not an Italian waiter – it was Michael Geraghty. Either the shock of this, or something else, woke her up.

She lay there for a moment staring at the ceiling, remembering where she was and why. The curtains were drawn and although it was gloomy she knew it was still daylight outside. She looked at the clock beside the bed. Ten past two. She had slept for about three hours and she could smell something cooking.

She found Larry in the kitchen, putting a casserole dish in the oven. She stood watching him from the open door, barefoot in her white bathrobe.

'What's that?' she said. 'Not mushrooms?'

He looked round and she saw the expression on his face when he saw her in her bathrobe and she felt a blush coming on.

'No. It's something called a Dublin Coddle,' he said. 'Cabbage and bacon and potatoes. It's kind of winter comfort food. Did you want mushrooms?'

'No,' she said. She didn't want a Dublin Coddle either from the sound of it. 'That will do fine,' she said as he headed for the fridge in search of orange juice. 'Is Ben here?'

'No. I said I'd pick him up later.'

He closed the oven door.

'How long will it take?' she said.

'Well, coddling means slow cooking but I guess we could have it in about half an hour if you're hungry.'

She walked up to him and put her arms around him. She felt

wonderfully relaxed and unusually confident. Maybe it was the clary sage she had put in the bath water.

'Half an hour will be just right,' she said.

In the event it took a little longer and she had to fake the orgasm. This did not surprise or disappoint her. It rarely happened the first time. She was either too nervous or too excited or both. In fact she was excited enough to make the right kind of noises without having to think about it. She didn't think he noticed the difference. He'd know when she had one for real, though.

Afterwards they had the Dublin Coddle. With champagne.

'It should be Guinness,' he said, 'or a strong cup of tea, but I thought champagne was more appropriate.'

'You were right,' she said. Guinness would have reminded her of Geraghty. He had never made her a Dublin Coddle.

'Do you have any Irish,' she said, 'in the family?'

'Not to my knowledge,' he said. 'But I do like Ireland.'

'So do I,' she said. 'But not everything that comes out of it.'

She watched him carry the two glasses of champagne over to their table and set them down very precisely – like candle sticks, she thought, at an altar – and sit down, almost as carefully, opposite her. He was a big man and his movements were self-consciously delicate as if he was always afraid of breaking something. Perhaps as a young boy he had knocked a lot of things over and learned a lifetime's caution. She saw him in an English school cap and blazer, in an old-fashioned hardware store with his mother, knocking over stacks of plates, plant pots, packets of budgerigar seed. Then she remembered that he had no mother; she'd left him before he went to school.

He picked up the champagne flute – carefully – by the stem and raised it to her.

'Cheers,' he said.

'Cheers,' she said, raising her own.

She was very happy.

*   *   *

228

She stayed happy for six whole days. Right through the New Year to January 4th. It helped having Ben with them; he was their catalyst. They planned trips with him. They had snow fights in the water garden where the snow lay white and unspoiled. They went sledging – on Hampstead Heath and at Crystal Palace where they inspected the huge model dinosaurs on the island in the park lake, among the snow and the trees. They went on the London Eye and saw the city spread out beneath them in the snow. They took a boat on the river up to Richmond and saw the deer in the park. They fed ducks on the lake. They went to a pantomime – *Cinderella*. Ben was the perfect child at a perfect age. In the evenings they put him to bed with a story at about eight o'clock and then they had supper and made love. Or made love and had supper, depending on how they felt about it. She stopped having to fake the orgasm.

One night, after they had made love, they talked about Michael. Larry wanted to know if any of the books in the apartment belonged to him. She thought it was a curious question, considering all the others he *might* have asked about the man she had married.

'No,' she told him. 'He wasn't a great reader and whatever books he had he took with him when he left. I think there were a couple of boxes, that's all.'

'Do you ever see him at all?' Larry asked.

'No. Not at all.'

'So it wasn't an amicable divorce?'

'We're not divorced yet – but no, there was, there *is* nothing amicable about it.'

She tried to tell him about Michael but it wasn't easy. She couldn't imagine now how she could ever have fallen in love with him, let alone endured the relationship for three bitter years.

When she had first met him, she told Larry, she had thought of Mr Rochester in *Jane Eyre*. A beautiful-ugly man, a Vulcan, a sculpture crudely hewn from granite (or perhaps something flintier, flakier). Always she would think this of Geraghty: that he was only half finished. And at first there was the expectation that he was progressing towards completion – even that *she* might be able to complete him. But it gradually dawned on her that this was it: you got what you saw. He was in a permanent state of being half completed – or permanently flawed. And with this came a sense of perennial dissatisfaction with himself and the world and everybody else in it, especially those unfortunate enough to be closest to him.

Geraghty at his best was kind, generous, exciting, intelligent, creative, a good lover, a good *cook* – Jo had once made a list of all these qualities, feeling the need to do so – but he was *damaged*. And in a way she could not mend.

He needed constant support and reassurance. He needed some-one who was willing to look after him, to bolster his ego, at whatever cost to her own. A nurse, a nanny. A Jane Eyre. (Though even the Blessed Jane could only cope with Rochester, Jo recalled, when he was blind and half crippled.) Geraghty needed someone so strong she did not fear being diminished by his demands. Or someone content to dwindle into a wife.

Jo was neither of these things.

She was critical of his writing and his opinions, especially about literature. She challenged him over his interpretation of scripts and characters. She drove him to a sullen fury of resentment.

Jo did not like this tendency in herself but there were times when she thought that Geraghty's ego was so big, his hunger for praise and attention so unremitting, that she had to puncture it to survive. It was only her critical faculty that stopped her from being eaten alive.

There was a story that Jo felt was a perfect analogy of her relationship with Geraghty. It was one of the old Bohemian folk tales her mother used to tell her as a child – the tale of Kuratko the Terrible.

Kuratko the Terrible was a rooster. Old Grandpa bought him from market when he was a little chicken but when he got back to the farm he quickly began to grow. And the more he grew the more he ate. He ate all the worms in the farmyard and then he ate all the hens. Then he ate the pig and the cow. And when he'd eaten all the farm animals he moved into the farmhouse and ate Grandpa and Grandma. He became the terror of the neighbourhood. The King sent a squad of soldiers to shoot him but Kuratko ate them all up, muskets, bayonets and all. Nothing could satisfy his monstrous appetite. He would have eaten the whole of Bohemia but one day he found Kotsor the Cat sleeping in front of the fire and gobbled her up as a light snack and Kotsor scratched and scratched at his crop with her sharp claws until he dropped down dead.

And then Kotsor the Cat crawled out of the hole she had made in Kuratko's crop and ate *him*.

Jo would sometimes tell this story to the children in her slow readers' group at the school in Southwark. She made up different versions to amuse them. She had Kuratko drinking all the beer in the brewery. She had him chasing the peasant girls. She had him strutting about on his dunghill singing rude songs and making everybody applaud and shout for more on pain of being eaten. She had him cock-a-doodle-doing outside the royal palace at three in the morning and beating up all the soldiers sent to shoot him. 'I'll fight every man in the house,' shouted Kuratko, in an Irish accent.

Disturbingly, the children seemed to rather like Kuratko. It was Kotsor the Cat who terrified them.

Jo could see that Larry was a little concerned about her, too.

'I'm not that fond of cats,' he said.

'Then don't eat them,' she said.

But she felt well eaten already and it didn't bother her anything like as much as she thought it would. She felt as if she was losing herself in him and for a while at least she was happy to do so. She had not phoned any of her friends to say she had come back early. She hadn't even phoned Meg, though she felt guilty about it. She didn't want to break the spell.

But a part of her knew it couldn't possibly last.

One afternoon they went to see the boat.

They stayed on the wharf. They didn't go any further because Ben was with them and he didn't like the look of the birds. They watched them out on the wooden piles, huddled against the cold. Gulls mostly with a couple of cormorants and a heron. A regular little bird sanctuary.

'They're very friendly, really,' Jo said. But she thought her voice lacked conviction. Ben said nothing.

'We're going to have to do something about this,' Larry said. 'They have courses at London Zoo for people like you. I know they do spiders and snakes. They get people to handle them. Maybe they do birds. Maybe we should buy you a parrot.'

Ben looked at him warily, not sure if he was joking.

Jo didn't mind the birds, whether they were friendly or not. What she didn't like the look of was the boat, even with its Christmas tree on the mast under a fine dust of snow. There was snow on the deck, too, and a delicate tracery of footprints from the birds.

'You *lived* on that thing?' she said.

'It's very cosy inside,' Larry assured her, 'when you get the stove going. It's even got central heating. A bit primitive but it works.'

But the mooring looked bleak and cold – and threatening in a way she found hard to comprehend. It was almost visceral – as if the place represented a threat to her *personally*. It was like this was a part of Larry she could not reach and the place knew it and was waiting for him, to take him back. She knew this was nonsense but she shuddered and put her arm around Ben, hugging him to her.

'Cold?' Larry put the back of his hand to her cheek. He was always warm. It was like he had his own stove inside, primitive central heating.

There were patches of snow on the penthouse roofs of the buildings and on the scaffolding where they were still doing conversions and there were Christmas trees on the cranes, all lit up with coloured lights. But it didn't look Christmasy. In fact the entire waterfront looked grim and brooding all of a sudden – and even a little dangerous – as if all the luxury, all the new wealth was so much designer stubble on the old sinner's face and it was still the secret haunt of Fagin and Bill Sikes and old Gaffer Hexam sculling for corpses on the turn of the tide.

'Let's go have lunch,' she said.

They walked along the river towards Wapping where they were having lunch. The pub was decorated for Christmas, with red candles on the tables, and the waiter brought them crackers to pull with Ben, but Jo felt sad all of a sudden and it was hard to shake it off, even with the wine.

'Is there anything you've left on the boat?' she asked Larry casually, as if it didn't matter.

'A few things. Some clothes and stuff. The collected works of Elizabeth Barrett Browning.'

'Sure,' she said. She was surprised he'd even *heard* of Elizabeth Barrett Browning. 'But seriously, if there is anything you're bothered about you ought to move it over to my place. It'll be all damp and mildewed.'

He nodded but said nothing and she found this threatening too.

Back in the apartment she asked him for the first time about Virginia Woolf. She had not seen him read either of the books he'd left at the bedside. He told her that Amy had asked him if he could take her Bloomsbury Walk over for a while and he was doing his homework.

'You know Amy?' she said. She still kept her voice casual but the alarm bells were trying to raise the dead.

'Only through Meg and Rob,' he said. 'I got talking to her about the walking tours one day. I was a guide on one of the pleasure boats when I was a student and I knew a bit about Jack the Ripper. So she introduced me to this kind of co-operative that runs them and they gave me a trial run.'

'So you're not really interested in the books,' she said.

'I think I could *get* interested. I'd rather do it than Jack the Ripper.' He looked as if he was about to say something else but she got in first.

'I meant in the novels, not the walk.' She was almost sharp with him and he looked up in surprise.

'I'm having a bit of trouble with the novels,' he admitted. 'I think she's an acquired taste.'

She nearly said, 'Yeah, you'd better stick to Jack the Ripper,' but didn't. She hated herself when she was like this but she couldn't help it. She was desperate now to ask him about Amy.

'Amy's tour is very good,' she said.

'You've been on it?'

She nodded. 'Have you?'

'No. I've only met her a few times.'

A *few* times, she thought. *Where?*

'I didn't even know she was an expert on the subject.'

One of several possible remarks sprang to mind, all equally bitchy, but she held her tongue.

He couldn't possibly have had an affair with Amy, not without knowing that she considered herself an expert on Virginia Woolf – even if she had as much difficulty finishing one of her novels as Larry apparently did. Jo sighed, not quite with relief. It was difficult for her to trust somebody, after Geraghty.

'She took us down to Sussex once,' she said, 'to see Charleston Manor where they all lived. And the house in Rodmell where Virginia Woolf drowned, in the river at the bottom of the garden.'

A small voice piped up.

'Why couldn't the ginger wolf swim?'

They both looked round to see where the voice came from. It was Ben, on the floor, playing with some toy cars. They'd almost forgotten he was there.

'What did you say?' said Larry.

'I said, why couldn't the ginger wolf swim?'

They didn't know what he was talking about for a moment. Then Jo began to laugh.

'He means Virginia Woolf,' she said.

Then they were both laughing and Ben looking at them, mystified.

Next day Larry took him back to his mother.

Jo was cooking supper when he came back. He was a little distant, as if he had something on his mind. She thought it was because he was missing Ben but it wasn't just that. He told her while he was opening a bottle of wine. He thought he should move back to the boat for a while, he said.

She felt as if she'd been punched in the stomach.

She carried on chopping onions for the pasta she was cooking. He was pouring the wine and talking like he was planning a trip to the off-licence or something.

'It's only just across the river. I could maybe stay there during the week and come back at the weekend. I don't want you to feel as if I've moved in permanently.' Then, as if aware how this might be construed, 'I mean, I don't want you to feel taken over.'

'I don't feel taken over,' she said. She kept her back to him.

'Well, that's good but, you know, you *might*, if I just stay on here – if I just *assume*, you know, like take it for granted.'

She said nothing now. She felt the way she had with Geraghty: give him enough rope, he'll hang himself. She felt the anger. They were like tomcats. Street cats. Crawling back when they wanted a bit of warmth, a nice tin of cat food. Maybe she should put in a cat flap.

She cut herself with the knife, just a small nick in her thumb.

He was over at once, all concerned, and then he saw the tears.

'What's the matter?' he said.

'Fucking onions,' she said. 'You fucking chop them.'

She stomped off into the bathroom to get a plaster, leaving him the knife.

CHAPTER TWENTY-TWO

The Royal Foetus

LARRY KNEW HE'D DONE the right thing but he wished he'd been able to explain it better. He could not possibly have moved in with her, just like that. It would have been an impossible strain on both of them.

He had the conversation with himself, instead of her. Every time she complained about him leaving the cap off a tube of toothpaste he'd have thought she wanted him out of her life. Not that he ever *left* the cap off the tube. Painters always put the caps back on. And cameramen, even ex-cameramen, were excellent people to live with. They were so meticulous about their equipment. But that wasn't the point. The point was that Larry wanted to enjoy their romance before it turned into a relationship – and to do that he needed his own base.

But it wasn't going to be the boat.

He knew that when he stood on the wharf, where he had stood twenty-four hours before with Ben and Jo. It's got a stove, he'd said, it's got central heating. But now he was appalled at the thought of sitting in that dark wheelhouse at night with a bottle for company, gazing over the river to where *she* lived. The sense of loneliness – worse than that, of *desolation* – was overwhelming. It wasn't just the boat. It was the part of him that was a part of *it*. The loner. The derelict. His dad. He could not bear the thought of the old cadaver creeping back in through the half-open door and wrapping itself around him. But he had to have somewhere.

He thought of the house. Could he?

He'd loved that house. He felt angry suddenly at the thought of what had happened – not to Rob – but to the *house*. Stained, for ever haunted by that one night. Last time he'd been there, when he'd cleaned up the blood, when he'd stood in the shower, he'd thought he could never live there again. But perhaps that was in the immediate aftermath of cleaning the remains of his best friend off the floor and walls. Perhaps it would not be so bad now. He'd have to change the shower, of course, and he couldn't imagine using the kitchen again – but could he sleep there? Could he use it as a base?

He had to give it a try. He'd never have Ben back again but – for the time being at least – he didn't need to. They could spend the weekends at Jo's – if she'd have them.

On the way through Spitalfields his eyes were caught by a headline slashed across a news-stand. *Hooker Lead Latest*. He bought the paper and found himself reading Stone's theory about the random female killer, almost word for word as he had expounded it to Larry in the pub. But there was nothing new. Inevitably they made the link with Jack the Ripper and quoted some tame analyst who went on about the female backlash – 'ridiculed by the feminists of the 1970s but never satisfactorily dismissed'.

He dumped it in a skip by the old flophouse.

It was almost dark when he arrived at the house. He had the keys in the side pocket of his shoulder bag. He looked up the street before he opened the door, checking it out. Empty except for a solitary figure rooting about among the used books in the box outside the bookshop, looking like a character out of Dickens with a long black scarf and a cap. He wiped a drip off his nose with the back of his hand and then dug in his pocket and pulled out a large grey handkerchief like a piece of rag and gave it a good blow. Larry thought you wouldn't want to buy a used book after he'd been using it.

Finally, but still unwillingly, Larry opened the door to his house.

It was the third time he'd been back since the murder, the first time without the blood. Instead, there was a smell of fresh paint and disinfectant. He checked all the rooms, lingering at the door to the bedroom.

There was a question mark hanging over the bedroom. Had Rob used it that night? Had he been in the bed, with a woman, when they heard the door bell ring? These were questions the police had asked. Larry thought the answer was No, because the bed had been made when he checked it with the police after the murder. It was impossible to imagine that the woman – and the killer – had made the bed *after* the murder. But not for the police, apparently. Forensics had taken away all the bedding to test for traces back in the lab. Larry hadn't had it back yet. He didn't actually want it back. He looked at the bed, stripped down to the mattress. He wouldn't be sleeping on the bed. He had been thinking about this on the way over here. He planned to sleep on a camp bed in the attic. It was the only place in the house – with the possible exception of Ben's room – where he felt he might be *able* to sleep. He planned to cook there, too. He was going to camp out in his own house.

He entered the bedroom and opened the wardrobe to find his sleeping bag and his rucksack. He was just leaving when he saw the book.

It was on the bookshelf by the bed, on its side in the gap between the top row of books and the top of the bookshelf and Larry could read the title and the author's name on the spine quite clearly from where he stood.

Orlando. Virginia Woolf.

Larry did not have any books by Virginia Woolf.

He put the rucksack and the sleeping bag on the floor and walked over to pick it up. Then he stopped. A sudden caution made him take a tissue out of his pocket and use it to hold the book by the corner of the spine. He put it down on the bedside table and used a pen to open the front cover. He knew what he would see there but he was hoping he wouldn't.

Josephine Connor, August 1981.

Larry had searched this room on the instructions of the police, looking for anything that was strange or out of order, and he hadn't noticed it. His eyes must have slid right over it without taking it in.

He sat down on the bed and ran through all the possibilities in his mind. Now he came to think of it, he was almost sure he had seen the book before. He might even have slipped it into the bookshelf himself without really thinking about it – weeks ago, weeks before the murder. *The last time Rob stayed here with a woman.* He'd known it wasn't Rob's book – Rob's literary tastes were even more lowbrow than Larry's – so he'd thought it was the woman's. But there was no particular significance in it at the time and it had slipped to the back of his mind, to lie there unacknowledged, like the book itself.

Impossible, he whispered. Jo could not have been here. She could not have been here and not told him. But there were things Larry had not told *her*. One thing in particular.

He would drive himself mad thinking about this. There were any number of explanations. She could have left it at Meg's and Rob had picked it up and started reading it – and then brought it round here. To read while he was waiting for the woman to turn up. Larry couldn't quite picture this but still . . .

Something else was troubling him but he couldn't quite put his finger on it. It was something somebody had said to him. Something to do with Virginia Woolf . . .

Then it came to him.

He phoned Jud but he couldn't reach him, either on his cell phone or at Amy's. Larry wondered if he'd find him at the Ten Bells. The pub was just round the corner, opposite Spitalfields Market. Jud usually held court there with fellow members of the Tours Committee, the people who arranged the schedule and the publicity and gave you the chop if they thought you weren't up to scratch – the Committee of Public Safety, as the other guides called them, in sardonic reference to the cabal that had instituted the Terror in Revolutionary Paris. Jud was Robespierre.

But tonight he wasn't here. Larry approached the two committee members who were – Trevor and Stan, the two he'd seen with Jud at the bar during the Christmas party – and asked them if they'd seen Jud around but they hadn't. Not since before Christmas, they said.

Larry asked them if they'd like a drink. They nodded as if they were doing him a big favour. Some of the guides bought the committee members drinks and generally sucked up to them in the hope of getting more work, or a better slot in the schedule, but Larry had been told that it was a waste of time and money. They had their own agenda. He took two pints over for them and one for himself and started by telling them that Amy had asked him to stand in for her on the Bloomsbury Walk – 'so long as it's OK with you guys, of course,' he added carefully.

They nodded, saying nothing.

'But Jud said something to me I didn't pick up at the time,' Larry continued in the same easy vein. 'Something about there being a link between Virginia Woolf and Jack the Ripper.'

The two men exchanged a brief sardonic look.

'One of Jud's half-arsed theories,' Trevor said, or was it Stan? 'For the punters.'

Larry thought he understood. All the guides had their own theories about the identity of the Ripper, which they expounded at the end of the walk. The punters expected it. When Larry had been understudying Jud on the tour he had heard Jud present three different theories – each with a royalist connection. One was that the Ripper was Queen Victoria's grandson, Albert, Duke of Clarence, who'd caught syphilis off a prostitute and desired revenge. Another was that he was Victoria's personal physician, Sir William Gull, who thought he was the Anti-Christ. And the third – easily the best in Larry's view and the one he had adopted for himself – was that it was a team of assassins *working* for Queen Victoria because young Albert had made one of the whores pregnant and was being blackmailed by her. The assassins knew it was one of five or six women but they didn't know which one exactly, so they kept killing them and ripping their wombs open until they found the one who was pregnant. All the other mutilations were intended as a blind, to put the police off the scent.

But Larry had never heard the Virginia Woolf theory.

'Don't tell me – he reckons Virginia Woolf was the Ripper?'

They seemed to think that was hilarious, though Larry couldn't see that it was much less plausible than the one about the royal foetus.

'Not Virginia Woolf,' said Trevor (Stan?) when he'd had his little chuckle. 'Her cousin Jem.'

Virginia Woolf's cousin Jem, Larry soon realised, was the man he had read about in the biography – J.K. Stephen, the 'tormented bull' of her childhood, the author of 'A Thought' and other misogynist poems. He had been a gifted student at Cambridge, they explained, and had become the tutor to the Duke of Clarence. But then he'd suffered a terrible accident. He'd been hit on the bonce – as Trevor–Stan put it – by a beam engine and become 'a bit of a nutter'.

Whether or not his nuttiness stretched to ripping five or six prostitutes apart with a set of surgical instruments was, they implied, a matter for conjecture. There appeared to be no actual 'evidence' other than the accumulated suspicions raised by the poems and his persistent abuse of Virginia Woolf and her sisters and a few dodgy entries in his diary which Jud might have made up, for all they knew.

'You know Jud,' said the one Larry had decided was Stan. 'It's probably a dig at Amy.'

'Mind you,' said Trevor, 'it *could* have been Virginia Woolf.'

'Oh yeah?' said Stan. 'Dressed as a man, you think?'

'No, no, dressed as a *woman*,' said Trevor. 'Think about it.'

'Cunning,' said Stan. 'That'd be how she caught them off their guard, then.'

'Too right it would. With the whole of London on the lookout for a *male* killer. I mean there's your tart stood there at the corner of the street and she sees this figure coming at her and she's thinking, Ay-up, could be the Ripper. Best scarper. But then she catches a glimpse of the face in the gaslight and she thinks, Oh, it's the author of *Mrs Dalloway*. A very good evening to you, Mrs Woolf, and how's the next one coming along? And quick as a flash out comes the old cleaver and she's grinning from ear to ear.'

They chuckled a bit more into their beers and then Stan said, 'How old would Virginia Woolf have been at the time of the Ripper?'

'Ooh about six and a half,' said Trevor.

'That fucks that one on the head, then,' said Stan, 'unless she was big for her age.'

'Good try though,' said Trevor.

They finished their pints and looked enquiringly at Larry to see if he was going to buy them another.

But Larry had had enough of them for one night. He'd got what he came for, even if it left him none the wiser about Jo.

He stood up. 'Well, if you see Jud around,' he said, 'tell him I was asking after him.'

He didn't fancy going straight back to the house. He was thinking the less time he spent there the better. He thought he'd have a curry in Brick Lane first. It didn't seem such a bright idea now, moving back in.

It seemed even less bright when he finally walked home at ten o'clock after a Chicken Madras and two pints of Kingfisher. His route took him along Princelet Street where the *real* silk-weavers' houses were – as opposed to his own silkworms' cottage. Most of them had been done up by the new owners, people who'd moved into the area in the last few years, not immigrants like most of the people who'd moved into Spitalfields in the more distant past, not asylum seekers. People in the media, Larry supposed, people in advertising, or interior design, artists who had been to art school a long time ago. Larry could only guess at their identity; he didn't know any of them. He knew only that they were rich, at least as rich as the people who had built the houses and a lot richer than any who had lived in them since. They had restored them to their former grandeur but it was a gaunt, grim-faced grandeur, a disciplined Calvinist *esprit*, renouncing frivolity or show. On the outside, at least. Most of the windows facing the street were shuttered with only the occasional crack of light revealing a life within. In one or two Larry caught a glimpse of an ornate plaster ceiling or the gilded frame of a painting. Those he had seen at other times revealed a determined antiquity, a studied display of taste and discrimination, old lamps for new.

There wasn't much light at street level and there was a hint of fog in the air, the ghost of a Victorian smog. This had been the very edge of the Ripper's killing fields but he'd done his best to leave as much blood here as in Whitechapel, disembowelling Annie Chapman in Hanbury Street and doing a complete butcher's job on Mary Kelly, his last victim, in Dorset Street, right opposite the market. The silk-weavers had long gone by then, taking their gentility with them, their houses turned into cheap lodgings for no-hopers, four or five to a room. But on a night like this it was not hard to imagine them as they had been in Victorian times, with the shutters up, as they were now, and the smell of fear in the streets.

And no one out in them, beside Larry, so far as he could see. Just a block or two from the bright lights of Brick Lane the streets were as quiet as a morgue, his solitary footsteps muffled by the mist. He turned into his own street, past the old flophouse on the corner, and approached the front door of his house. He had left the lights on, naturally, but it did not look welcoming. He studied it for a moment, from a few steps away, from top to bottom. No signs of forced entry, not at least from the front. He tried the key in the door and it was still double-locked.

He stood in the hall, looking into the kitchen. He imagined Rob sitting there at the table, with a bottle of wine. As once he'd found him, on his return from some trip or other, with that ironic smile on his face, the unrepentant villain caught in some mischief. 'Grab yourself a glass,' he'd said, 'pour yourself a drink.' He'd borrowed the place while Larry was away, to do some entertaining, he said. Cock Robin. Larry missed him.

He carried the TV up from the living room to the attic and switched between movies until two in the morning, until he was tired enough to fall asleep. Surprisingly he slept well, waking just after eight o'clock to hear the pigeons on the roof. He lay there for a while, more comfortably than he could have imagined, watching the sky turning through various shades of ink to sepia. Finally he reached for the remote to watch the breakfast news and after five minutes they had an update of the main headlines. Larry missed most of the detail in the flood of adrenalin. Even the name meant nothing to him at first until they said he was a playwright.

CHAPTER TWENTY-THREE

Death of a Playwright

GERAGHTY HAD BEEN A handsome man – not even the drink seemed to change that – but this had. A hook, they told her, honed to an edge on the inside of the curve. She could not have identified him from his face but there were certain marks she remembered. Older, more innocent wounds. A crescent-shaped scar on the bottom of his right foot from when he was six years old and he'd trodden on some glass on the beach. Another on the fleshy pad of his thumb from when he was a student at Queen's and someone tried to bottle him in a Belfast bar. She remembered turning his hand over in her own and asking him about it, shortly after they met, and then lifting it to her mouth and kissing it. He had used the same hand, less effectively, to ward off a blow from the hook and it had taken off two of his fingers.

'More like a scythe, really, but thicker and with a pointed tip,' Stone told her conversationally, but watching her slyly, noting her reactions.

She asked if he seriously believed a woman could have done what had been done to Michael. He seemed surprised at the question.

'If she was angry enough,' he said. 'A woman scorned.'

Then he inclined his head as if something else had just occurred to him. Like a large bird, she thought, listening for worms moving under the ground.

'Unless he was a friend of Dorothy's. Gay,' he added, in case it needed explaining. 'Wasn't gay, was he, or bisexual?'

She knew she was being provoked but didn't care. 'No,' she said, 'not to my knowledge – but I suppose he might have been.'

Her responses were dull, even stupid. Surprisingly he didn't ask the right questions so she didn't have to lie too much. The nuns would have called these sins of omission. After a few hours he told her she could go and she found Larry waiting for her in the lobby. She let him take her over. She felt like a parcel he'd come to pick up. She noticed it was dark but didn't bother to look at the time. She leaned against him in the cab on the way home and he put his arm around her but neither of them spoke.

There were messages for her on her voicemail. Two from Meg, one from Liz. She wouldn't answer them just yet. The first thing she needed to do was take a bath.

After a few minutes she called Larry in. He brought a glass of wine for her and she told him to stay so he went back for the bottle. When he came back she'd already finished the glass and he filled it up again. Then she told him about it – as much as she could.

'He rented a flat in Notting Hill, at the bottom end of Ladbroke Grove . . .'

She had an idea he'd had it before they split up, a place to take his women if they didn't have somewhere of their own, or couldn't use for whatever reason . . .

'They know he left the theatre just before nine o'clock. He'd been rehearsing his new play and afterwards he had a few pints in the bar with the cast. As usual. They said they thought he was going to meet someone. A woman. Not that he said. He wouldn't, he'd just hint. So even if he'd walked back he'd have been at the flat at around nine-thirty.'

She held the cold glass against her cheek remembering how Geraghty used to climb into the bath with her sometimes with a bottle of wine and a couple of glasses. He'd lie there, at the opposite end, with his legs on either side of her, and he'd be going on at her about something or other – poking sticks in his usual way – and she'd watch him through the glass, through one eye, as if it was the sights of a gun. Bang, you're dead. You're dead meat, buster. She saw him now walking back from the pub, with his dark curls and his blue eyes, God's gift, with a bellyful of booze, on his way to meet a woman for the night.

'Just after midnight one of his neighbours came home – the guy in the flat below – and he sees this wet patch on the ceiling and it's dripping down and it looks like blood. He knocked on the door and didn't get an answer so he called the police. They say he died between ten and eleven o'clock.

'They wanted to know where I was, of course.'

She paused, waiting for him to ask but he didn't.

'And, *of course*, it was the first Thursday of the month and there was a meeting of the Used Women's Book Club. The usual suspects. Me, Liz, Amy and Meg. You can imagine what Stone made of that.'

She gave him the details as she had given them to Stone, in the same dull, flat tone. Take it or leave it.

'It was at Liz's house. I was there between eight-thirty and eleven-thirty. I drove straight home and arrived at five to twelve. The night porter saw me come in.'

'You don't have to tell me this,' he said.

'I know. However . . . What I didn't tell Stone is that at about nine o'clock Meg said she wasn't feeling well and she decided to go home. She was going to take a taxi but Amy insisted on driving her back, to make sure she was all right.'

He was sitting on the closed lid of the toilet watching her, with the bottle of wine at his feet.

'I didn't tell him because he didn't ask. I just said I was at a meeting of the book club with all three of them. I didn't say anyone left. Maybe they'll tell him – or he'll find out some other way. I know what he'll think. He thinks it already. He thinks we had a deal. I kill Meg's husband and she kills mine.'

'Why would you want to do that?'

'You name it.'

'Revenge?'

'That's one.'

He sighed as if he really didn't want to waste his time with this. 'Revenge for what?'

'He betrayed me. Over and over again. He humiliated me. He might have hit me.' She saw his expression. 'You don't know.'

'I don't think so. Look what you did to the last guy who tried it.'

'Oh, yes, that's another thing. Stone knows about that, too. We know what you're capable of, he said.'

'If he thinks you're his hooker, why didn't you use the hook?'

'I didn't happen to have it with me on that particular occasion, so I just broke his foot.'

'I wouldn't take Stone too seriously,' he said. 'Up until yesterday he was banging on about the random female killer. So now he thinks it was a conspiracy. Tomorrow he'll have another theory.'

He came over and filled her glass. She wondered vaguely if he was trying to get her drunk, to loosen her tongue – that's what Geraghty would have done – but she didn't care any more. He stayed kneeling at the side of the bath with his hand resting on her shoulder, stroking the side of her face with the back of his finger. She leant her head against it briefly, squeezing it to her shoulder. She wondered if she could trust him but she was beginning not to care about that either. Maybe it was the wine.

'There's something else,' she said. 'I owed him money. One hundred thousand pounds. For this place. When we split up we had it valued and it cost me two hundred to buy him out. I raised half of it and owed him the rest. I had to find it by the end of the year – the year just gone – or I had to sell. I told everyone I couldn't bear to sell this place. Now I don't have to.'

He leant forward and kissed her forehead. She closed her eyes. It upset her that she hadn't been able to cry.

'I'll get out now,' she said.

He held the towel and she wrapped it round her and sat on the edge of the bath.

'What was the matter with Meg?'

She looked at him sharply.

'Meg?'

'You said she didn't feel well.'

'That's what she said.'

She stood up and walked past him into the bedroom. She felt a little unsteady on her feet and very tired – the bath had been too hot. She took off the towel and climbed into bed. He stood watching her from the doorway.

'Tell me about Meg not feeling well,' he said.

She lay back, looking up at the ceiling. 'She had a headache but she wouldn't take anything for it. She said she just wanted to go home and lie down. Liz said she'd been fine when she arrived – she was the first there – like she was looking forward to seeing us. We talked about it later, when they'd gone, and Liz said she'd told her about you and me.'

'You told Liz?'

She glanced at him from under her eyelids without moving her head.

'Was there any reason why I shouldn't?'

He didn't answer but he came into the room and sat on the end of the bed.

'I phoned her when you left. I needed to talk to some-body. Normally it would have been Meg but because of Rob, you know ... I mean, I didn't even phone her to say I'd come back early from Boston. We thought she might have been pissed off with me. I know it sounds a bit schoolgirl but ...'

'But that's not really the problem, is it?'

'How d'you mean?'

He spelled it out for her. 'She wasn't there after nine o'clock and you haven't told Stone.'

'No.' She put her head back and the sigh was more of a groan and then, without looking at him, she told him the other problem.

'She wasn't there when Rob was killed either.'

He was silent. She levered herself up on her elbows. 'You mustn't tell anybody this. Promise.'

She really did feel like a schoolgirl now, sharing secrets in the dorm, except he was the wrong sex. And they had never shared secrets like this.

'If anyone does, it's got to be me. Or Meg herself.'

'All right.'

She lay back again with a sigh. It was easier when she didn't look at him.

'The book club usually meets at seven-thirty. But on the night Rob died Meg didn't arrive until just after eight. When the police contacted her – to tell her what had happened – she phoned me – at work – and asked me to say she was there at seven-thirty. And to get Liz to say the same thing. She said she'd explain later.'

'And did she?'

'No. Not really. She just said she was confused when the police asked her where she was and she gave the time she was *supposed* to get there, not the time she actually did. And she reckoned if she went back on that it might seem a bit odd.'

He looked thoughtful, as well he might. Jo had thought about little else for weeks. 'So she didn't tell you *why* she was late?'

'No – but she told me she left her own house at five o'clock. So what was she doing for three hours? Apparently *not* wandering around the Tate Modern.'

'You don't think she killed Rob, do you?' he said.

'No. I've gone over it over and over again in my mind and it always comes back to that. I don't believe she could have done it.' She spoke the words slowly and precisely as if to the slow readers' group. 'But where *was* she?'

'She was with me.'

Jo said nothing for a moment. And then she said, 'Oh.'

Just that. She closed her eyes.

'Jo,' he said.

Why had she not realised? There were so many clues. She wondered how long it had been going on. Months, years?

'We met for a drink,' he said. 'At a wine bar in Clerkenwell. I thought she wanted to talk about Rob and she did, kind of. But we both knew what we really wanted to talk about and where it was heading. There's always been this – I don't know, expectation, *fear*? – that it could happen. We talked about it. We both *wanted* it to happen. But, we agreed, we couldn't.'

'Not until after the A levels,' she said.

'We didn't put a date to it.'

'But you'd like to?'

'Not now.'

'Liar.' She said it without anger, too numbed, too weary for anger.

She felt him move along the bed until he was lying beside her outside the covers with his hand on her shoulder, his mouth close to her ear, and she moved her head away.

'Jo, listen, I wanted to go to bed with Meg, OK. I can't change that, no matter how bad I feel about it. If Rob hadn't died the way he had, or if I wasn't in love with you, I might still want to go to bed with her. I might *already* have been to bed with her. Who knows? But it didn't happen and now it never will.'

Jo found this less than satisfactory but she had a shrewd idea it was probably as good as she was ever going to get. It occurred to her, too, that he had probably just told her that he loved her and she'd nearly missed it.

She opened her eyes.

'Did she know where Rob was at the time and what he was doing?'

'No. At least, *I* didn't tell her. And she didn't give me any indication that she did.'

'When did you meet?'

'At five-thirty.'

'And when did she leave?'

'I don't know. I can't remember. I know, I know, I know . . .' He was shaking his head. 'I wish I did but I don't. I've thought and thought about it. It couldn't have been earlier than seven. It might have been as late as half-past but I honestly couldn't say for sure.'

'I don't suppose you were thinking about the time,' she said. Then, after a moment, 'How long would it take to get from Clerkenwell to your place?'

'Walking? About a quarter of an hour.'

'So if she left at seven . . .'

'She could have just about got there. But she'd have had to move pretty fast to do what . . . was done, and get to your place by eight.'

'Just after,' said Jo.

She put her hand up to her head where the ache was coming from.

'It wasn't Meg,' he said.

'Well, you ought to know.'

'Jo, I wanted to tell you. I've been wanting to tell you all week, but it would have seemed like I was making too much of it.'

'And you didn't tell the police, either?'

'No. I thought I should leave that to her.'

'Such a gentleman.'

'Look, even though nothing happened between us, we were with each other on the night Rob was murdered. Can you imagine how I feel about that?'

'I don't know that I can,' she said. 'Tell me how you feel.'

She took her hand away from her head, where it was shielding her eyes from the light, and his.

'We're doomed,' she said. 'You know that, don't you?'

'It's going to be hard to handle,' he said. 'But I wouldn't have said doomed.'

'I don't feel tired any more,' she said. 'Or else I'm past tired. I can't go to sleep anyway. I'm going to get up. I think I might go for a walk.'

It was a quarter to seven.

He left her to get dressed. When she came into the kitchen he had made a pot of coffee and some toast. Surprisingly, she felt very hungry all of a sudden. He sat opposite her, watching her spreading jam on the toast.

'There's something else I need to talk to you about,' he said.

'Great,' she said.

He bent down under the table and took something out of his bag and put it on the table. It was a book in a plastic folder. *Orlando* by Virginia Woolf.

'I went back to the house,' he said, 'and I found this in the bedroom. It's got your name inside.'

It took her a moment. Then she said, 'What was it doing in your house?'

'Well, I gather *you* didn't leave it there.'

'I've never been to your house,' she said. 'Well, I've never been *in* it.'

He frowned at her, puzzled at the distinction. She told him about timing the route from his place to hers. 'To see if it could be done in the time,' she said. She deliberately didn't say, to see if *Meg* could do it in the time.

'So how did this book get there?'

She reached out for it.

'Don't take it out of the folder,' he said.

She looked at him, not understanding. For a second she thought it was to keep it clean – if only everyone was so careful of her books – and that reminded her.

'Amy,' she said. 'I lent it to Amy.'

'*Amy?*'

'You don't think she'd buy her own books on Virginia Woolf, do you? Not when she could borrow them from me. She never even *reads* them. I can't believe she read this one. She probably just carried it around with her to impress people.' Then she thought about it. 'Has Amy ever been to your house?'

'Not as far as I know. Certainly not while I've been there. When did you lend Amy the book?'

'God, let me think. About two or three months ago, I suppose. You're not thinking she was there with Rob . . . ?'

'Well, obviously not on the night he died.'

He saw the expression on her face.

'Jo? She was with *you* on the night he died . . . ?'

'She didn't get here until after Meg,' Jo said. 'Well, after eight o'clock.'

'Oh Christ,' he said. 'So both times . . . And she knew *both* men.'

'No.' She was shaking her head. 'It's impossible. Lots of people knew Rob and Michael. They moved in the same circles. Kind of. Rob went to at least two of his plays and he went to the parties afterwards. They were both womanisers. There might be an actress they both knew . . .' She caught his eye. He didn't have to say that Amy was an actress.

'She had a part in Geraghty's new play,' he told her. 'At the Gate. That's why she wanted me to take over the Bloomsbury walks.'

'No.' She was shaking her head. Because she didn't believe it, or didn't want to? 'She didn't tell *me* that. She didn't have *any* work, she was telling us on Thursday – she hadn't had any work for ages, not as an actress. She was pissed off about it.'

'Well, she had a recall, then – but she was counting on it.'

'They'd cast it already. They were rehearsing. He was drinking with the cast on Thursday night,' she reminded him.

He got up from the table and went into the other room and came back with another book. It was one of her Virginia Woolf biographies.

He opened it and took out a postcard that had been stuck inside and handed it across to her. There was a list of names and dates written on the back.

'What's this?' she said.

'It's not yours then?'

'No. It's not my handwriting.' The hand was neat, almost crabbed, the letters all sloping the same way. Hers were all over the place.

Larry looked at Jo's signature at the front of the book. 'Of course not,' he said, and she heard the relief in his voice. 'I should have noticed. Jesus. So did you lend this to Amy, too?'

'I can't remember. I might have.' She flicked through it and saw the pencilled notes, the dog-eared pages. 'It does look as if she's borrowed it at some time or another – unless *you* did this.'

He shook his head.

She picked up the postcard again with its list of names. 'What *is* this? Do these names mean anything to you?'

He told her.

'But why would Amy be interested in the victims of Jack the Ripper?'

Larry told her Jud's theory about Virginia Woolf's cousin Jem.

'It doesn't mean anything,' Jo said.

He tapped the other book in its plastic folder.

'But this does. It will have her fingerprints on it.'

'And mine, too,' she said.

'But if it has *Amy's*, it links her to Rob – and the house.'

'You're going to give it to the police?'

'They said if I found anything in the house that wasn't mine . . . I'd looked but I'd missed it until yesterday.'

She was shaking her head.

'I've never really trusted Amy,' she said, 'but I'd never have said she was violent. I mean, what you're saying is . . .' But if she put it into words it would somehow make it real. 'And with Michael – just because he didn't give her a part *in his play*?'

'I *didn't* say it.'

'But you *think* it.'

'So do you?'

'No I don't.'

She stood up. 'I'm going for a walk,' she said.

He sat there while she put her coat on.

'Are you coming?' she said to him, finally.

He looked surprised. 'I didn't know you wanted me to.'

'Oh, for heaven's sake.' She threw him his coat.

Jo leant on the rail by the old Anchor Inn at St Mary's Overy and stared into the black water. It was one of her favourite spots on the river – in winter, at least; in summer it got too crowded. She loved the name, St Mary's Overy. It was named after an old church that had once stood here. When Jo first discovered it, shortly after she moved to London, she thought it was St Mary's *Ovaries*. Despite the spelling she still thought there must be a connection. Only the English could come up with a name like that. There was a small inlet from the Thames with a lock gate and a replica of Francis Drake's *Golden Hind*. You could hire it for parties. Next time she had something to celebrate she was going to have a party there, she told people. They'd been waiting a long time.

The tide was up, the water lapping almost at her feet. They'd walked nearly a mile without speaking.

Now she said, 'She'd have to be very, very disturbed.'

'Well, yes,' he said.

'I mean, she couldn't just – *go* like that. There'd be a history. A mental history.'

'Maybe there is,' he said.

'That we'd *know* about.'

She stared at the water beneath her feet. The dark river, the great dark pool . . . a *thick, sticky substance which closed over her head*. What is the significance of water in the writing of Virginia Woolf? Discuss.

'Why couldn't the ginger wolf swim?' she said.

'I'm sorry?'

She had not been speaking to him – she had been musing to herself – but now she repeated the words more loudly and confidently as the memory returned. 'Why *couldn't* the ginger wolf swim?' As if she really wanted to know.

'Because she had a stone in her pocket?' His voice was sardonic as if this was some inappropriate game she wanted to play.

'But *why*? Why did she want to drown herself?'

'You tell me.'

'I'm just about to, if you let me think. It was 1941. She was scared the Nazis were going to invade England and they'd all be in concentration camps. Leonard was a Jew. She . . . but there was something else. Something to do with Sigmund Freud . . .'

'Why are we talking about Virginia Woolf?'

'Because Amy is obsessed with Virginia Woolf and there's a link, if only you'll shut the fuck up and let me think.'

But it was no good, it was gone. She had to go back and look at the books. She practically raced him all the way back along the river.

She found the biography where they'd left it on the kitchen table and looked for the relevant chapter.

'She'd just met Sigmund Freud. He came over to London in 1939. They talked about her childhood – and then she started to read his books. She was reading them right up to her death – she wrote about it in her journal – and he seems to have convinced her that the child abuse was fantasy. Wish fulfilment.'

'J. K. Stephen?'

'Not just him. He was nothing compared to the brothers – the *step*-brothers – Gerald and George. Especially Gerald. I mean she described it in her letters – to Vanessa and Clive Bell, Vita, Violet Dickinson, Adrian Stephen her brother, her *real* brother. All kinds of people. She wrote it in her memoirs. I mean, listen to this . . . This is when she's about eight with Gerald and he's about eighteen or nineteen. He lifts her up on to this ledge, or shelf, in the hall, where the maids used to stack dishes, and there's a mirror . . . Here it is.'

It had been marked with a line down the side of the page. Jo read aloud:

*As I sat there he began to explore my body. I can remember
the feel of his hand going under my clothes; going firmly and
steadily lower and lower. I remember how I hoped that he
would stop; how I stiffened and wriggled and wriggled as his
hand approached my private parts but it did not stop!*

'There's more. He comes to her bed at night. She's terrified. I
mean, if it's true what she describes then she's systematically
abused by her step-brothers for years and no one does anything
about it. Leonard Woolf said they'd spoiled her life before it had
fairly begun.'

She turned over the page.

*I dreamt that I was looking in a glass when a horrible face –
the face of an animal – suddenly showed over my shoulder. I
cannot be sure if this was a dream or if it happened.*

The last sentence had been underscored so violently it had gone
through the paper.

'That's the face she sees in the mirror in the hall. But did it
happen to her or did she make it up? That's the thing. Freud
seems to have convinced her that it was all in her mind – fantasy,
false memory syndrome – it wasn't what *happened*; it was what
she *wanted* to happen. It was devastating for her. I mean, she
despised these men. She was so ashamed by what they'd done
to her – and now she finds it's all fantasy. Or she thinks it *might
have been*. No wonder she's in despair. She described Gerald as
an obese alligator. And George as a fat louse, beady eyes like a
rat, an overfed pug dog ... and listen to this ... *swollen with
flesh that one wants to slice*.'

'OK, so Virginia Woolf wanted to cut up her stepbrothers –
but what does this have to do with Amy?'

'History. You said there had to be a history. Well, there is.
The reason Amy is obsessed with Virginia Woolf is because of
something that happened to *her*.'

'Like what?'

'I don't know. I've forgotten.'

'You've *forgotten*?'

'It was just something Liz said to me. Ages ago. I didn't take it all in and she wasn't that keen to go into details anyway – she just said the reason Amy's got this thing about Virginia Woolf is because she identifies with her. Something to do with being abused as a child.'

'Sexually abused? By her stepbrother?'

'I don't know. She wouldn't say. I mean, she was obviously sorry she'd mentioned it.'

'I know her stepbrother,' Larry said. 'His name's Jud – and it wouldn't be him. She has a reasonably good relationship with him.'

Jo stood up.

'I'm going to talk to Liz.'

'Tonight?'

'I'll ring her.'

She left the room to use the phone and when she came back she said, 'She's coming over.'

'What – right now?'

'I know. I mean, I didn't say much. I just said I wanted to talk to her about Amy and she said she'd come over right away. I think she must have been worrying about it herself.'

He looked at his watch. It was half-past eight. 'D'you want me to stay?'

'I don't know. What d'you think?'

'I think you'll get more out of her if you're by yourself.'

'I think so, too. Where'll you go?'

'I'll go back to the house.'

She started to object.

'Don't worry, I'll come back later. I just want to put this back where I found it.' He picked up the book in its plastic cover. 'If I do tell the police I don't want them to know I've moved it.'

She told him to take her car.

CHAPTER TWENTY-FOUR

The History

WHEN LARRY LEFT JO felt a sense of panic. There was loneliness in it, so desolate it felt as if she could hardly breathe; it felt as if she was dying. And there was fear, too, but not for herself. She wanted to run after him and tell him to stay. This was not in character. She put it down to the shock of Michael's death, of seeing him in the morgue. If they had still been married, properly married, she would have been in hospital now, or at least under sedation, in the care of friends. The imminent arrival of Liz was not as reassuring as it might have been.

Jo had been surprised, and not a little disturbed, by the way Liz had reacted to her phone call. She had half expected her to be caustic, even angry. Liz often had a go at Amy – to her face – but she could be very protective of her, too. She always defended her, often quite aggressively, when she was under attack from anyone else. But on the telephone she had sounded alarmed. Especially when Jo had told her about the book.

Jo worried now that maybe she should not have mentioned the book. Not until she had gauged the exact nature of Liz's concern. What if she wanted Jo to destroy it?

Liz could be quite intimidating at times, especially when she was angry. Physically intimidating. In an argument she soon began to shout.

Surely, Jo thought, I am not frightened of Liz?

She almost rang her to tell her not to come; she did not feel up to it, to leave it until tomorrow. She even started to dial the number but did not finish. The silence oppressed her. The apartment oppressed her. For the first time since Michael had moved out she did not want to be alone here. She put her head in her hands, kneading her fingers into the eyeballs as if she could squeeze out the image of him as she had last seen him in the police morgue.

She thought about his family in Belfast, wondered if she should ring them. But she had only met them once. Catholics from the Falls Road, his two sisters and his two brothers in Sinn Fein, another brother shot dead by the Army at a roadblock, in the 1980s, with an Armalite in the boot of his car, planted, the family said. His mother had never got over it; she had died within a year, of cancer. Now they had lost Michael, too, the only one of them to get out in one piece, as his father had said to her.

She lifted her head from her hands and saw the demons.

'I like them,' she had told Larry when she first saw them there and he had asked her if she minded. 'No, leave them where they are.'

But now they bothered her. She felt they were watching her, malignant, sneering, knowing something she did not. They had been there, in Larry's house, when Rob was killed. She felt they were bad luck, an evil omen. She picked up the phone again but then the doorbell rang, making her jump.

She heard Liz's voice on the intercom and told her to come on up. She remembered that the last time she had said this to Liz was on the night Rob died, when they had held the book club here. Liz usually arrived with Amy but not that night. She had been the only one to arrive on time and they had sat here in the kitchen sharing a bottle of wine, waiting for the others.

For an instant, just before she opened the door, Jo thought she might have Amy with her now. But she was alone.

Liz put her arms around her and hugged her almost fiercely, then held her back, at arm's length, looking seriously into her face.

'How do you feel?'

'I'll live . . .' and then, because that sounded so awful, 'I can't pretend I still loved him but I did once and seeing him like that . . .'

Liz hugged her again and then she said, 'Is anyone else here?'

Jo told her there were just the two of them.

'The police have been on to me,' Liz said. 'About last night. I didn't know what to say. I didn't know what anyone else had said.'

Jo wondered if this was why Liz had come over so fast. She wanted to find out what Jo had told them. She would be too careful to talk on the phone. Jo wondered if the police were watching her apartment, noting who came and went. This did not seem unlikely.

'So what *did* you say?' Jo asked her.

'I said you'd all got there at around seven-thirty and that you stayed until after eleven but the other two left some time earlier. They wanted to know how *much* earlier but I said I couldn't be sure. I just didn't know what to say. What did *you* say?'

'Much the same.'

'So when did he die?'

'They think some time between ten and eleven.'

'And have you spoken to Meg?'

'No. She's left a message on the answer machine but I haven't phoned her back yet.'

'If she wants us to lie for her again . . .' Liz left the sentence unfinished.

'She asked us to lie the last time because she was with Larry,' Jo told her. She explained about the meeting at the wine bar in Clerkenwell.

'So why didn't she say?'

'She was embarrassed.'

'*Embarrassed?*' She could practically see the progression of Liz's thoughts. 'So they were having an affair?'

'No. Just talking.'

'Uh huh. They were having an affair.'

Jo didn't bother to deny it. How could she, anyway? She didn't know for sure.

'So they could have done it together,' Liz said slowly. 'Or Larry could . . .' with more enthusiasm. 'He was the only one who knew where Rob was.'

'And Michael? Did Larry kill him too?'

'How should *I* know?' She peered sharply at Jo. 'How do you know all this? Did Meg tell you?'

'No. Larry did.'

'Larry did,' Liz repeated drily. 'And Larry found the book?' She saw the Virginia Woolf biography lying on the kitchen table and reached out for it and then stopped herself, as if it was hot.

'Is that it?'

Jo told her no, it was one of the novels – *Orlando* – and that Larry had taken it home to put back where he had found it.

She could see that Liz wanted to ask her how come she and Larry were so close all of a sudden but there were more pressing matters on her mind.

'Is there any reason to think Amy was ever at Larry's?'

Jo shook her head. 'None that *I* know of. Can you think of any?'

'Of course not. It's bollocks.'

But there was a trace of uncertainty in her eyes. Of defensiveness perhaps.

'And Rob and Amy?' Jo pressed her. 'You ever thought there might be something going on there?'

At first Jo thought she was going to deny it. But then she said, 'I don't know.'

'But you had your suspicions?'

'I saw them together at a party. A first night. About two or three months back. Rob was there but not Meg. There was something about the way Amy was behaving with him. I just wondered. I just thought – you wouldn't, you *couldn't* – but the thought did run through my head.'

'You didn't ask her?'

'No, but she just had that look about her, you know. The cat with the canary look. Kind of guilty but pleased with herself, too. I've seen her like that before.'

'And what about Michael?'

'No . . .' Liz shook her head firmly. 'I'm sure she wasn't screwing around with Michael.'

Jo told her about Michael's play.

'You think she killed him because he didn't give her a part in his play? Jo, are you crazy?'

They were both silent for a moment. Liz was staring at the book on the table and Jo could see she was still bothered about something. It was the other book that troubled her, Jo thought, the book Larry had.

'What happened to Amy when she was a kid?' Jo asked her. 'You started to tell me once.'

Still Liz said nothing but she looked as if she was struggling to keep it back. Then she said, 'She was raped. By her stepbrother.'

'Oh my God. You mean Jud?'

'Not Jud. There was another. I don't know his name. Jud's older brother.'

'Did *she* tell you this?' This is Amy, Jo was thinking, this is the fantasy factory.

Liz nodded.

'And you believe her?'

She looked cross then. 'Is that the kind of thing you lie about?'

'Amy might.'

Liz looked as if she might contest this but then she nodded again and said, 'True. Amy might. Or imagine it. But I know she had a bad time. She never knew her old man. He pissed off when she was a few months old, or it may have been before she was born. So there's just her and her mum, in this council flat in Hounslow. Practically on the airport runway, she says.

Then they moved round a bit. Her mum was like a New Age Traveller. They lived in a bus for a while. Did Glastonbury and that, joined convoys.'

'Amy lived on a bus?'

'I know. Maybe this is all bullshit, I don't know. But I reckon she was telling the truth about the rest of it. In as much as you can believe anything Amy ever tells you. Anyway, when she's about ten or eleven her mum meets this guy. Someone in the music business, quite rich, whose wife had died. He had two kids – boys. One a few years older than Amy, the other a bit younger. Anyway they all shacked up together and the older kid raped her.'

'Did she tell anyone at the time?'

'No, she says she was too scared. He threatened to cut her tits off.'

'She had tits at ten?'

'For Christ's sake, Jo, do you want to hear this or don't you? I'm telling you what she told me.'

'Sorry.'

'She might have been older than ten. Anyway, she's terrified of him and it carries on. She's like, having to do whatever he wants with her. But the younger brother, Jud, he *knows*. He and Amy are real close and she tells him and he's real cut up about it. And what happens, when the older brother's nineteen he dies in a car crash. He's just learned to drive and he spins off the road, hits a truck or something. The police say the brakes have been tampered with, the brake fluid drained off or something, and there's a suspicion the other kids did it.'

'Amy and Jud?'

'Yeah. There's never any evidence but the parents obviously think there's something in it. They send Amy off to boarding school and they take Jud off to America with them.'

'*Did* they tamper with the brakes? Did Amy tell you?'

'I didn't get a straight answer but I got the impression they probably did.'

'Oh Christ.'

'This doesn't prove anything, Jo.'

'Only that she's a total . . .'

'Psycho? She's not a psycho. What would you do if someone raped you?'

'This is the trouble, Liz.'

'OK, but I swear to God, Jo, Amy is not a violent person.'

'You mean you've never *seen* her violent.'

'I'm going to ring her.'

Jo was alarmed.

'What are you going to say?'

'I'm just going to ask her about the book. I'm going to tell her Larry's got it and he's going to give it to the police. We've got to warn her.' She saw that Jo was about to object. 'She didn't do it, Jo, I'm sure as hell she didn't – sure as either of us didn't. But if she was fooling around with Rob she'd better have a story ready. Maybe she lent him the fucking book.'

Jo listened to her end of the call. It did not sound as if she was handling it very well. Liz covered the mouthpiece and said to Jo, 'She says she never had *Orlando*. It must have been another book you lent her.'

'Let me talk to her.' Jo reached for the phone and practically tore it out of Liz's hands. 'Listen to me, Amy,' she said, 'you know as well as I do that I lent you that goddamn book and whatever you say your prints are going to be all over it.'

She took the phone from her ear and looked at Liz.

'I didn't do that very well,' she said.

'What's she say?'

'Nothing,' said Jo. 'She hung up.'

CHAPTER TWENTY-FIVE

The Christmas Tree

AS LARRY DROVE ACROSS Tower Bridge on his way back to the house he remembered the Christmas tree. It was Twelfth Night and the Christmas tree was still on top of the mast on the tug.

'Fuck,' he said.

He stopped the car on the north end of the bridge and thought about it. It was raining. Not too badly but still . . . Did he believe it was bad luck to leave the Christmas tree up after Twelfth Night? No he did not. It could stay there until next Christmas as far as he was concerned. But there was his dad to be considered. His dad thought it was bad luck. His dad would be seriously displeased if Larry left it there. You'd have thought that after a lifetime of bad luck he wouldn't care so much, but he would. There was a fair chance he'd been watching all day from the Bermondsey Wall, fretting in case Larry forgot to take it down. In fact, he was probably sitting in his flat right this minute going on about it to Auntie Ethel, threatening to come down and do it himself. Just so he could feel a martyr about it.

Larry swore again. Then he started the car and drove to Hermitage Wharf. The tide was on the ebb but the barges hadn't settled on the mud yet. He stepped across them with extreme caution knowing that if he fell in he wouldn't stand a chance with the speed the river was running. That and the cold. There were still patches of snow and ice on the decks and they were greasy with rain. He was cursing out loud as he struggled to wedge the gangplank into position. He looked up at the mast, squinting against the rain. The little Christmas tree seemed to mock him. It seemed so long ago that he had pulled it out of the river.

The rain was heavier now. Larry could see it streaming down in the lights from the waterfront. There was no way he was going to climb a mast in this just to take down a Christmas tree.

He opened up the wheelhouse and switched on the lights and the heater. He switched on the deck lighting, too, so he wouldn't have to take a torch. He found a sharp knife in one of the lockers and a yellow waterproof. He thought about wearing a lifejacket. But even if he did slip, he was unlikely to fall into the water. He left the lifejacket where it was in the locker and went back on deck.

He climbed the ladder to the roof of the wheelhouse. He should have brought gloves. The metal rungs were cold as ice. When he looked up he could hardly see for the rain in his eyes. The base of the tree was about three metres above the roof of the wheelhouse, too high for him to reach. He went up the narrow ratlines hand over hand and wedged an arm through them while he sawed through the rope with the knife. It didn't take long. He let the tree topple past him on to the roof of the wheelhouse and then went down after it and tossed it into the river. The tide took it away in an instant, into the cold and the dark.

Ben would have wanted a more satisfactory ending.

When Larry reached the wheelhouse he decided to make some coffee. Then he thought he might as well pack up the few things he'd left here. There wasn't much.

Then his phone rang.

It was Jo.

'Where are you?' she said.

'On the boat,' he told her. 'I had to take down the Christmas tree.'

There was a brief pause. Obviously she was thinking about this. Then she said, 'What – at the Hermitage?'

'Well, no one's moved it lately,' he said. He was surprised she remembered the name of the wharf.

'Sorry, I'm not thinking straight. Have you still got the book with you?'

'Of course,' he said. In fact he'd left it in the car.

'Don't move,' she said. 'Don't do anything. I'll be right over.'

CHAPTER TWENTY-SIX

Voice Male

THEY WERE STILL ARGUING about it when they heard the doorbell.

They looked at each other.

'Maybe it's Larry,' said Jo.

But it wasn't Larry. It was Amy.

'It can't be,' Liz said. 'We only just spoke to her.'

Jo pressed the button to let her into the lobby.

'You can open the door,' she told Liz.

'All right, I will.'

But Jo could see she wasn't happy about it. She followed her into the hall to watch.

Liz opened the door in one quick movement, pressing herself back into the wall. It was Amy. She stood in the open doorway, wearing a black plastic raincoat, shiny with rain, and carrying a black plastic shoulder bag.

'Oh Jo,' she said. She walked in and threw her arms round her. 'Oh Jo, I'm so, so sorry.'

'How the fuck did *you* get here?' said Liz.

Amy looked round and seemed to see her for the first time.

'Liz,' she said. She opened her arms to her but Liz was still holding the door.

'I phoned you at home,' Liz said. 'How did you get from Peckham to here in ten minutes? Fucking jet skates?'

'What you on about?' Amy asked her. 'What's she on about?' she said to Jo.

'Why did you come here?' said Jo.

'To see you. The police told me about Michael. I'm so, so sorry.' She began to cry.

'Oh God,' she said. 'Oh God, it's such a mess.'

Liz and Jo looked at each other.

'Tell me about it,' said Jo.

Liz closed the door.

It took a while but eventually they began to get some sense out of her.

First they told her about the book Larry had found. She looked at them with her big blue eyes, scared but scheming, Jo thought.

'So who were you seeing?' Liz asked her. 'Larry or Rob?'

'Larry of course,' she said.

'Liar,' said Jo. She wished she was as convinced as she sounded. 'Why would Larry tell me about the book if it was him?'

Amy looked down and said in a small voice: 'Well, OK it was Rob.'

Liz swore.

'Well, I'm sorry but I wasn't exactly the first. I mean, it wasn't as if I was planning to take him away from her.'

'You don't get it, do you?' Liz raged at her. 'The guy's fucking dead. And you were having an affair with him.'

'Not at the time, I wasn't. I hadn't seen him for about three weeks.'

They let that pass.

'You weren't with him that night?'

'Of course not. I was here with you.'

They reminded her that she hadn't arrived until after eight o' clock.

'Well, I was a bit late. I'm often a bit late.'

This was true.

'So OK,' said Liz, with heavy patience, 'before we get any further into this, who was I talking to just now?'

'When?'

'When I phoned your house and I thought I was talking to you.'

Amy looked down at the table again.

'It must have been Jud,' she said in the same small voice.

'Jud?'

'He sometimes takes me off on the phone.'

Liz and Jo looked at each other.

'He takes you off?'

'You know – impersonates me. He's amazing, really. He can do anybody. That's why he does so many voice-overs. You'd never know it wasn't me. It's a bit of a worry, actually.'

'For Christ's sake, Amy,' said Jo.

'Well, it started as a sort of a joke. But then it got a bit out of hand.'

But they could see the panic in her eyes.

'What do you mean, *out of hand*?' Liz asked her.

'Well, if any men rang.'

'What if any men rang?'

'He'd make arrangements with them. Pretending to be me. So they'd turn up – and I wouldn't.'

'But why?' They both spoke together.

Amy shrugged. 'I don't know. Jealous, I suppose. Or just to be funny. We fell out about it but I thought he'd stopped. But then . . .' She didn't finish.

'Go on,' said Jo.

'Well, I did wonder why Rob hadn't phoned me. I mean, I wondered if he *had*. And Jud had answered, pretending to be me.'

'And arranged to meet him,' said Jo.

'Oh God,' said Liz. 'I told him Larry had the book.'

CHAPTER TWENTY-SEVEN

The Lady Jane

WHILE HE WAS WAITING for Jo, Larry decided to pack the clothes and things he'd left here. Jo was right, they felt damp already. He didn't have a suitcase but he found a black dustbin liner that would do. He'd just started when Jo rang again.

'Where are you?' she said. He could hear the stress in her voice.

'On the boat,' he said. 'Where are *you*?'

'At the apartment.' She sounded mystified. 'What are you doing on the boat?' she asked him.

Larry frowned. 'Waiting for you,' he said. He wondered if it was the stress getting through to her. He reminded her of her last phone call.

'I didn't call you,' she said. Her voice, normally quite low, sounded almost strident. 'I thought you were at the house.'

He heard some kind of discussion on the other end of the line. 'What's going on?' he said. 'Who's with you?'

When Jo came back on she sounded calmer but her voice was urgent. 'Listen to me, Larry, you have got to get off the boat.'

'What do you mean, get off the boat? You just told me, don't move until you got here.'

'That wasn't me.'

'What do you mean, it wasn't you? I didn't imagine it.'

'I'll explain later. But please, just for me, just get off the boat as fast as you can.'

'*Then* what do you want me to do?'

'Larry, I'm serious. What's the name of that pub by the mooring? On the road.'

'The Town of Ramsgate,' he told her, 'but –'

'Wait for me there. I'll be ten minutes.'

He stood there with the phone in his hand, wondering what was wrong with her. It must be delayed shock, he thought.

He finished packing his clothes, then he pulled the drawers open to make sure there was nothing he'd left in them. All he found was a blue photograph docket with some stills he'd taken last time he was on location with Rob. Larry remembered throwing them into the top of the bag when he'd packed back at the house, under police supervision, shortly after they'd taken the body away. It seemed an odd thing to do now, to pack these when he'd left so much else behind. He wondered what had been going through his head. Something to remember him by, something to give Meg? He looked through them now. They'd been down in Cornwall, doing some historical re-enactments on the old square-riggers at Charleston Harbour, their last job together before he went to art school. The camera assistant had taken a couple of Larry and Rob, Larry looking through the viewfinder as usual and Rob looking over his shoulder. They were standing very close and Rob looked as if he was about to say something in Larry's ear. Without the camera it would have been curiously intimate. Curiously, because in all the years they had known each other, they had rarely touched, not since they were children and then only to wrestle. They never hugged. Their fathers hadn't hugged *them* and they didn't hug each other. Larry would have said that until Ben was born there was no other human being he had ever felt so close to – not even his aunts when he was a child, not Ruth – and yet they had hardly touched each other physically in thirty years.

Larry sat down on one of the bench seats in the saloon, holding the photographs in his hand but not looking at them. Instead he looked around the saloon, taking it all in. The old black stove, the table and seating, the bleak walls, the single bookshelf. What was he doing here? The Christmas tree now seemed more of an excuse than a reason and now he was looking for excuses to stay. There was nothing for him here. It was cold, it was damp, it was miserable . . . *and he didn't have to care about it.*

He had always known there was a part of him that belonged here. That didn't belong anywhere else, or *to* anyone else. It was the part of him that didn't want to engage, to get involved, with other people, with life. The part that preferred to view the world through the viewfinder of a camera. One of Larry's favourite old movies was *The Horse's Mouth* with Alec Guinness in the role of the painter-tramp Gully Jimson. Gully didn't need a home, he didn't need people. He just wanted to paint. He painted anything. He liked a challenge. In the end he had started painting a giant fresco on the side of an old ship, a rotting hulk out in the Thames where no one would bother him. There was a part of Larry that wanted to be old Gully. Or even his dad – Gully Jimson without the talent.

Larry imagined living here through the seasons with his paints and his canvases, painting in the wheelhouse, stacking them up, unseen, in the for'ard cabin. Joining his dad for a drink at Sunday lunchtime in the Judge Jeffreys, watching the odd football match with him on Sky. Auntie Ethel fixing something to eat for when they got back. No effort required. He had always been better in a threesome. Larry and the two aunts. Larry, his dad and Auntie Ethel. Larry, Rob and Meg . . . The friendly witness to whatever they had going for them and the arbiter of their disputes, and it had worked, in a strange kind of way, until he and Meg spoiled it. There was a lesson, if he ever needed it – far, far better not to get involved.

But what about Ben?

Ben was the problem, of course. He could never run away from Ben as his mother had run away from him. He couldn't imagine a life without him – and it scared him half to death.

And Jo?

Larry thought about the five or six days before he had left

her to go back to the house – before Michael Geraghty died – but would it ever be like that again? Larry didn't think so. He foresaw the inevitable decline. So much better to forestall it.

He could almost think himself into it, but not quite.

'You have to take a risk with your feelings,' Ruth had said to him once, probably just before they split up. 'Sometimes you just have to dive in, and you never will.'

Why not? he thought. Just for once, why not? You could only drown.

He dropped the photographs into the dustbin liner and tied the neck and carried it up to the wheelhouse. He was impatient now to get to the Town of Ramsgate. She should be there by now, waiting for him.

He switched all the lights off and locked up the wheelhouse. He hoped it would be for the last time. When he turned round she was standing a few feet away, near the gangplank. For a brief moment, he thought it was Jo, come to find him. Then she stepped forward and he saw her face.

CHAPTER TWENTY-EIGHT

The River

THEY TOOK AMY'S CAR because Jo had lent hers to Larry and Liz had come in one of her vans. Jo sat next to Amy guiding her but she got lost in the warren of streets north of Tower Bridge. She was starting to panic, peering through the windscreen wipers and the rain. Liz sat in the back, trying to give directions, having no idea where they were or where they were going.

'I don't know why we have to meet him anyway,' she grumbled. 'Why didn't you just phone him and tell him to come back to your place?'

Jo couldn't explain. It was partly because she didn't think he'd take any notice unless she told him the whole story and she didn't want to do that on the phone. But it was also because she felt she had to get to him as fast as possible, or something terrible would happen.

And now they were lost.

'Just get to the river,' she told Amy. If she could get to the river she'd run along the riverside walk until she found it.

'Go back to Tower Bridge,' she said.

But then they turned another corner and she saw the police station at Wapping, the headquarters of the river police.

'It's just along here,' she said.

They stopped outside the Town of Ramsgate and she ran into the pub. But he wasn't there. She asked the barmaid if she'd seen him.

'Not tonight, love,' she said. 'In fact, he's not been here since Christmas.'

Jo ran outside, barging into Liz coming in.

'He must be on the boat still,' she told her.

She led them down the side of the pub to the river. Liz looked at the bridge of barges through the rain.

'You've got to be joking,' she said.

But Jo was already going down the steps.

He was still alive when they found him, slumped against the side of the wheelhouse like a drunk in a pool of liquor. Jo slipped in it getting to him. Only then, as she knelt down beside him, did she see the hook sticking out of his neck.

His eyes were open and when he saw her he seemed to be trying to smile but it didn't come out like that. There was blood on his teeth. He was breathing through his mouth: short, sharp breaths that seemed to give him pain, like he was breathing needles. Jo didn't know what to do. She heard Liz on her mobile phone, calling for an ambulance and the police.

There was so much blood. She was kneeling in it. She knew she had to stop it but she didn't know how. She began to undo the buttons of his coat, gently, as if she was getting a child ready for bed. The hook had gone through his collar and she saw with relief that it was more in his shoulder than his neck. There didn't seem to be too much blood coming out. Not enough to explain the pool she was kneeling in. Then she felt the wet on her hand and saw the other wound in his chest and that was where the blood was coming from.

She took off her coat and then her sweater and bunched it in her fist and pressed it against the wound. She didn't know what else to do.

'They're on their way,' Liz said.

'Where's Jud?' said Amy.

Jo had forgotten she was there, forgotten Jud until now.

'Gone,' she heard Larry say.

'Gone?' Amy looked around the deck and Jo looked too and

saw the blue light of the ambulance crossing Tower Bridge, heard the siren across the water. 'Gone where?'

'In the river.' He spoke thickly as if his tongue was too big for his mouth and looking back, Jo saw the frothy bubble of blood.

'Don't try to speak,' she said, but he had been thinking about it for a while and there was never going to be a better time. She had to lean closer to hear him and she felt the spray of blood on her cheek.

She drew back, putting her hand to her face.

'What's he say?' Amy asked.

'That's not even funny,' Jo said.

'What did he say?' Amy was shouting at her now.

Jo heard the panic in her voice and hated her then because Larry was dying and all she could think of was Jud. Jo's voice was brutal.

'Men shouldn't wear high heels,' she said, 'on boats.'

CHAPTER TWENTY-NINE

Dead Man's Hole

THEY FOUND THE BODY at Dead Man's Hole, exactly where Larry had said it would be. Jo was impressed.

'They usually turn up there,' he said. 'But I was wrong about Monks.'

She had no idea what he was talking about but didn't ask. On the way to the hospital he'd been babbling all kinds of nonsense at her. *I will come back for you . . . I haven't begun to miss you yet . . .* He told her later they were quotes from films and he'd thought that as long as he could keep remembering them and saying them out loud he wouldn't pass out and die – but the paramedics had got bored with him and given him a shot.

He was lucky to be alive, the doctors said. They'd shown Jo the X-rays. The knife had punctured the left lung and stopped just short of the heart; the hook had missed a main artery by about half a centimetre. Jud, it turned out, was practised in the use of both. He had once played Captain Hook in *Peter Pan*. Sergeant Harris must be feeling smug, Larry said.

They were learning a lot about Jud but as most of it came from Amy there was no telling how much of it was true. He'd never really got over the death of his mother, she said. And when he found out what his brother had done to Amy he'd tampered with the brakes on his car. He'd been in and out of mental hospital ever since and in between times he lived with her. He was obsessed with her. He 'identified' with her, she said. He'd speak in her voice, dress in her clothes . . . He became very angry if he thought she was being 'fucked about', as she put it, by some bloke.

Her affair with Rob had apparently come under that category.

Rob had been using her, she said. He derived a particular satisfaction from screwing Meg's friends. It was as if he were out to prove a point – and when he'd proved it, he dumped them. This had made Jud very angry. But it was only after Michael Geraghty was killed that Amy began to have her suspicions.

She'd only been to bed once with Michael, she said, but he had as good as promised her the lead in his latest play and then given it to someone else. This had made Jud very angry, too.

Amy advanced the theory that Jud had taken it upon himself to avenge the rights of *all* used women. He would sometimes walk the streets at night, she said, dressed in her clothes, inviting attack – but she swore she had no idea he had ever seriously hurt anyone. She thought he was just play-acting, in his role as the Avenging Angel.

'I knew all along it couldn't possibly be a woman,' Larry said, when he heard all this.

'Oh sure,' Jo mocked him. '*No one* believed it could *possibly* be a woman.'

She was aware that some people continued to believe it. Lady Macbeth might not have held the dagger but she had made damned sure Macbeth would.

Even Liz had voiced this suspicion to Jo.

'It might not have been in the forefront of Amy's mind,' she said, 'but she knew damn well what would happen if she told Jud some man had been giving her a hard time. She's known it since he killed his own brother.'

Jo considered whether to pass this observation on to Larry but decided against it. There was no proof. Let Amy bury her dead. Let them all bury their dead.

There was still a half-hour of visiting time left but Jo had arranged to meet Meg for dinner in Soho – on neutral territory. There were bridges to be mended. She had a feeling, though, that it was an exercise in damage limitation. They would never be as close as they had been in the hills above Amalfi. And there would never be another meeting of the Used Women's Book Club.

She leaned over the bed to kiss Larry goodnight. He was in a private room for the time being so the police could take a statement from him, but he was being moved into a general ward in the morning, and if he continued to improve he could be out by the weekend. Jo had insisted he came back to the apartment and so far he'd made no violent objection.

His options, however, were by no means as limited as Jo had imagined.

He was surrounded by Get Well cards and four vases of flowers. Thinking of him as a loner, Jo was surprised to find he had so many friends and slightly disconcerted to find that such a high proportion of them were women.

She was determined not to let this trouble her, but as she was leaving the hospital she noticed a young woman in reception and something about her made her think this was one of Larry's well-wishers. She had a bunch of flowers – red roses – which she laid across the reception desk and as Jo passed by – closer than she needed to – she heard her ask for Larry Hunter.

Jo hovered near the exit so she could see the woman's face. She was an attractive blonde, perhaps a little older than Jo had first thought – Jo's age, or a year or two younger. Her coat was open and as she turned away from the desk, Jo caught a glimpse of a white T-shirt with a picture on the front and a logo. She couldn't read it all but she caught the words *rough girls* just before the woman headed down the corridor towards the room where Larry was lying.

A NOTE ON THE AUTHOR

Paul Bryers is the author of many fine novels, the most recent of which is *The Prayer of the Bone*. He is a TV and film director when he is not writing and he lives in London.

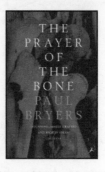